A MURDER TOO SOON

Michael Jecks

CRÈME de la CRIME

This first world edition published 2017
in Great Britain and the USA by
Crème de la Crime, an imprint of
SEVERN HOUSE PUBLISHERS LTD of
Eardley House, 4 Uxbridge Street, London W8 7SY.
Trade paperback edition first published
in Great Britain and the USA 2018 by
SEVERN HOUSE PUBLISHERS LTD.

British Library Cataloguing in Publication Data
A CIP catalogue record for this title is available from the British Library.

ISBN-13: 978-1-78029-098-0 (cased)
ISBN-13: 978-1-78029-581-7 (trade paper)
ISBN-13: 978-1-78010-898-8 (e-book)

Typeset by Palimpsest Book Production Ltd.,
Falkirk, Stirlingshire, Scotland.

A MURDER TOO SOON

Recent Titles from Michael Jecks

The Jack Blackjack Mysteries

REBELLION'S MESSAGE *
A MURDER TOO SOON *

The Medieval West Country Mysteries

NO LAW IN THE LAND
THE BISHOP MUST DIE
THE OATH
KING'S GOLD
CITY OF FIENDS
TEMPLAR'S ACRE

Vintener Trilogy

FIELDS OF GLORY
BLOOD ON THE SAND
BLOOD OF THE INNOCENTS

* *available from Severn House*

This is for Alison and Angus of Tiverton Castle, the owners of one of the most delightful castles – and homes – which has inspired many of my books, this one included.

In loving memory of Roy George (Peter) Jecks
A wonderful father.
1920-2017

PROLOGUE

I t has been said, so I have heard, that a man's good name is his most precious possession; it should be more highly prized than silver or gold, rubies or diamonds.

That sounds fine, but I've always felt that my own most important and valuable assets are my good looks and my pelt, and I am very closely attached to both. I dislike the idea of spoiling or losing either of them.

Which is why, when I was suddenly confronted by Thomas Falkes in a dim, dingy alleyway that smelled of hog shit and rotten entrails, out near the shambles beside Smithfield, my inclination was just to turn and run, especially when I saw his mouth open in a broad grin. There was a lot in that grin: malice, vindictiveness and a complete lack of feeling for his fellow man. Mostly, it showed he was looking forward to inflicting pain on me.

And I would have bolted, too, were it not for the two men who had appeared behind me. Individually, they were large – as wide as the alley, almost, and tall as a house, or so it seemed. It felt as if I was confronted by a wall of muscle.

'I want a word with you,' Falkes said, while I cricked my neck looking up at their faces.

I turned to face him. It's better, I reckon, to see what is about to happen rather than guessing, and, besides, I would never break through those two. I was inclined to think that if I were to escape, it would be around Thomas.

'Hello, Thomas,' I said airily. Then I saw the size of the knife in his hand.

He smiled. 'I'm going to cut your ballocks off and feed them to you.'

Not the most favourable beginning, but Thomas Falkes was not one of the world's light-hearted conversationalists. One of the most famous thief-takers and crooked men in the whole of London, if you ignore the politicians and lawyers, Falkes was a swindler, blackmailer, procurer of whores and fence of stolen goods. There was no crime so small that he wouldn't deign to corner it. I'd heard that he had once robbed his own mother of her pewter. Another man told me he killed his own father, but I think that was Falkes boasting. I doubt he ever knew his father.

He had a problem with me, and it wasn't necessarily my approach to business.

When my life suddenly changed for the better, with a house in the fashionable area near the Moor Gate and a new suit of clothes (which included a rather lovely new jack in cream with a splendid reddish lining), many people grew jealous. Wherever gossips would meet, you would hear my name mentioned.

I was sworn to secrecy. Not that it was needed. I could hardly walk abroad and announce my new post. Many were the rumours about me. I heard some of them in the street as I passed by, and it seemed a grand ruse to live up to them – apart from the one that said I had sold myself as a bardash to some rich duke or earl who had more interest in a he-whore than his own wife. I didn't want *that* reputation.

My master, John Blount, expressed himself plainly when he heard the stories about me, but there was little *I* could do to stem the flow. People saw me in my finery and in my new house, and came to their own conclusions. At first he sought to accuse me of boastfulness, but it was his own fault. After all, it was Master John himself who had made my name so prominent in recent weeks. A man can scarce keep his entire life hidden when his fortune changes, and John Blount was paying me well. Only weeks before, I had been a poor, destitute fellow, living with purse-snatchers and pilferers, and all those who knew me were surprised to learn that I was now living in a house not far from the Moor Gate. Those who saw me were convinced that I must have robbed the Queen herself to be able to live in such a grand style. Well might they guess.

Still, my problem today lay in the fact that Thomas Falkes did not listen to those who suggested I was a sodomite. No: he had good reason to believe that I was not that way inclined.

While he was a gross brute of a man, with the face and manner of a degenerate alehouse-keeper, his wife was formed from a very different mould. Jen was slender, pale, with red-gold hair that was so abundant its weight seemed to keep her chin tilted upwards. She had blue eyes, full lips that were always on the verge of smiling, and a pair of bosoms that a man could pillow on for a lifetime and die happy.

I had grown to know young Jen, you see, and Thomas had come to believe that she was bestowing her favours on me. I don't know; perhaps if Jen had charged me a fee, Thomas would have been happier (if she had shared it with him). Be that as it may, she did visit me a few times. She was impressed with the style in which I lived. Perhaps she considered that she could throw over one husband for a richer one. Whatever her reasons were, I was happy to share my time with her. She was a pretty thing, and the sight of her coming tripping through my door was always enough to make me raise a smile – and something else besides.

Perhaps the necklace was an error, though. I was feeling expansive and happy after an afternoon's gambling at the Bear Pit, where I had made a good profit. I knew I was to be rogering Jen half the night, and on my way home I saw a necklace in a merchant's and bought it for her on the spur of the moment. I know: silly behaviour. What if her husband saw it? Still, she seemed ridiculously touched, and a day or two later she gave me a little pewter flask in return. It was tiny – no good to anyone – but I promised I would hold it with me at all times. She swore it would bring me good luck. Some luck!

To be honest, I had expected the little strumpet to sell the necklace almost immediately. She had the heart of a wanton, and money was money, while a necklace could lead to embarrassing questions from Thomas, but the silly bawd couldn't help herself. She liked it. I heard later that she wore it when she was out with him, and he asked where it came from.

So that was why I was now standing in a dark alleyway, with two of his heavier brutes behind and him before me, dangling a long, thin blade around the area of my ballocks.

It was not a comforting experience.

*   *   *

As soon as I heard Thomas had come to the cuckold's conclusion, it was clear that I was in trouble. If he decided to assault me in the deep, dark dead of night, I would stand little chance against him, and that was intolerable. I refused to remain closeted in my new home – I was used to walking the streets – but I am no brawler. If there is to be a fight, I prefer to land a blow with a cudgel and run. Not for me the excitement of a long-drawn dagger tournament.

I tried the bluff approach. 'Why, Thomas, what have I done to upset you?'

He grinned evilly. 'She may be a little tart, but she's *my* little tart. I won't have other men dipping their wicks—'

'Oi! What's goin' on in there? Hey, you!'

I have never been so grateful to hear a constable's voice. This was a large, roistering fellow with thick lips, cheeks like a cider-drinker's, and the belly of a bishop. He bore a heavy-looking staff, and as he approached us from behind Falkes, he brought this down into the quarter-staff, as if it was a lance he was pointing at us.

One of the men said something, and Falkes quickly shoved his dagger away and turned, with a smarmy friendliness in his tone. 'How can we help you, Constable?'

'What are you lot doing here?'

'I am with Sir Thomas Parry's household,' I said, pushing past Falkes quickly. 'I would be grateful if you could tell me the way to St Paul's. I am new to London.'

'You must be if you come walking down alleys in this area,' he said, eyeing the other three. 'These with you?'

'Yes,' said Falkes, just as I gave the opposite response.

'We were walking together, but now our paths diverge,' I said, looking at Falkes.

The constable gave me rough directions, which I ignored in favour of sticking to busier thoroughfares, and in that way made my way to a wherry, where I caught a boat for the south side of the river, past the bear pits, and out to the Cardinal's Hat, my favourite stew, brimful of little harlots who would do almost anything for a decent purse. However, today I had no need of feminine companionship; it was more Piers, the door-guard, and his blackthorn cudgel that I craved.

Soon I was sitting inside Piers's little chamber, sipping a strong, spiced wine and contemplating my future. It was a bleak prospect.

If I could see no remedy – and other than paying a dubious fellow a large sum to slaughter Thomas, I could see none – I would have to take a lengthy holiday from London. It was not a thought to fill me with delight, but there seemed little alternative. I would have to think of an excuse to leave the city for a few weeks; I would have to escape.

Which is why when John Blount told me he wanted me to go to that Godforsaken hovel, the palace of Woodstock, I leapt at the chance.

Even though he told me he wanted me to murder some woman who had done me no harm.

Yes, it came as a surprise to me, too. I'd never even heard of her.

The interview with Master Blount was infuriating. Most of my discussions with Master Blount are, I find, but this was even worse than usual. It is not every day a man is told he must commit murder – although Blount would term it an 'assassination', and called it 'expedient', as if those words could remove the horror.

I had no inkling of this when I knocked on Blount's door. He lived in a small house not far south of St Paul's Cathedral, one of those narrow, three-storey buildings with prominent beams and limewash over walls and timbers. His fair-haired servant opened the door, waving me through to his parlour. His rooms were all plain and sober enough, just like him. There was little to upset even Queen Mary's prudish tastes.

It was a smallish chamber, and bare, apart from a table, chair, stool and a number of candles. A simple wooden cross hung from a nail in the wall. There was only one window, and that gave a clear view of the Fleet river. Outside all was grey and dull. Low clouds had appeared and were threatening rain at any moment. I had felt sure it would piss on my head as soon as I set off homewards. Not that I was in any great rush. I was very aware of Thomas Falkes and his stated desire to see me gelded before taking more drastic action. Dark streets and overcast clouds made for dangerous walking when a man like Falkes wanted to hurt a fellow.

When I entered, John Blount was already standing with his left hand on his sword hilt, his right on the chair's back, keeping his distance from me. His second companion, Will – whom I still thought of as the Bear, because of his dark hair and enormous size – was behind my master as he spoke.

'The Lady Elizabeth is at Woodstock,' he said, as though I heard nothing of her position. 'You will come with me and we shall see what we may of the area.'

I was nothing loath. Any excuse to leave London just now was welcome. 'Woodstock?'

He gave me a cold look. 'Yes. The Queen's palace. It's only two or three days' journey, up the other side of Oxford,' he said.

'Why do you want me there?'

'It is an old palace. Four hundred years it has stood there, they say. First as a hunting lodge, then as a royal palace, and now mostly as a prison.'

I shrugged. I also noted that he had not answered my question. 'The journey will do me good. When do we leave?'

'You are eager,' he said, and his face darkened into a frown as he spoke.

'What of it?'

'There will be a task for you when we arrive,' he said.

'Yes? So?'

He took a deep breath and eyed me. 'It is time you repaid your debt. Master Parry has invested a great deal in you. Now it is time you returned his favours.'

God's teeth, but that was a painful thought. Parry, so I had learned, was Blount's master, a jovial, portly gentleman with a pleasant, smiling demeanour. But that did not hide the fact that he was as political as any bishop, and twice as dangerous.

'Return them?'

Blount bared his teeth in a smile. I hated that expression on his face. I suddenly understood what he meant. You see, as I have mentioned, I had been in trouble during the rebellion. Somehow I managed to upset all forms of rich and influential people, and the upshot of it was, I was induced by this same Parry to be his hireling: he was to pay my rent and board, and in return I was to do his bidding. Specifically, I was to be his own personal executioner: an assassin.

At the time, it had seemed an easy choice. I had lost my home and friends during the rebellion, and to be offered a house and clothing, as well as full board and spending money, was too good an offer for me to reject. However, there was the other perspective. It occurred to me in a flash that my position was not one to make a thinking man jealous. Yes, I would have board and lodging, but equally, were I to refuse him, Blount may be instructed to find another man to take on my job, whose first task it would be to ensure that my mouth was stopped permanently. It was not a happy reflection.

I won't go into the reasons how or why Parry decided to select me from the weeping boil that is London. You can see my comments in the earlier chapter of my chronicles. Suffice it to say, he felt he had good reason to believe that I was capable and willing to do his will in this, and the more I thought about it, the more certain I was that I would be able to enjoy the good life for a while, and then disappear into London's underworld. It wasn't as if Parry or Blount would be able to announce to the populace why I owed them money, after all.

But now I was to be presented with a victim, and I was sure of one thing: be it a cat, dog, cony or human, I would not be able to kill it. My hands were made for other things.

Of course, the obvious and best course was to do as I had planned: I should swiftly leave home and find a new refuge in the city. However, Thomas Falkes was a hideously ever-present concern. At the thought of him, my hands went clammy and my brow beaded with sweat.

Blount was still talking. I tried to calm my fluttering nerves and listened.

'Lady Elizabeth has been held in appalling conditions since the rebellion. Just now she languishes in Woodstock, surrounded by her enemies. She has a gaoler, Sir Henry Bedingfield, who has restricted her movements, and everything she does is watched and noted in case it can be used against her. The

Queen still believes her to have been associated with the rebellion, and I believe she will have Elizabeth's head if she can do so with impunity.'

I forgot: I haven't mentioned Lady Elizabeth and her plight, have I?

You must remember that these were the days after the attempted rebellion. That damned fool Wyatt and his merry men of Kent sought to persuade our Queen Mary that she may not marry her Spanish Prince; but the rebellion failed, miraculously, at the gates of London, and in a few hours the whole of Wyatt's company was captured, with many of them soon to be dismembered and set out on every available spike, or left dangling in chains from gallows as a dissuasive example to the rest of the country.

However, Queen Mary had a firm conviction that others were involved. Poor Lady Jane Grey and her husband were speedily executed, and then Mary began to cast about for other plotters. Her eye alighted on her own half-sister, Elizabeth, and there it fixed. It was unfair, of course, but life often is. The two had never been close, since as soon as Elizabeth was born, Mary was declared illegitimate, and I don't think it was easy for Mary to accept her change in status while Elizabeth was feted as their daddy's 'little princess'.

Now the boot was on the other foot, and Queen Mary was metaphorically pressing her dainty toe into Lady Elizabeth's face and grinding it hard.

So, although it's hard to remember now, Lady Elizabeth then, in 1554, was a prisoner. A twenty-year-old lady, she had been held in the Tower immediately after the rebellion, but one month or more ago, in May, she had been transported to Woodstock, where she was kept under close guard to prevent any possibility of further plots and schemes. Queen Mary and her advisors were convinced that her younger half-sibling must be trying to rob her of her throne, and the Queen's Council sought to ensure that no one else could again make such an attempt, and especially not someone who was committed to the English Church. Mary and her clique wanted to bring Britain back to the Roman yoke: one and all were papists.

They sought to keep Elizabeth locked up like a rabid hound until she could be safely removed.

That was the feeling among the folk of London, anyway, and many were the stories of Elizabeth's saintliness in the face of her persecution. Somewhere in London it was noted that when people called out, 'God save Princess Elizabeth', they heard a voice from the heavens echoing their cry, or so it was said, but when others called, 'God save the Queen', their entreaties failed to rouse the angels. It was the cause of much comment for a few days. Then a less superstitious and much more suspicious bailiff investigated and found a woman in an upper chamber.

I heard later that the young woman who had provided the echoing voice had been punished for her temerity. There was little new in that. People were beginning to learn that the new Queen was her father's daughter, and unforgiving towards those who questioned her right to rule. It was later that she turned her attention towards those who flouted her will on matters of religion.

That was when everything went to hell for the kingdom, although, of course, things were already bad enough in that month of June, when I was locked up inside Woodstock, suspected of a murder I couldn't have committed.

It was shocking to think that the Queen could be plotting to kill her own half-sister, but no one gambled poorly when they wagered on the cruelty of the House of Tudor. Even so, had I considered the situation more carefully before we undertook the journey to Woodstock, I might have realized how this tale of the Princess's situation was not likely to be good news for me. Unfortunately, my mind at the time was still filled with the dangers of meeting Thomas Falkes down a darkened alleyway. Any escape from London seemed a glorious relief. 'Have her head?' I repeated.

'You do not care that the Princess is held like a common criminal, watched over and persecuted?'

This was one of those difficult moments. In short, no. I didn't care. I was more concerned about holding my hide together against any possible threat from Falkes, but I could hardly say that.

Blount took my silence as confirmation that I had remembered my place. He cast a disapproving eye over me nonetheless as he continued, 'She is permitted only three ladies-in-waiting and three manservants. It is inadequate for her needs. And now Bedingfield has imposed a new woman on her. He has installed a spy within her household. It is repugnant to think that she must acquiesce, but she has no choice. One of her most loyal ladies has been removed, and Lady Margery Throcklehampton installed in her place. She is not to be trusted. Not only is she a spy, but she has even removed Lady Elizabeth's seal, so now all correspondence must be viewed by her. The Princess has no privacy, no security. It must be awful for her.'

'For Lady Elizabeth?'

'Yes. You must kill Lady Margery.'

'Eh?'

'She is a serious threat to the security and safety of the Princess. You must kill her.'

'Me?' I squeaked.

He looked at me doubtfully, and forbore to remind me that I was supposed to be an assassin.

'A woman? I was not hired to kill women.'

'You were hired to do Sir Thomas Percy's bidding.'

That was not something I could dispute. 'Who is she? Her family, I mean?'

'Lady Margery Throcklehampton? She is daughter of the Nevilles up at the Scottish March. Her father used to be an important man in the days of King Henry. The Percies were popular at court for a while, but now? She made a bad marriage to Throcklehampton, who plainly married her for her money and influence, while she took him for his lands, so I heard. That and his position. She was always ambitious, and her husband is a political animal. He's one of those snakes who thinks only in terms of destroying others to further his career. I have no doubt he angled for his wife to be granted this position to strengthen his own situation. Lady Margery will be glad to help him. Her first husband died young, and her son needs a stable future. She will hope that her husband will be able to ingratiate himself with the Queen's Court and produce a worthwhile legacy for her son, with contacts among the rich. She will be passing on everything she can to Sir Walter, and he will tell the Queen's allies in order to destroy Princess Elizabeth. Then the Queen will have no bars to her ambition.'

'What ambition? She's the Queen!' I protested.

He looked at me in the sorrowful manner of a tutor whose pupil has made an elementary mistake at algebra. 'All monarchs want to leave their mark. Queen Mary wishes only to see the country sold to the Pope and undo all the work of her father. King Harry tore down the Catholic Church in this kingdom. He took away all the fripperies and extravagances so that the public could worship as God intended, in sober equality. She would do away with that and take us back to rule by the Roman Church. She must be prevented.'

'Her husband is Spanish.'

'But *we* are English,' he snapped.

It was curious. I had never seen him so emotional. He was angry about my response, as though he thought I had no soul. I nodded as if in agreement. 'But what could I do? Even if we were to travel to Woodstock, I would be unlikely to meet the woman. How could I kill her? There are walls about the palace, I suppose? You expect me to climb the battlements, killing sentries *en route*, and find my way in the dark to her bedchamber, avoiding all this Sir Henry Bedingfield's men, and creep into Princess Elizabeth's chambers to find one lady among all the others, and somehow . . .'

'You do not need to worry about that. We have an arrangement. You and I are to be messengers. Sir Henry Bedingfield refused to allow the Princess's chamberlain, our master, Sir Thomas Parry, to visit her and, since Lady Margery has deprived her of her own seal, and all correspondence must be sent with Lady Margery's approval, the Princess has need of safe messengers. We must witness any confidential reports or communications from her and take them to Sir Thomas Parry. She has much business to be conducted. The Princess has extensive estates, and their value would be depreciated, were her farmers and yeomen not made fully aware that she wanted their rents. Too many will try to hide on hearing that their landlord has been arrested and held. They reason that with the landlord out of the way, they can hold on to their money for longer. But she needs her money still. So does Bedingfield.'

'What do you mean?'

Blount gave a short, irritable gesture with his hand as though I should have been more interested in the affairs of such people, rather than the tarts at the stews. 'Bedingfield can't afford to support the Princess in the style she expects. He has little money. Even manning the palace will be costing him dear. So many men-at-arms cost a great deal to maintain. So he ensured that she should pay for all the guards and their food, as well as her own little entourage. Princess Elizabeth is being held against her will, and she must pay for the privilege. That means that her letters and legal documents must be taken to her, and also that money must be brought in order that she might give some to Bedingfield for the upkeep of the palace.'

'That must be a sore annoyance to her.'

'Yes . . . and no. It means she can keep in constant contact with her chamberlain, Sir Thomas Parry, who even now stays at the nearest inn. And we must go there, take his messages to Princess Elizabeth and her responses back to Parry. It gives you plenty of time in the palace to get to know it, learn where Lady Margery resides, and execute her.'

'I see.'

What could I say? I had the temporary embarrassment of Thomas Falkes who wanted to personally skin me alive – and he was not a slave to metaphor – so I could not flee from Blount and remain in the city with any security. He would want to find me if I disappeared. The money I owned came from him, as did the house and food and even the new jack on my back. He was ruthless, and if he thought I was running away after taking his money, my life would be in peril from him as well as Thomas Falkes. Then again, to leap into this palace with instructions to murder a lady-in-waiting was hardly congenial. There were dangers there, and I could already feel the strange roiling in my belly at the thought of killing a woman. It was wrong.

'You must go and pack.'

Yes, the idea of stabbing a woman was repellent. I could

not do it. It was a foul, cowardly act. I opened my mouth to tell him, when a crash from the road outside made me leap into the air like a startled deer.

At the window, Blount stared out. 'A cart's lost its axle,' he said.

'Oh!' I said. In my mind was a horribly clear picture of Falkes's face. It bore a leer, and he held a knife in his hand. Suddenly, Woodstock seemed a most appealing alternative.

'Very well. When do we leave?'

In the end the journey took us four days but with the changes in dialect we might have gone to a new land. The people were so uncouth! It showed why it was so easy to take the money from peasants when they arrived in London. They had hardly the sense they were born with.

As an example: two days from London I became tangled in a game of dice. One man demanded to know the cause of my good fortune.

'Beginner's luck,' I said, but he was not placated.

I didn't want any trouble, and Master Blount was glaring at me, so I said that I had a lucky potion and I showed him the little flask Jen had given me. I explained it was a gift and I could not help the fact that it was so efficacious.

Next morning, he appeared and pressed a fat purse into my hand. He and his comrades had clubbed together. I stared at the silver, dumbfounded. I could scarcely believe that they had found so much without recourse to theft, but be that as it may, I could not leave their silver. I kept it and passed over my small pewter pot of water. At least they hadn't realised I was using shaved dice.

It was a relief to reach Woodstock at last and escape dull-witted churls like them. Or so I thought.

DAY ONE

I have no fond memories of Woodstock.

Dilapidated, odorous, damp, and suffused with a chill that ate into the bones, it was a depressing pile of semi-rotted timbers and cold stone, grey as a winter's day before snow. Some said the atmosphere was caused by the marshes all about. Personally, I think that malignant spirits infested the place. I was not to be disabused of that notion.

The first intimation I had of its danger to me was in a quiet chamber off the hall on the first day of arriving there.

I recall that room very clearly: dark, dingy, ill-lit, small, with stairs climbing to the next floor immediately on the right. A door to the left, outlined by daylight, led to the outer courtyard, while a second, behind the staircase, gave into an inner passageway. I had been passing my time in the company of Sal, Kitty and Meg, three delightful maids who were clearing the rushes in the hall. Joking and trying my luck with them, I was startled to hear a loud clattering noise and came out to seek the source. I had thought a clumsy servant had dropped the jug of wine and cups I had demanded, and was preparing to laugh at his foolishness. Instead I found myself tumbling over a large obstruction, and fell swearing to the stone flags into what felt like a slippery pool of oil.

When you are knocked to all fours in the relative darkness of a gloomy chamber, it can be confusing. My knees were badly scraped and bruised, and my right hand had fallen with full force on to a pebble that jabbed painfully at my palm. I remained there some moments, jarred, my lips pursed as a pulse of anguish stabbed at my hand like a burn, unable to take in my surroundings. I was still there on my knees when I heard the first scream. Turning, I was confronted by the sight of a maid in the doorway with her mouth wide. It was Sal, and she was staring down beyond me. Something in her expression made me follow the direction of her glance.

I stood hurriedly, gaping. I had not expected to find this. I backed away, until the handrail of the stairs prodded me in the back. Shortly afterwards, the finely honed blade of a long ballock knife tickled my Adam's apple, pushing me against it harder.

There was, I am sure, a man holding the knife, but at the time my eyes were fixed on the steel rather than his eyes. The cold prick of the tip at my throat was most compelling.

I was, you might say, in a difficult position at that moment. It was not only the man before me and the knife in his hand. There was also the matter of the body lying on the floor at my side.

That body was unsettling.

It was the body of a woman in her early thirties, with glorious auburn hair that flowed unrestrained over the floor, much as did the blood from the wound in her throat. More precisely, it was Lady Margery Throcklehampton, the woman whom I had been instructed to murder.

Events like these colour a man's views. No, I do not like Woodstock.

The man before me looked more like an assassin than me, I have to say.

He was shorter and had a wall eye. A scar reached from his chin to up over his left ear, pulling the left side of his mouth into a sardonic grin. I didn't like the look it gave him, but then again, with his knifepoint all but puncturing my gizzard, I was not likely to think of him as a glorious example of manhood.

'I know this looks bad,' I said. His knifepoint pressed harder.

'Guards!' he bellowed.

'*Shite!* Wait!' I said, trying to keep my throat still while I desperately sought for something to say. I shot a look towards the doorway, but Sal had fled.

'Why?'

'This wasn't me!' I said, and held up my hands to show my innocence.

His eyes fell to my palms and his face hardened. When I glanced down, I saw that they were covered in gore.

'Piss on you!' he snapped, and from that I took it that he wasn't interested in any delaying tactics I might attempt. Yes, my hands were smothered in it. When I fell, it was into a pool of her blood. I had a fleeting moment of relief when I saw that none had splashed on my new jack, before the horror of the situation overwhelmed me.

It was apparent that One-Eye and I were unlikely to fall into a comradely discussion about the body and speculate as to who the killer may be. He, for his part, seemed pretty convinced he knew who it was. Rather than meet his accusing glare, I looked down at her.

She was lying on her back with her throat cut. Blood had splashed over the walls and on the floor, and lay like a heavy apron down the front of her expensive gown. When I looked at her, I saw what looked like expensive rubies glittering at her breast in the light from a dingy window. Now I realize that they were clots of blood. The thought made me shiver. There were marks at her throat as well, paler lines in the foulness, and I wondered whether she tried to grasp the knife. They looked like fingermarks in the blood, as though someone had grabbed at her flesh. But that thought was soon washed away by feelings of confusion and nausea.

It was plain enough that while I was standing and staring at her, my wall-eyed friend had walked into the chamber. He took in the scene in one glance and came to the immediate (and wrong) conclusion that I must be responsible. I should not condemn him; the sight was enough to unman me. However, I do have a strong streak of vindictiveness in me, and his assumption of my guilt was hurtful. I resented it, and him.

Never mind all that. I could feel the blood trickling from where his blade had pinked me, running down my neck to the little pocket above my collar bone. If he pressed a little harder, it would puncture my spine, I was sure.

'Please,' I began, hoping to persuade my companion to remove his dagger from my throat, and as I did so, I saw a shadow. A figure detached itself from behind the stairs, stepped up stealthily and, even as the clamour of rushing armour clattered towards us from passages and through the hall, I saw a club strike my captor on the side of his head. His one good eye glared at me, and I suddenly realized that he was about to collapse. I squeaked while I could, thinking that at any time my throat would be seriously stabbed, and jerked an arm up to knock his blade away. Even as his expression took on a mildly bemused air, his eye rolled up into his brow, and he slowly toppled like a great oak reluctantly yielding to the axe.

I was preparing to throw up when her voice came to me, insistent and imperative.

'Come with me! At once!'

I have had my fair share of adventures in the last few months. What with hiding from Thomas Falkes after he learned about his wife visiting me, and only weeks before that the murderous period of the rebellion, when everyone seemed determined to kill me, I've had more than enough excitement for the next ten years. Seeing a matron before me with a stout club in her hand and fire in her eye, I was tempted for a moment to remain where I was. Only a moment, yes, because the sound of approaching guards was growing closer.

She whirled about and fled, and I followed her, rushing over my captor (I kicked his cods from pure viciousness as I passed) and in through the door behind the stairs. She latched it, propping a besom against it when I was past, and then she led me along a passageway, through another chamber, up some stairs in a circular tower, and out along a roof, not pausing to catch her breath until we had entered another tower and I could fall to my knees like a supplicant.

My liberator was a middling-sized woman with a bosom like a barge. She wore a slightly threadbare gown of dark velvet, and her hair was mostly hidden beneath a clean linen coif, although some strands of reddish gold had straggled appealingly at her temples. She was no young strumpet, but a maid of some five-and-thirty summers, I would guess.

I gave her my most winning smile. 'Mistress, I am most grateful—'

'Aye, you'll be grateful enough when I crown you with my

stick,' she said, and hefted the weapon in both hands in an alarmingly competent manner, which all too closely resembled a woodsman gripping his axe. I retreated, hands aloft to show I meant her no harm. Which is ironic, bearing in mind her actions so far that day.

'Wait, please, Mistress! I've done nothing to deserve your buffets!'

'You'd best keep it that way,' she snapped. 'Who are you?'

'I am called Jack Faithful.' Yes, I am, sometimes. 'I'm only recently arrived from London.'

'From London? Why are you here?'

'I came with my master, John Blount. He is here to meet with Princess Elizabeth, for he has messages and reports of her manors for her. There are documents to sign.'

'Princess, eh? I thought she was to be referred to as "Lady", not "Princess".'

'I am only a servant!' I protested. 'How would I know the correct form of address?'

Few enough did. Since the old King, Henry, had divorced his first wife to marry his second, the realm was confused. Our Queen, Mary, had been raised as a princess and then discarded when her mother's marriage was declared void. Now that she was Queen, she had declared that her mother's marriage was legal, and thus her half-sister Elizabeth was a bastard and, as such, no princess. Or, not any longer. Confusing? Yes.

'What were you doing down there?'

'In the passageway? I was in the hall with some people and heard a noise. I went out there and all but fell over the maid.'

'Did you see a man there who could have killed her?' She hefted her weapon again, and it struck me that she was peering closely at me.

'I saw nothing, until I stumbled across her, and that Catholic brute with a wall eye tried to prick my throat for me!'

Sometimes I may not be as observant as I should be. It was only after speaking my piece that I noticed the rosary that dangled from this lady's belt. Perhaps I should keep my views on religion to myself, I thought.

'Hmm.' She contemplated me for a moment. In the light

from a high window, I could see that she had the most glorious green eyes. After what seemed like an age, she gradually allowed the weapon to fall slightly, as though she was inclined to believe I represented little danger to her.

'You can speak with my master, John Blount. He works for—'

'I know of him,' she said, and it appeared that the name did not endear me to her.

'He works for Sir Thomas Parry,' I added.

She spat at the floor. '*Him*?'

I concluded that his name too was unfavourably received.

'And you are?' I asked.

'If you must know, I am the one who saved your life. Do not rely on me to do so again!' she snapped, and slipped through the door back to the walls. The door closed with a positive snap like a gaol's.

For a little while I stood there, staring at the door, and then I stepped to the wall and slid down it until my buttocks were on the ground. Suddenly, I felt a great lassitude washing over me, and all I craved at that moment was ale, and plenty of it.

Just now, I thought, my friend Piers would be drinking his fourth pint of the day and preparing the rooms at the brothel for the clients. Looking out through the window at the landscape here, I mourned the narrow lanes and streets of London. They seemed so much safer.

Then I reflected that at least Thomas Falkes was nowhere near. That was some consolation.

I stepped into the chamber where the woman's body lay and made myself known to the men inside.

There were several of them. Guards, servants gazing fearfully, maids sobbing quietly. My friends Sal and Kitty were in there, although Meg had been taken away. There was a small pool of sick where she had been. Apart from them, there were the steward, a shortish, grey-haired and grey-faced churl, who looked me up and down and didn't appear to like what he saw; Blount, who stood staring at me with a curious fixity; near him, a sallow-faced man with grim, dangerous features and an expression of glowering suspicion; beside him, a younger lad with a fair thatch and the build of a bull. On Blount's other side there was a querulous old fellow with hair more white than grey, and thin, pallid features, who stood with his hands clutched in front of him as though he was pleading for a loan from an Italian; and, finally, an enormous belly like a barrel. Looking hard, I saw that there was a shrewd-looking face above it. This individual wore garb that looked vaguely ecclesiastical, almost like one of the cathedral canons from St Paul's, with thick black cloak and cap.

As I entered, I took this all in. Then, 'I was the First Finder, I think,' said I, and instantly was the focus of all attention.

'Why did you run away? What were you thinking?' demanded the anxious, older man.

'How did you find her?' said the steward.

The big man with the belly was the man with the keenest mind. He lowered his head to gaze at me. 'Did *you* kill her?'

All these questions and many more were fired at me, until my head began to ache. The questions flew thick and fast as pigeons from stubble, and soon I felt that my head was spinning like a top, and I had to hold up my hands to slow my interrogators. The only consolation was the quieter, doleful tone at the back of the room that kept demanding, 'How did you knock me down, you bastard?'

Blount left, giving me a sour stare, just before Sal happily told all who would listen that I had been with her and her friends when we heard the rattle of plates on the stone floor. The woman was dead before I opened the door. I was innocent, there were witnesses to prove the fact, and I was safe.

It was a relief to leave that chamber and gather my reserves. First, I went to the trough by the stables and washed my hands vigorously, trying to remove as much of the blood as I could. I scrubbed and rubbed at them, scraping them on the stone of the trough until there was no more. It was a relief to see that at least my jack was unmarked. Then, weary, I went to sit at the hall's bench between two buttresses. This old wall was not as strong as it should be, and there were regular supports to maintain it.

All I wanted then was a warm ale and a chance to close my eyes. Seeing Sal, I asked her to fetch me a drink, thanking her for her speedy assurances of my innocence. Soon she was back, and I emptied the first quart in no time. I was glad that my innocence had been so easy to demonstrate. I was safe for now.

That was my first thought. Whoever was guilty of this murder, it was plainly not me. For once I was safe.

After a while, the ale worked its magic and I closed my eyes. Not for the last time, I became aware of a sense of dislocation and loss. This wasn't my sort of place; it wasn't London.

While about me the palace bustled, it was a different busyness compared with home. That was what I missed. All of it: the noisy streets, the alleys filled with garbage, the sows ruffling and snuffling in the corners of the walls, chickens squawking as children ran by trying to catch a cat, the shrieks and cat calls from rejected whores, the curses from urchins refused money, the rumble of heavy wagons, the singing and dancing and merriment. It made my eyes moist just to think of it. Here, there was the sound of birdsong, of calm whistling, of dogs grumbling while they waited near a fire. It was weird.

All I wanted was to be whisked home. Instead, I was stuck in this doleful manor with my master and, of course, a murderer.

Not that the presence of a murderer was a problem for me. The man who slew Lady Margery Throcklehampton was plainly on the same side as my master, even if I was unsure whose side that was. Still, my master wanted this woman dead, and now dead she was. The enemy of my enemy is my friend, and all that. With luck, my own position would be eased, for with the target of Master Blount's hatred slain, there was no need for me to remain. I could hope instead to be permitted to vacate the premises and return to London – slowly. Perhaps Falkes would by then have forgotten my misdemeanours and be more concerned with matters other than me and his wife. I could go back to life in my house near the Moor Gate, or down at the stews with Piers and the wenches in the Cardinal's Hat. That made me perk up a bit.

A spasm passed through my back at the thought of the wenches at the Hat. It was pure nostalgia, a poignant memory of all the things I missed, and it was enough to spur me to leave this horrible place. I should walk to the gates and pass through without delay. *Now!* Falkes or no Falkes, London was calling to me.

I opened my eyes to the thin sunlight.

The yard was full of a constipated urgency and excitement. Men ran and tried to look eager and busy, but I could see that they were hurrying back and forth, never going far, always remaining within a short distance of the door as though they were bound by invisible cords. I have seen the same behaviour at home, when peasants will hang around near a scene of disaster, hoping to catch a glimpse of distressed families or bludgeoned burglars. Here in the yard, the men-at-arms and guards mingled with the grooms and maids, all remaining near enough to the hall that they might see the body, or witness the capture of the killer, or, better still, both. There was that restrained thrill that comes of a disaster that has struck someone else.

I saw no sign of my one-eyed friend, which was a relief. The man's instant assumption of my personal involvement was disconcerting. If anyone were to learn of my instructions as Master Blount's assassin, they could become painfully serious rather than merely embarrassing.

Amidst the huddles of men who stood conferring, the women gossiping freely, there were two who caught my eye.

One was the younger fair-haired man I had seen in the room. In the daylight, I could see he was a well-built man of perhaps two-and-twenty summers, a bold, strong fellow with a square, open face, and wearing the sort of expression that women think of as endearing, but which makes me think of a dim version of lap dog favoured by rich ladies. You know the sort: fawning and slobbery. He looked rather like that. And altogether too careful about his dress, I thought, too. He had very tight hosen to show off his thighs and calves to best effect, and a richly slashed jack that left little of the expensive silk lining to be imagined. Personally, I thought he looked a frivolous and feckless individual.

The man with him was a different character entirely. He was the one with the sallow complexion and grimly glowering

demeanour. About him there was something of the look of a
bold adventurer, like those merchants who kept trawling the
seas in search of new lands to conquer. He and the younger
fellow stood in the shadow of a buttress supporting the hall's
wall, and, as I watched, the older man prodded the other in
the chest with a stern finger.

I would not have tried such an act. In London, behaviour
like that would result in a broken finger – or worse. The
younger man did not take it well, unsurprisingly. He rose on
the balls of his feet and his head jutted forward, while he said
something that was clearly brief and to the point. The finger
rose and poked once more.

It was a mistake. There was a short, blurred movement, and
the sallow-faced man was left holding one hand in the other
while his face turned a gentle green colour. The younger man
leaned down, spat something rude in his face, and pushed him
away with both hands, contempt oozing from every pore,
before he made his way over across the court.

When he came level with the open door to the chamber, I
saw his eye glance through it. From where I was, I could see
inside: the bright splashes of scarlet dulling to a clotted brown,
the gleam of auburn hair, the shoulder of a green velvet dress.
I looked at the man and saw him blench at the sight. Then he
was barging people from his path as he strode away.

The other man was clearly made of stronger stuff than I had
imagined. He held his damaged hand still, but he did not run
away to demand assistance. Instead, he stood massaging it,
watching while the younger man marched off, heading for the
door that led to some of the guests' chambers. He'd probably
only had it bent back and dislocated, not broken.

I was surprised that the younger man was stationed in the
guest chambers. Most had to share their sleeping spaces with
the servants in the hall, but the more privileged few were
granted their own rooms, like my master, and this fellow was
obviously similarly honoured.

A shout came from the chamber where the body lay. It
sounded like a woman's cry, or perhaps a child's. Whichever
it was, I saw Sallow-Features turn and stare, a look of sudden

alarm or concern on his face, before it hardened into a crisp shell of determination, and he hurried to the gates, where he spoke to the porter.

I cared little. It was nothing to do with me. But as I turned to face the door, I noticed the keen-minded fellow from the chamber. Outside, he looked even more enormous, this one. He was tall, with a thatch of fair hair and amiable features. With his semi-religious garb, he looked like a giant Friar Tuck. His attention was fixed firmly on the man with the porter. As I observed him, his face turned to the door through which the fair man had disappeared. I followed his gaze, and when I looked back at him, he was gone.

What of it? Three men, and all irrelevant to me, so I thought. I had more urgent things to consider, such as how to disappear from this place, and that quickly.

There was a shout, more calls, and men were bellowed at to '*Get back to work!*' as the door to the little chamber with its repellent bloody decoration was firmly closed. I span on my heel to fetch my gear before leaving, only to find that the giant was standing right behind me. He gave me a broad smile, tipping his head, and then, shoving his hands into his belt, walked away, whistling.

His sudden appearance behind me and his knowing look both inspired a feeling of deep trepidation. I decided there and then to escape this place.

But before I could, I was accosted by the querulous old man from the chamber.

'I would speak with you, Master Blackjack,' he said as a servant ran to him and spoke of a message from the Queen's Coroner.

That was when I first realized that the fellow was Sir Henry Bedingfield, the seneschal of this palace.

He was a nervous old soul, I have to say. As he spoke, his fingers were pulling at threads on his jack, tugging at his bottom lip or the hair at his temple, or rubbing his chin. He was never still, and his eyes darted about the yard like a bird fearing a cat.

'Yes?'

'What exactly are you doing here?'

'I am Master John Blount's servant.'

'And what is *he* doing here?'

'We are here bringing messages from Sir Thomas Parry. I don't know more than that.'

'Tell me again how you found her.'

So once more I told him that I was in the hall with Sal, Kitty and Meg, we heard the noise, I dashed out, tripped, and was found there by One-Eye.

Sir Henry stood nodding to himself.

I said, 'Of course, I've never met the woman. Not like you: many will think you had a hand in her death.'

His mouth fell open. 'Me? Why me?'

'All must know that Lady Margery was put there to keep a close eye on the Princess. But suppose she didn't bring you the information you wanted,' I mused. 'Others may think you sought to punish her.' Sheer nonsense, of course, but I intended to stop him thinking about me for a while.

I failed.

A shrewd light came into his eyes. 'Most will think it more likely that the First Finder was the killer. You tried to put the blame on to others,' he said.

This was expected. A stranger to the house like me was easier to accuse than someone known to all and sundry in the jury. Yes, it was expected, but it still made my bowels lurch uncomfortably. 'Why should I? I don't know the woman! I only arrived here today.'

'Oh, I see. Yes, I suppose there are always some who will believe the worst of anyone,' he said.

Then he shocked me by saying, 'I have heard you are a dangerous man, Master Blackjack. This lady who has died, it might be thought that she was an enemy of the Lady Elizabeth, so an enemy of your master. It would scarcely be a surprise if you were thought to have slain the woman.'

I felt as though he had punched me in the gut. 'An enemy? Surely not! Who says such a thing?'

'Many. And as a lady-in-waiting to the Lady Elizabeth, who took an interest in that lady's affairs, some say Lady Elizabeth's friends could have wanted poor Lady Margery removed.'

'Well, I had nothing to do with it!'

Perhaps the heat of my denial was convincing, for he looked away fretfully and muttered, 'Who ever heard such a thing as this? A poor woman murdered, and for what? Perhaps for politics, perhaps a jealous . . . but no matter.'

'This is outrageous,' I blustered. 'I'll have to tell my master.'

'Do so. You will not be the only man suspected,' he said, and pulled a thread from his felted coat in an abstracted manner. 'She managed to upset many about the palace. But she was a good servant to the Queen, I have no doubt, if painfully difficult to deal with. I shall have to call the Coroner, of course. We shall see what he can find.'

He stumbled away soon after that. And if my resolution to depart had not been determined already, that conversation would have convinced me. I turned away, and over at the far side of the court, I saw my Friar Tuck once more. He was staring at me, hard.

I am no dullard when it comes to danger. Although I craved peace and a place to sit quietly and think, it was obvious I had no time to waste. Instead, I hurried to the hall where my pack lay. Most of my belongings were still at the inn at Woodstock, but I had some few items that I'd brought to the palace. I had expected to be here only for one day, after all. However, I could not find my pack. I hunted through satchels, packs and saddle gear where I thought I had left my bag, but it was gone.

As I searched, from all parts of the palace there came the sound of shouts and clatterings of armour. The palace was being searched for the murderer, as if there was some foreigner with a bloody dagger in his hand, hiding in a cupboard and waiting to be found. Well, I had no desire to be tested once more. That last interview had been enough for me.

Hoping that perhaps Master Blount had already had the same idea, and had taken my pack for me, I determined to scuttle out of the palace as quickly as I may. After all, Blount had ordered me to murder the woman and now she was dead. I wanted to get clear away and keep my head low. I did not fear that my alibi could fail, but an innocent man could be broken on the rack as easily as a guilty one for plotting the murder of a lady above his station. Many could be keen to learn why I had been determined to assassinate the poor woman . . . indeed, whether I had succeeded or not.

So I squared my shoulders and strode out into the yard and towards the gate like a clerk who's discovered a theft from his bishop's wine stores, intending to make my way down the muddy road towards Woodstock itself and thence somewhere else. I had no idea *where* just now, but I hoped that by putting distance between me and Woodstock, the 'somewhere' would occur to me.

Except that when I approached the welcoming, wide-open gates, they began to swing shut. I would have hurried and attempted to bluster my way through, but even as I did so, the fair-haired young man was there already. After removing the peremptory finger jabbed in his broad chest, he was keen to leave the palace as well.

Now I was closer, I could study him in more detail. He had the sort of thick neck muscles that compensate for an empty skull. You see these pretty fellows in London near the court often enough. Men with brawn but very little brain, who prefer to spend their time finding the best hair-stylist and the best supplier of fine silks and hosen to show off a perfectly turned leg. As well as fair hair, he had a fine, straight nose, and cheekbones that any woman would crave for herself, but his language, as he was pushed away from the gates, was not the kind I would expect from a lady.

'You pox-ridden cock-bawd! Open that gate for me, at once!'

The porter, whom I had seen earlier in the day, was an amiable enough fellow. He stood now, a half-foot shorter than the fair man, and stuck his thumbs in his belt in a friendly enough manner. 'Ah, now, my apologies, Squire, but there has been a murder, so I've heard, and you know full well that means I have to lock the house while we wait for the Coroner to come.'

'The Coroner? What do I care about this murder! Open the gates! I have an urgent mission.'

'You can have an order from the Archbishop, for all I know, but the gates stay shut.'

'Open the gates, you addled whoreson; open them, I say, or I'll run you through!'

The porter shook his head and made no effort to move. The fair man shrugged his cloak aside and grabbed his sword hilt. With a slither of steel, he pulled the blade free of the sheath, but before he could point it at the porter, one of the gate's guards, who had been watching with interest, brought his staff on to the man's head with full force. The fair man seemed to hesitate, and then took a half-step forward and turned. I saw him smile with a confused air, like a man on his second gallon of strong ale trying to remember his joke's ending, before he toppled slowly into the mud.

It was enough to lighten my mood, but my day was about to turn black. I noticed John Blount watching me from the top of a short flight of stairs some yards from the gates. The steps led up to a door that opened into a room built into the outer wall. It served as a chamber for my master. He beckoned me.

I obeyed. It was not as though I was going to be able to get back to the inn where I was staying. I took one final, sad look at the gates as the last of the enormous bolts was slid across, two guards turning and standing in that slouching, bored stance of the professional soldier set to perform a tedious task.

At least I could be hopeful that my master would let me sleep on his floor since I couldn't get back to my own bed.

'Have you got my pack?' I asked as I approached.

John Blount was the sort of man who few would try to argue with or fight. He invariably dressed in black: a dark jerkin, with dark scarlet decorations, belt, grey hosen and boots of some soft, soot-coloured leather, all set off with a broad-brimmed hat that left his face in shadow. His figure beneath the shades of black was hard to discern, but there was something in his careful economy of movement that spoke of strength. Yet few would guess how hard his body was. I'd learned soon enough that he was as tough as cured leather, his muscles quick and hardy as a smith's, and his mind as relentless as any man of politics and deceit. He could strike like an adder, with no warning. I'd seen it.

Now he gave me a cold stare: 'Is it my place to look after the pack of a careless ruffian?'

His face was strong. Clean-shaven, he was moderately good-looking, with grey, serious eyes under a strong brow. Together with his down-turned mouth, his expression was invariably fixed in a glower, although whether of concentration or active dislike I was never sure. Generally, when his eye lit upon me, I was confident that it was mostly disgust.

'You have done magnificently well,' he said with hissed malevolence when I was near enough. He pulled me into his small room. It smelled of old horses. Saddles and bridles were stored on racks and hooks, and there were blankets piled on a shelf. A low bed was over on the right, and a small stool. There were two benches, and on one sat Blount's servant Will. Blount pushed me against the blankets and glared. 'Do you recall my orders? To kill her quietly, to make it look like an accident, and under no circumstances bring attention to yourself?'

'Yes, but—'

'So what did you do? You killed her here, in a public space, with great violence, and raised such an outcry that even the blockhead Bedingfield was alarmed!' He was not shouting, but somehow his hissed words carried more emphasis than a bellow.

'You blame *me*?' I said, outraged.

'You killed her, didn't you?' he demanded.

This was a tricky one. I didn't wish to admit immediately that I had failed in his command, but then again I didn't want to accept the blame for this atrocious murder. I held my tongue as he continued.

'I ordered you to kill Lady Margery, but I said you should keep it low-key, so that as few people as possible would be perturbed. I said I wanted her to disappear without fuss, didn't I? And instead, what did you do? Caused the whole palace to come to uproar, and the gate to be closed so we're locked in!'

'It's not my fault!'

'I suppose it was someone else's? Whose? The man who found the body?'

'He found me there. It wasn't—'

'"It wasn't me!" "It's not my fault!"' he mimicked. There was no need for that.

'I was going to say—' I began, but he cut me off.

'I shall have to give you an alibi,' he said. 'Else you'll never leave here alive. You were so incautious that they'll have to keep the gates shut until the Coroner's been to visit.'

'Where shall I sleep? I have a room at the inn at the town. If they hold me here, I'll have nowhere to rest!'

'Will can do it. You were gambling, understand? You were in the orchard with Will here, if anyone asks you. He will corroborate your story.'

I glanced at Will. My nickname suited him, for he truly was a bear of a man, with a thick black beard and the build of a wrestler. At his side was Blount's other companion, a shorter, wiry fellow with fair hair and a constant smile. I didn't trust either of them.

'What of all the people who didn't see us there?' I asked sourly.

'Don't be a fool! I was in the yard a little before the woman was killed and saw no one who could deny you. There was no one in the orchard.'

'You think *me* the fool?' I said. 'We are here, locked in this palace until the Coroner can come, and you seem unconcerned, yet you could be accused of her killing!'

'Me?'

'You have told others to commit this assassination!'

'Not I,' he said with a quiet smile.

I glared at him. There was nothing written, and although a man could be tortured into a confession, Blount would no doubt be safe. He had friends.

'What shall I do while we wait?' I said, pointedly looking at the bed and two benches in the chamber.

'If you're worried about your bed, you can sleep in the hall. Or there are plenty of haylofts, if you don't mind the rats.'

Neither was overly appealing.

'So you remember the story? You were . . .'

'Did you not listen? The tale of sitting in the orchard cannot work.'

'Why not?'

'Because I was not there, and many can confirm it. You assume that I would be foolish enough not to have thought of an alibi,' I said with hauteur. It was meant to sting. 'You don't want to know my genuine alibi, then?'

He opened his mouth to speak, but no words came. Will roared with laughter and slapped his thigh, and glanced at me with an expression of near admiration. 'Master John, you didn't expect that, did you?'

Blount glowered. 'You had this planned all along? That is good. What is your alibi, then?'

'I was in the hall with three of the maids. We heard a noise, I ran to it, and found the body of the woman.'

'That sounds well. So three people can confirm that you were with them while you were killing Lady Margery. Excellent. You are quite sure that they are reliable?'

I grunted my agreement. 'I was with them until after we heard the noise. I went with one of them and found the body. She went to raise the alarm and a moment later this one-eyed man came in, saw me and the woman, and assumed I'd killed her.'

'Yes, that works,' Blount said. He was seemingly content with my tale, although he clearly believed it to be a fiction.

I was dismissed, plainly. He turned away and sat at Will's side near the small hearth. I stood undecided, looking from one to another.

'You want something more?' Blount asked. He was pouring wine. It looked rich and flavoursome.

'Well, I . . .'

'Shut the door when you leave.'

I left Master Blount's chamber and stood at the steps, leaving the door ajar, hoping the next breeze would open it wide. Sadly, the noise it made scraping on the flagged floor was enough to convince me that it would take a strong Whitstable wind to move it, and the sort of mild breaths of wind that were to be found here, so far inland, would be inadequate for the task.

A pair of carters were arguing with the porter, demanding to be released, but the porter and his men were obdurate. Two servants were helping the fair-haired man over to a bench as I watched. The poor fellow was obviously still mazed from the knock on his head, and he shook his locks dazedly from time to time, then sat and covered his face in his hands. I cast a glance at him, and then at the two at the gates as I descended the steps from Blount's room, but there was little to gain by waiting there. They were not going to open the gates for me, it was clear. Instead, seeing the door open to the chamber where I had fallen over Lady Throcklehampton's corpse, I went over and was about to peer inside when I heard voices.

I could hear them before I could see anything in that malodorous little room: a man and a woman. Leaning against the nearest buttress, I found myself concealed in its shadow from the people in the yard, while also hidden from those inside. I listened intently.

'Well? What should we do? In the name of God, that I should have had such an affair!' Ah! I recognized that voice. It was Sir Henry again, I realized.

'Please, you must keep a firm grip on yourself!' I jerked back from the door. I knew that voice too. It belonged to the lady who had clubbed One-Eye with her stick and threatened to do the same to me!

'Why not, Maid? In the name of all that's holy, it was my damned idea to bring her here! I was the man who pushed out the other noisome woman!'

I felt the blood drain from my face. Had I heard that right? Bedingfield had killed the woman who was here before Lady Margery?

'Mistress Sands? You had to remove her. She was too deeply engaged in manipulating people here. And you know full well that she was concealing correspondence from Lady Elizabeth. Lady Elizabeth is a clever woman, and she knew how to get what she wanted at all times. You know that.'

So he had! They wanted to remove an impediment to their spying on the Queen's sister.

'I am glad she left the place,' he continued, and I sagged with relief to hear that he had not ordered her death. It's one thing to know that Lady Margery's killer remained at large,

without thinking that this apparently harmless old fool was also
a murderer.

'Good!' the woman said.

I could hear him tutting. He continued, 'I've heard she is
living in France now.'

'They are welcome to her.'

I mused over that. This woman Sands had been loyal to the
Princess, so she was evicted in favour of Lady Margery, who
would be more compliant about spying.

'Lady Elizabeth has me twisted so tightly about her little
finger, it's a miracle my backbone is unbroken,' Bedingfield
said.

It was intriguing listening to him. He sounded full of
remorse, and deeply affected by the death of Lady Margery.
Perhaps he was a decent enough fellow. The woman, on the
other hand, was composed of sterner stuff.

'You must be firm with her. Do not submit to any more
embarrassments. Lady Elizabeth is a strong woman, and she
will use any laxity in the regime here as a sign of weakness.
The fact that she has somehow managed to effect the murder
of this poor woman is a proof of her deviousness and danger.'

'What of the man who did this?'

My ears pricked.

'We don't know who it was,' she said.

I felt a thrill of relief. I had thought someone could have
accused me.

She continued, 'There was one poor fool in here – the First
Finder – but he didn't have the intellect to harm her, nor anyone
else. I did question him, but he barely had the brain to understand my meaning.'

I thrilled with a very different emotion.

'Who, then, could be responsible for this?'

'I would think someone who has recently arrived at the
palace and who is already engaged with Lady Elizabeth.
The man I spoke with arrived here earlier with the messenger
for the Lady. The messenger's name is Blount, I think. I would
have him watched to prevent him from escaping.'

'What now?'

'You have done all you should. You have locked the gates,

you have ordered all those within the walls to remain here, and you have sent for the Coroner and a strong force to help keep the palace secure.'

'Secure!' The man gave a hollow laugh. He sounded utterly defeated. 'How can we be secure when forces gather outside all the while? There will be an assault on the palace before long. With no possible means of locking the doors, how can we prevent their intrusion?'

'Please do not be so defeatist. You sound like a man who has seen the conquering army on the hilltops all about. There is no one here yet – only a few wandering brigands who are held back by our walls. When the Coroner arrives with the Sheriff's force, we shall be better able to guard the buildings – and *her*!'

I was thinking about this, when I heard footsteps approaching from inside the room. Stepping quickly to the other side of the buttress, I waited. Bedingfield and the woman came out and hesitated in the sudden bright sunshine, then walked off towards the kitchens, Bedingfield bemoaning his troubles and difficulties, while the woman at his side patted his arm and spoke soothingly.

It occurred to me that I should see whether I could learn more from them, and perhaps I should pursue them and try to overhear their conversation, but discretion prevailed. Even as I was considering how best to follow them, the giant appeared – the one like Friar Tuck. He ambled along behind the two, his head down, hands hooked in his belt once more, oblivious to others in the court, I thought. Just then he turned and stared back in my direction.

There was no accusation in his eyes, but I was transfixed by that look. It was like a priest at the altar bellowing about fire and brimstone, and pointing at me, saying, 'Yes! I mean you!' It happened to me once, and I could feel the rest of the congregation shuffling away from me. This time, there was no one else watching. I turned away from him, but as I walked away, I could feel his eyes boring into my back like a pair of awls.

I was to be stuck there for some days, and I suppose this is as good a time as any to describe Woodstock, because so many have said it was thus or not thus: that it was a richly decorated, lovely palace or a crumbling hovel Queen Mary wouldn't have used for her pigs.

Neither was entirely true. The house did have many failings: only four doors held locks or bolts, so many guards were needed to prevent rascals from entering at will; the slates of the roofs were old, and in the winter many had slipped, so one of the first sights to confront me when I entered the chamber where my master was to be installed was a bucket where drops from leaks were collected. The wind seemed to howl in about the house, because even when the doors were closed, the leads in the windows were so ill-maintained that glass was perpetually falling and smashing.

Yet, for all that, it was a strong building.

Blount had told me it was first built as a hunting lodge. That was in the day of Henry I. He had a wall set about it, too, of some seven miles in circumference, in which he could hold his collection of lions and leopards. Well, not much of the original wall survived by the time I reached the place, but there were still plenty of vicious animals stalking the grounds. These walked on two legs rather than four.

I'll never forget my first view of the palace as we rode along the single road from Woodstock itself.

It became visible glimpsed only dimly, a pale ochre viewed between trees, no more than a yellowish haze at first that served to define the woods. But then, as you approached the oaks and chestnuts, you began to make out details.

First to be seen were the chimneys. Initially they looked like tall tree stumps, as if a small wood on a hill had been cut across by a giant's scythe. Then the hill resolved itself into a series of roofs, some tiled, some with grey wood shingles, that rose haphazardly; over generations, different blocks had been added as they were needed, much like a miniature town, and now the roofs sprawled like those in London or York.

Finally, when you passed through the enclosing woods and could see the building, you were struck by the gatehouse.

It was a sturdy, square block with castellations and four small windows that gave a good view of the road, but for an attacker it was a daunting sight: strong, imposing, threatening.

Walking under this, the visitor entered the outer court. On the left were the stables, while ahead was the hall – a great block as large as a church, with a stone arcade dividing it along the centre so that was left as two aisles. Beyond this hall, on the left, was the chapel – a large chamber with the ability to see to the souls of all the household. To the right stood the kitchens, standing a short way from the hall with an alley between them to serve as a guard against fire, while storehouses of all kinds were set into the encircling wall. This outer court was at least two hundred yards square, and at all hours of the day it was full of wagons and carts, merchants haggling and arguing, and men-at-arms walking about with faces like stuffed frogs as they tried to ignore the rude local populace and pretend that they had serious work to perform.

Of course, most of them didn't.

Behind the hall there was a second, smaller courtyard, of perhaps only one hundred square yards, and beyond that lay more buildings. Each served some purpose, but during my time there I spent little time investigating. Like most guests, my time was spent in the hall and larger courtyard. We weren't welcomed in the rest of the palace.

In our section, the walls stank of mould and damp, but they were yet solid. It was more sound than the house where my father raised me – and smelled more wholesome than the odour of recently tanned leathers. Even so, Woodstock had what to me felt like a malignant atmosphere. It was the sort of place where a man would walk along a dark corridor and hear . . . *things*. Steps behind you that stopped when you stopped. Candles and rushlights would gutter and flare and puff into glowing cinders in an instant for no apparent reason, and the air felt as cold as the charity at a prison's gate.

The surroundings were interesting. I come from Whitstable, but had lived in London from the moment I could leave my home, and the sight of the town of Woodstock did not impress. It was a poor collection of peasants' houses, three or four better homes where merchants and burgesses lived, the Bull, where I had expected to be housed, and which had a good series of chambers for travellers, and the other essential – a church. The priest there had adopted the new English religion with alacrity, and now had converted back to the Roman faith with equal speed, so I heard. He kept his head when many others were losing theirs. Literally.

Connecting the royal palace and the inn was a single road. It led, pretty straight, across marshland on a causeway, and I had been told that leaving the causeway was suicidal. A traveller attempting that would soon be up to his belly in the mire. Not that there was any need to leave the road. A man on it would have an easy walk along the valley there.

The chambers set aside for the young Princess Elizabeth were over the gate itself. She had four good rooms, all hung with her own tapestries or painted, and all her permitted belongings were with her. Thus she had a warm lodging, cosy in the winter, with good views and many comforts. However, for all that, this place was to be her prison for a twelvemonth. And no number of delightful distractions can compensate for a young person's loss of freedom, especially when the young person is a princess.

At the gates, my fair-haired friend of earlier had managed to clamber to his feet and was again berating the gatekeeper, although somewhat more politely and cautiously, a hand to his head. Seeing a groom engaged in the time-honoured English task of leaning on a dung fork, watching and enjoying the show, I crossed to him.

'Who is that?'

'Him? What of him?'

'What's he in such a hurry about?'

'He's Squire George of Carlisle. Don't you know him?' the groom sneered. He wanted to show that he moved in better circles than me. He probably did.

'But why's he in such a hurry?'

The man glanced back at the young fellow. 'Who knows? He's young and rich and doesn't want to be caged up here with the likes of some of the others around here.' At this point he eyed me from scuffed boot to unkempt hair. 'No doubt he has his reasons.'

I was tempted to make a cutting comment, but the fellow did have a useful weapon in his hands and I had no desire to be accused of brawling in a royal palace. 'What sort of reason could he have?'

'It's said he was carrying on with the woman who died.'

'What?'

He sneered at my innocence. 'The squire's young; she was rich and beautiful. It's hardly surprising.'

That was interesting. I wondered whether the squire could have been so keen on leaving because he had killed the woman. Or, perhaps, if he was having an affair with her, he feared reprisals. Perhaps he had a rival in love, and that was why she was killed?

And perhaps pigs could sprout wings and fly at will. It was none of my affair.

'It's shocking to hear that she's been killed, even if she did have an affair.'

'Her husband wasn't happy.'

'How do you know?'

He sneered and shook his head as if in disbelief at my stupidity. 'Because Kitty, the chambermaid, heard them arguing two days ago.'

'What were they saying?'

He shrugged. 'He wanted her to obey him, demanded something or other. Probably that she stopped throwing herself at any man who was available.'

'Kitty heard all this?'

'Something like it. They were shouting so half the palace could hear them. He often bullied her and beat her. That time, Kitty saw him strike her, and she fell. He reached for her, and Kitty thought he was going to punch her, but he just shook his fist in her face and stalked off.'

'Hardly a marriage of love, then,' I said. They were rare enough, surely, but it was sad to hear that a man regularly beat his wife. Even marriages of convenience, with money or power shared between two families, did not commonly result in physical battles. They formed their own households and went their own ways.

I was about to walk away when I had another thought. 'Have you been out here all morning?'

'There's a lot of shit in the stables.'

'Were you here when the woman was killed?'

'What if I was?'

'The door over there, past the hall, leads to the room where she was killed. Did you see the squire around there after the murder?'

He considered. 'Just before the hue and cry there were a few fellows out hereabouts. The man in the chamber up there,' he said, nodding towards John Blount's room, 'and I saw the squire, and Sir Walter Throcklehampton, too.'

The woman's husband, I guessed. It was interesting to know that there were at least two men who could be viewed as suspects, and amusing to hear that one of them was my own master, a man who had wanted me to kill her for him. Then my earlier thought returned to me: if this Sir Walter got wind of his wife's adultery, that might lead him to punish her and seek compensation from her lover.

I left the groom leaning on his pronged staff and made my way to the hall, aware of an unpleasant feeling in the pit of my belly. At first I was not sure what the cause was, but soon I understood. It was this place: it was steeped in misery and deceit, and all those who stayed here grew infected with it.

As soon as I could, I would leave this melancholy manor, I decided, glancing again at the gates.

I would look longingly at those blasted gates many more times before I could finally escape.

At the time of the evening meal, I saw Blount and his companions making their way to the hall. I followed them.

'I have heard that two others were seen in the court when Lady Margery died,' I said.

We were in the corner of the great hall. Servants had been busy. Earlier, when I was flirting with Sal, Kitty and Meg, it had been empty, with the trestle tables stored behind tapestries on the north wall. These had been brought out and erected in three rows along the hall, and cloths set on them. Dishes were brought in now, and plain bread trenchers placed before each diner. I was looking forward to this, for I had a keen appetite. On the dais sat Sir Henry Bedingfield, gloomily getting outside a large jug of wine – his second since the meal had begun.

He did not look happy. At his side was an empty chair, and every so often he cast an eye at it as if remonstrating with a ghost. At his other side was another space. One, I assumed, was for the Lady Elizabeth in case she deigned to join us; the other, I thought, was for Lady Margery Throcklehampton, although it seemed curious to leave her place set out. She was dead, after all, and wasn't likely to return to the meal now.

'What of it?' Blount said. His voice was low and he didn't look at me as he spoke, but kept his attention on the other people in the hall. 'They are not your concern. For now, you need only concentrate on your story and make sure that your confederates do, too. Women can be unreliable on occasion. I still wish you had listened to me when I said that you needed to make the death quiet. Still, I suppose sometimes victims will throw plans off course. Did she fight back? No, don't tell me. I don't need to know. The less I know, the easier it will be to deny all knowledge later.'

'But I—'

'Enough. I shall speak with you later. We'll all be locked in here until the Coroner arrives, in any case.' He nodded to me, wearing that insufferable look on his features that said he felt he had done a good job in picking me. It made me bitter.

A servant brought a large bowl for our mess and set it on the table between us. Blount took the flesh hook and served himself first, and then the other two did the same before I was allowed my share. I sat back grumpily while Will helped himself, hoping that there might be something left for me when he was done. At least Blount's fair-haired servant was less greedy. He took a small portion and passed the bowl to me. There was little left but the gravy. I poured it into my plate and took a hunk of bread.

Just then I saw a familiar face and pointed. 'That woman there! Who is she?'

Blount looked over his shoulder. My friend the club-wielder had entered and now she passed down the middle of the hall as elegant and regal as a swan on the water. 'She's too good for you. Keep your tarse in your cods, man!' he said.

'No! I mean it! Who is she?'

'She is Lady Anne. Daughter of the castellan, Sir Henry

Bedingfield. So keep your hands and prick away from her, unless you want them all cut off. Sir Henry has more than enough on his mind already, without some London sex-fiend attempting his daughter's virginity.'

He leaned down to his food, his expression returning to its customary grimace of disgust, and I sank back on my bench and stared at this Lady Anne. She glanced at me briefly, and it was as if I was invisible. Her gaze swept past me and on to Blount and the others, but her nose was high to keep the smell of commoners like us from her nostrils, and she continued to her father, sitting sedately at his side in the empty chair. He made no comment, but gave her a short nod as she took the seat I had assumed was for Lady Margery.

I had no idea why she had decided to help me, but I was glad she had. The one-eyed man was convinced that I was in a conspiracy to injure Lady Elizabeth, and if I'd been taken by the guards he called, things might not have gone so well. It was fortunate that I had the words of three maids to support me, because else I would find myself in difficulties, and since all were to be kept under house arrest until the Coroner arrived, I could not escape.

However, although I knew I was safe from accusations of murder, there was the other aspect of Lady Margery's death that was giving me pause for thought: if *I* had not killed her, then the man who had done so was still here, inside the palace. The squire had been nearby, as had Blount.

Blount. He had commanded me to kill the woman. If he had killed her himself, he might think he could pass the blame for her murder on to me.

I did not like that consideration.

I spent much of that evening in deep reflection. I saw the squire at another table, but he did not appear to be in the mood for a conversation from the way he ignored those about him. He looked bleakly all around, and I wondered if this was the sad demeanour of a man who has lost his lover. I chose to leave him to his ruminations. Certainly, from the looks he cast about him, an opportunity to box a man about the head would have been welcome to him. I desired to give him no reason to select me as his personal punchbag.

Rather than risk his ire, I sought out a quieter place, and finally found myself in a small chamber that was little more than a recess in the wall, not far from the buttery. A curtain was drawn back, and I could sit behind it and drink the palace's strong ale without being disturbed. A large candle in the passageway threw out a strong light, leaving my spot in shadow, and I leaned back on a moderately comfortable low barrel with my back resting against the wall, assured that I was concealed.

I was content. The other people did not appeal to me. I wanted solitude and ale. The palace had grown uncongenial. I did not enjoy seeing attractive women stabbed to death, especially when I had already myself been instructed to slay them. Nor did I like having one-eyed men thrusting daggers at my throat. It was still sore where he had broken the skin. I found myself wondering whether Blount had told anyone else that he wanted this Lady Margery dead, and indeed whether he had told anyone else that he had his own hired assassin. It was a thought that made my scalp crawl. At any moment someone could come to the same conclusion as One-Eye, and this time with more justification.

There was, somewhere in this palace, a man who had wanted this woman dead, I reasoned. Blount had explained *his* reasons, but I wondered now how Blount could be so certain of the fact that Lady Margery was spying. If he was right, then anyone who was keen to support the Lady Elizabeth, or who disliked or mistrusted the Queen, would have a good reason to want Lady Margery removed. That meant Lady Elizabeth, one of the two other ladies-in-waiting, or one of her three manservants. They were almost certainly devoted to her, since she had insisted on bringing these fellows with her, so it was likely that they would obey her commands, no matter how ill-framed. I was reminded of the old King who had demanded that someone might rid him of his troublesome priest, and three knights went and murdered Becket thinking he was ordering them. Fools! A king doesn't behave in so plain a manner. He is more likely to insinuate slyly that a certain fellow has earned his displeasure, and wait for his chamberlain to discover proof of treachery so that all the legal niceties can be followed. Much easier to have an executioner use his axe by the order of the courts than send a trio of dull-witted men to hack a priest to death at his own altar.

But my problem was clear. If anyone should come to the conclusion that I might have had a motive to slay Lady Margery, my life would not be worth the purse at my hip – and that was depressingly light.

Oh, for the happy days of my poverty in London! All I cared for then was the opportunity to meet with a decent cony and foist him. There were times I had made a good return by dipping into strangers' purses. Of course, I would often get little (like the time I won a purse of wooden tokens worth less than a dog's turd), but the life was at least free and easy. A man could breathe the fresh London air and hurry to the nearest alehouse or brothel and live well for an evening.

Here, however, I was trapped. No one could leave the palace until the Coroner had arrived and listened to the evidence so it could be recorded.

I wondered again about Blount. He had, by his own admission, been in the court when the murder happened. Perhaps he had been in the room, slew the lady, and decided to leave me to be accused. I knew Blount. He was ruthless enough. A player of chess will oftentimes sacrifice a pawn in order to achieve a better position on the board. I could not convince myself that Blount could even look at me as anything more than a pawn waiting to be discarded.

There were steps in the passage, and I listened with half an ear. I was feeling lonely and slightly maudlin drunk. I didn't wish for company. The steps went into the buttery, and then I heard soft footfalls approaching my cell. The curtain was moved, but I remained where I was, wishing the man to go away. I think that the candle must have blinded him, for although I watched his feet, I soon heard him speaking in a low voice.

'There's no one here, Sir.'

'Good.'

The two stepped into the buttery, I thought, and I could

scarce hear them. Not that I was interested. I was still thinking about Lady Margery.

One-Eye had been close by. He got there miraculously quickly, now that I thought about it. Perhaps he had killed her, was scared away by the noise but could not escape far, and when I hurtled in, he sprang out from the doorway and held me up? He certainly appeared from the doorway that led inside the palace. According to the groom, Squire George and Blount had been in the yard. Either could have committed the crime and darted outside, to all appearance merely aimlessly wandering.

No, I didn't think it was likely, but just now I was seeking any explanation. And then I heard a snippet of the conversation from the buttery and nearly fell from my perch.

'Close your mouth and keep it shut, or you'll have it permanently silenced! Or do you want to go the way of the bawdy-basket?'

You can be sure that I concentrated hard, even after several strong ales, on hearing that. To describe the dead woman as a pedlar and whore when she was still warm spoke of someone who had a serious dislike of her.

'You can threaten me all you like, but I know: I saw you out there.'

I recognized that voice. Last time I saw him, he was shouting for help to hold me, just before Lady Anne Bedingfield ended his excitement for the day. It was my friend One-Eye.

The other voice was silky smooth and very calm. It sounded like a razor being stropped to hair-halving perfection. 'I don't threaten, Matthew. I make statements of fact. If you speak to anyone of seeing me just before Lady Margery died, I will cut out your liver and make you eat it.'

I wanted to learn who this new man was, and was about to peer past the curtain when he said this, and I swear the tone of his voice would have frozen the fires of hell. All at once my desire to see his face retreated.

'Don't threaten me!' One-Eye said, but there was a lack of conviction in his voice.

'I'm not threatening anyone. But if you say you saw someone

leaving a room, what will that benefit you? Whereas if you find her little seal, I will pay you richly. It's more likely to work to your advantage.'

'Yes . . . well, I looked soon as I could. She didn't have it, I swear. Not about her neck. No necklace, nothing.'

'Her necklace was gone? Then the man you found in there – this "Blackjack". He was at her body, you said?'

'Him? He's just a fool from London. A useless wastrel with fewer wits than a beaten cur. He squeaked like a pig when I caught him.'

I bridled on hearing that. It has been said that a man should never listen at doors in case he learns something of how others view him, but to hear One-Eye speaking so disparagingly of me, shortly after hearing the same from Lady Anne and Sir Henry, was enough to make me grind my teeth.

'He must be the man responsible,' Razor-Voice said. 'Follow him. Learn all you can of him and tell me. Perhaps he stole it. If he did . . . Hush!'

There was a scraping of a door, and steps approached.

If this was a man's voice rather than his feet, he would be slurring like a peasant after the harvest feast. He sounded as though he had been drowned in a barrel of brandy. The feet dragged and slid, and I heard a crunch, as of a man stumbling into a table and knocking it against the panels. There was a loud giggle, then a snort, and the man belched.

'Oh! 'Scuse me, friends! Just need a . . . need a refill of my pot. Lemme push pasht . . . past you, sir.'

'We were just leaving.'

'Z'right. Good, good evening, then . . . Jusht . . . just need a quick . . . Think I need . . . You know.'

The two pairs of feet rapidly disappeared along the passageway, and I stood and peered after them. It was easy to recognize One-Eye, but the other man with the dangerous voice was not someone I knew. I watched as they reached the door to the hall. There, the second man turned and glanced back, and I recognized the sallow features of the man who liked to prod young squires in the chest. I hoped his finger was still painful.

The two passed through the doorway. As they did so, I

saw a man lean through the buttery's doorway. A man clad all in black.

I didn't need to see his face to know this was my master. Quietly, so he wouldn't hear me, I drew back into my little chamber and sat down.

What was Master Blount doing in here? Plainly, he was spying on those two because there was one thing quite certain to me: he was no more drunk than a nun at her initiation. But also, what was it they were looking for? A seal, Razor-Voice had said, and mentioned a necklace too, although that was of less interest. What sort of seal, and why was it worth killing the woman for it? It must be worth a lot of money, surely.

Then the ice formed in my bowels again. It was a familiar, horrible sensation. Razor-Voice had told the man to watch me, and then there was a significant '*if*' about whether I'd taken it. I didn't like that 'if'. It sounded as if there would be consequences, were they to suspect me.

I really, really wanted to get away from this cold, damp palace.

DAY TWO

The Coroner, Sir Richard of Cowley, was a tall, rangy man with a cold, haughty manner. His mouth was pursed and twisted in permanent pain, as if he had just spent a long journey on horseback with only a bad collection of piles to keep him company. His face was greying like his hair, and he wore a permanent scowl as though blaming the world for his being summoned to this Godforsaken spot. For all that he had a paunch like a cardinal, he rode with a straight enough back – no slouching there.

No matter what he personally looked like, when he arrived, bellowing for assistance at the gate, he brought with him a small cavalcade of men. While the Coroner sat on his beast, his eyes searching about him with permanent suspicion, the others bustled. There were clerks, servants, guards and some men-at-arms who were to remain at the palace for the better protection, so it was said, of the Lady Elizabeth.

'Come on, you flat-footed, flat-arsed apple-squires! Get your belongings from the carts and form up!'

This was all from a short, barrel-chested sergeant who strode about like a game-cock, organizing his troops. They were a mixed bag. One was as tall as me with a boy on my shoulders, but most were short, clumsy-looking peasant types. Some were young, but most, I saw, were older and experienced.

Their sergeant marched along their front, eyeing his men without pleasure. 'We've been called here because a lady has been cruelly murdered. She was in Lady Elizabeth's retinue, and the man who did it is likely not to be bothered about hurting others too. So we're here to protect people. The man stabbed her, and the gates were shut immediately, so the killer remains on the premises. That means he's still a threat to Lady Elizabeth. Your job is to make sure that the Lady Elizabeth is safe, no matter what. You understand me?'

'Yes, Sergeant!' the men chorused. They sounded bored.

The sergeant dismissed them and stood shaking his head. Seeing me, he pulled a twisted grin. 'What can you do with stock like that, eh?'

'They'll do their duty, I'm sure,' I said.

'As long as they aren't too wasted with ale. I'll have to speak with the bottler and make sure they get no more than their ration,' he muttered, and hurried off to the hall.

It made me wonder, watching the men as they milled about. Lady Elizabeth did not have many people with her. According to Blount, she was allowed three ladies and three manservants for all her needs, and with the death of Lady Margery, that number had reduced to only two ladies-in-waiting. Not ideal for a lady of such power, but Queen Mary had at least allocated all these men to help guard her. Or were they only to ensure that Lady Elizabeth did not escape?

The Coroner and his men dismounted at the gate, and I saw him turn and look up at the gatehouse where Lady Elizabeth was held. He stood staring for a long time before making his way across the court to the main hall, his clerks and guards hurrying along behind him while the servants began breaking into the wagons and carts of essentials.

I had nothing to occupy me, so I remained there, idling my time away as the porter and his men went to the gates to bar them. They were swinging the ancient timbers shut when a shout came, and a final cart entered, a smiling, scruffy tranter kneeling on the board. He waved a hand happily at the porter and doffed his cap.

The porter smiled back, but asked this last carter to go and set his goods with all the rest before busying himself with the bars and bolts.

To my surprise, the carter took his pony behind the other beasts of the Coroner's party and carried on. He caught my eye and smiled broadly, and a horrible feeling of having been there before struck me like a wet frog in the face.

It was Dick Atwood.

I am well aware that men like Atwood do not appear for no reason. He is like one of those mares that come to a man in his dreams, bringing lunacy and mayhem in their wake. I last saw Atwood as the rebellion was collapsing, and while all the others involved were captured or surrendered themselves to their fate, this one man managed somehow to avoid the gallows that he so richly deserved.

If I was a little more innocent, it is likely Atwood would have killed me earlier in the year. Luckily, I am not as innocent as my face seems and I lived to tell the tale.

However, seeing him there was as pleasant as sitting in a bath tub and finding the last occupant left behind a turd. I stirred myself and hurried after him as he clattered his way over the mud and cobbles towards the kitchens, before I was fully alive to the dangers of my position. He was already down from the cart and pulling a heavy canvas from the back of the wagon when I caught up with him.

'What are you doing here?' I demanded.

'Don't be alarmed, my friend!' he said, holding up both hands in a sign of peace. 'What do you think I'm here for? After the rebellion was quashed, there was nothing for me in London, was there? I had to escape and find a new life. So, here I am!'

'I don't believe you! You're a soldier of fortune – anyone's fortune, if you can snatch it,' I declared hotly. I was in no good mood with this fellow, as you can tell.

He looked hurt. 'That is a vile calumny, Jack. I've always been a friend to you.'

I was so astonished by the untruth of his words that I could not speak for a moment, and he continued unabashed. 'You see before you a poor victim of circumstance, Jack. I have been reduced to this: the job of a simple carter. It is the only occupation left to me.'

'You're lucky to be alive, man! You were a traitor to the Queen and would have seen Wyatt's rebels oust her from the throne, wouldn't you?'

He smiled amiably. 'You wouldn't want to talk about that, now, would you, Jack? After all, if we were to begin to discuss our positions, your own would interest people strangely, wouldn't it?'

I did not want to pursue that. During the rebellion, you see, I had been unfortunate enough to acquire a message that had been destined for others. The Queen would have liked to get hold of it, as would the Princess Elizabeth. It was intended for the rebels, and I was told that it assured them of support from someone well-born. Atwood knew all about the message, and looking into his eyes now, I saw that the affable light was being drenched by sharp calculation.

'You tell people of that, and I won't be the only man arrested,' I blurted. Even to my own ears, I sounded like a petulant infant.

Atwood stepped closer to me. I retreated. He wore a smile on his face, but that didn't fool me. I knew him. Violence was always to be preferred in his world. 'Do you mean to threaten me?' he said.

'I was only trying to explain that—'

'Because if you try to threaten me, just remember that I have a long memory, and a lot of friends who would take pleasure in pulling apart a man who helped thwart the rebellion.'

He drew back, and this time his smile looked almost genuine. He clapped me across the back and nodded to me, like an uncle who's just given sweetmeats to a cherished nephew.

'So we both have an interest in keeping our mouths closed, don't we, Jack?' he said, and then, certain of my compliance, he turned back to the cart and began to unload it.

I stood behind him, thinking that if I were a real assassin, I would strike now. If I were as bold and courageous as Blount thought, I would pull out my knife swiftly and stab him there, in the middle of the left side of his torso, a couple of inches from his spine. He would be dead before he hit the ground.

One stab and at least some of my problems would be over. Unless he realized and got his blow in first. And he was quick. I knew that.

I left him to it.

Atwood made a poor situation worse. I repaired to the buttery and had a scruffy knave draw me a quart of the strong ale. He was reluctant, muttering that it was early in the day for the strongest ales to be served, but I ignored him. I had need of it.

I carried my leather pot outside and took my ease on an old bench.

Why was I here? This was no place for me. I grumpily sank my first half blackjack and stared at the leatherwork glumly. I should be back at home, in Whitstable, with my father, the miserable old pizzle. He wanted me to follow him into the trade, becoming his apprentice so that I could take on the business and become a leatherworker like him. But as a young lad, that was the last thing I wanted. Any man who has lived with the odour of leathers tanned in dogshit and piss will understand why I was reluctant. No, he wasn't a tanner, but the leather arrived with the stink of the tannery. I hated it.

After that, he had advised me to join an army, but that was little better to my way of thinking. The idea of standing in a rank of men while other men shot at me or tried to dissect me alive was less than enticing. So I left him and home, and went to London to try my luck. There, I thought, I would soon make myself a fortune. Instead, I found myself lured into ever more dubious activities, until my swiftness at taking purses and dipping into their contents brought me to this present pass.

It was not fair.

I saw a woman walk past. She caught sight of me at the same time and a broad smile spread over her features. It was Sal, one of the maids with whom I had been talking, impressing them with my knowledge of London and fashion, while Lady Margery died one door away. I patted the bench beside me, but she lifted an eyebrow and indicated that she had been sent on a duty. She disappeared through a door near the kitchens, and I settled back to grimly enumerate the many injustices I had suffered, including this latest rejection, but before I could set her among the many disappointments in my life, she was back. She took my ale from me and drank deeply, wiping her hand over her mouth.

'You want a cup of your own?' I asked.

'No, I'm happy to share yours,' she said. There was a cheeky gleam in her eye. She was a comely little wench, with big hips, big bosom and trim little waist. Her hair was mostly confined in a linen coif, but the strands that had strayed were a delightful auburn that went with her pale hazel eyes perfectly.

'Last time I saw you was when the lady was murdered,' I said.

'And then the one-eyed fool accused you of killing her,' she said with a giggle. 'You didn't need to hit him, though. Not that hard. You nearly knocked his brains out through his ears, so I heard.'

I shrugged. 'You think he has brains to lose?' There was no need to mention Lady Anne at that point. Especially since Sal seemed to think that my courage in besting One-Eye was admirable. 'He was a dolt.'

'Yes,' she said. 'He always tries to pinch our backsides when we go past him. Last time I had to kick his shin hard to stop him.'

'Has he been here long?'

'No. He's only come since the Lady Elizabeth arrived.'

'Really? I assumed he was a long-standing member of the household.'

'Nah! He got here only two weeks before Lady Throcklehampton.'

I feigned disinterest. 'No one seems to know much about her.'

'There are many could tell a tale about her,' she said.

'What sort of tale?'

'Well, her husband is here now, but before he arrived, she was friendly with many of the servants. She has had to cool her ardour since he got here.'

I pretended to be shocked. 'You don't mean that she was waggling her buttocks at other men? Who?'

She told me of a number of men about whom suspicions had circled, but refused to give any details. It was interesting that I had heard the same about her with the squire, but I didn't see that it would aid me in finding the way to Sal's bedchamber.

'Did you see her with any of these other men?' I asked, leading the conversation back towards that subject. I was being subtle, you see.

'No.'

'Oh.' I leaned a little closer to her. 'I've heard that doors on the women's chambers are very strong. They have to be barred because of the attractiveness of the servants.'

'Some of us have no locks at all,' she said, wide-eyed. 'It

makes us feel very fearful at night. I need to have a strong man to protect me.'

'I would be honoured to serve you,' I said, and grinned.

'Stop leering! You look like my father when he eyed the wench at the alehouse,' she said, punching my arm. She must have been as strong as an ox. That blow hurt like a buffet from a hammer. I tried to rub it surreptitiously as she continued, 'Or more, you look like Sir Walter when he eyes us maids.'

'How could a man not admire such beauty?' I said, my hand on my thigh.

'He doesn't *admire* us; he just takes what he wants,' she said, standing quickly before my hand strayed far, sadly. 'He's one of those knights who thinks that any woman is his by right. If he tried that with me, he'd regret it!'

'Tried what?'

She looked at me, then said, 'A week ago he tried to get Meg into his bed. His wife was with Lady Elizabeth and he wanted a woman to warm his bed, he said. He offered her a penny or two. Well, she told him where he could shove his pennies, and he tried to hit her. She's fast, luckily, but he tried to catch her, and she thought he'd rape her for sure. He's not a nice man.'

She had given me something to think about. A man who was desperate and wanted to pick a maid from the palace's staff was not rare, but it was odd, I thought, when his wife was so near. Why didn't he demand his conjugal rights from her if he was after some? From what I had seen and heard, Lady Margery was not a quiet, meek woman. She had been flirting with other men – perhaps he was scared of her? If he was, he would be wary of trying his wandering hands with Meg or the other girls in case he was discovered. More likely he thought that his wife would refuse him. I don't know many of the rich or famous, but they do have some strange ideas. Could it be that while she was in the service of the Princess, Lady Margery was not supposed to lie even with her own husband? That did not match the story I had heard of her flirting with other men either, though.

No, I thought that it more likely that he was a forceful man who had his wife terrified. That would explain why she sought affection elsewhere, and why he dared to seek out servants who would see to his natural desires.

Another thought came to me: the groom had said that Sir Walter Throcklehampton had been outside the chamber when his wife was murdered. If he was a bullying, cruel husband, he might have decided that he had endured his wife's company long enough. Or he had demanded that she should let him into her bedchamber, she had refused, and he had killed her from some misguided passion.

Why would a man behave like that? I could not comprehend such behaviour. I know that some men of money and wealth will occasionally act in such ways, but it was hard to believe. I would try to consider him and learn what kind of man he was. If he was the kind of man to commit murder, I wanted to know for my own protection.

There were calls. A loud bellow told everyone that those who had any information should go immediately and attend the Coroner's inquest. I finished my ale and made my way to the hall.

The hall was filled to bursting. The entire household was there to attend the inquest.

There were a lot of grand people. From the left, I saw a number of maids and servants, who really had no place there, but I suppose the wenches might as well witness the inquest since there would be little work achieved that day. Sal was there, and Meg too. Meg was a chubby, sweet, small bawd, with honey-gold hair and a mouth that was full and prone to smiling. She looked the sort who would enjoy a horizontal grapple, I thought. It was hardly surprising Sir Walter would have tried his luck with her.

In front of them was the jury, a select group of men and boys, while a short distance from them sat a woman on a chair of her own, with two women at her side and two men behind her. Guards stood only a pace or two away, and there was a watchfulness about them that snagged my interest. I realized that this must be the Lady Elizabeth, the woman who had kindled the fires of rebellion, according to some.

She was a trim little thing, with a pale complexion and fine, good features. Not like her sister, who even then had become dumpy. No, Lady Elizabeth had the sort of looks that would make you cross a street to have a closer inspection. You'll have seen pictures of her, I have little doubt, but they don't do her justice. The fact is, she impressed me most favourably. She was slim, high-breasted, with hair that gleamed, her face regular and even. Even here, with so many men who were determined to keep her prisoner, she was serene. In fact, she appeared relaxed almost to the point of being languid. Certainly, her attitude could have been described as intensely bored with proceedings. Her face was turned upwards towards the ceiling, and I could easily imagine that she was counting the stones under the limewash.

My eyes were drawn away from her, towards the shape on the ground. Someone had brought Lady Margery Throcklehampton in on a trestle and left her on the floor under a sheet like discarded trash. She made a sad sight there, like a wilted rose. I never liked the sight of death, but to see a woman in her prime, like Lady Margery, murdered before her time, was very sad.

Others were still filing into the room. I saw Blount, standing almost behind a pillar at the back of the room, watching and listening, no doubt, while keeping his face concealed. Then others marched in, a child of eight or nine with them. This latest was snivelling and boo-hooing like a banker who sees his profits fail – he was making so loud a racket it almost broke my pate, and I wanted to tan his hide for him. This boy was holding on to the hand of the sallow-faced man who had been talking to One-Eye in the buttery. He glanced at the wrapped body briefly now, but soon looked up again and caught my eye. He looked away with a curl of his lip as though I didn't merit his attention.

More serious-faced men came in. One in particular piqued my interest: he was dressed in expensive clothes, overdoing the velvet, I thought. It was a little too flamboyant for London, and I sneered to see how he had mingled the fashions of the last three or four years. He had no idea. Looking at him, I got the strong impression that he was a yokel who had heard of the way people dressed at court, but who had not been to see it for many years. Then he looked up and I realized it was Bedingfield. He must have dressed in his best for the inquest; he really was an embarrassment. As he passed Lady Elizabeth, he bowed, but the lady scorned to recognize his respects, and then he stood with a scowl like a youth rejected by his leman.

And then I saw her again. It was the woman who had knocked down One-Eye, saving me from his knife: Lady Anne Bedingfield, daughter of the custodian of this place. She saw me, too, but she barely acknowledged me, instead raising an eyebrow and looking at me in the way she would have glanced at a turd on the rushes. I felt cowed. Worse, I felt challenged: humiliated and bested in that one glance.

I looked away, back towards Blount, and as I did so, I saw the giant once again. He stood a yard or two behind Blount, and was watching my master and me with great interest. Catching my eye, his mouth drew into a broad grin, and I was relieved by an interruption. The Friar, as I was coming to think of him, had a most unsettling grin.

But interruption there came.

With a sudden flurry of sound, the grim-faced Coroner appeared in the doorway. He stood there a moment, his eyes ranging over the jury, the crowds, and then the Lady Elizabeth. She refused to acknowledge him either, beyond a vague tilt of the head as if nodding.

The room fell silent, and some people began to shuffle their feet uncomfortably, everyone aware of the tension between these two, but then the Coroner stepped forward and into the chamber, crossing the floor to a large table on the dais. He peered down at the body as he passed it. Clerks and guards followed in his wake like cygnets trailing after a swan, their feet padding quietly across the rushes.

'Everyone here?' the Coroner demanded of Bedingfield.

'Yes, Sir Richard.'

The Coroner stood before Bedingfield's chair on the dais, and then nodded to the people in the room, cast a look at the jury, and finally allowed his eyes to rest on Princess Elizabeth.

'We shall begin, then.'

*   *   *

The Coroner peered down. 'This is the body?'

On hearing the confirmation, the Coroner began to instruct his clerk, opening his inquest with a loud bellow to all in the room to be silent, glaring at any who continued to mutter.

'We are here today to hold inquest into the death of this woman here,' he said, indicating the shrouded figure. He pointed at two servants. 'You two! Bare her face.'

The men obeyed. One was the groom who had been conspicuously contemptuous of me while he was so busily occupied leaning on his fork. He stepped forward with considerably less enthusiasm than the other, and the two pulled the wrapping from Lady Margery's face.

'Who can recognize this woman?'

'I can,' Sir Henry said, and so did Sallow-Features, who quietly stated that he was her husband.

She was still clothed, and the Coroner commanded that she be stripped naked. The men started to unbutton Lady Margery's gown, but when the groom reached for the kirtle, a pair of matrons bustled forward at Lady Elizabeth's peremptory command. Before the groom could attempt to continue, he was pushed away. The two ladies tenderly removed her clothing until she was entirely naked.

She was a well-built woman, I thought. Past her prime, perhaps, and with the marks of stretching at her belly where she had once carried a child, but it was her throat that everyone was staring at. The blood had pumped thickly, and she was stained all over her breast with blood.

At a signal from the Coroner, a bucket of water was brought and the two women washed away the worst of it.

'Jury, I want you to notice that the woman has not been molested. This was no rape. See? No bruising or bleeding about her groin. There is but one wound: the great slash about her throat.'

The wailing from the child grew louder.

'Will someone remove that squalling brat?' the Coroner demanded testily. The boy was taken by my friend Meg, and the sound of his despair gradually faded.

I could see the wound clearly. Whoever did this was not

planning on making a mistake. The knife had entered below Lady Margery's left ear and swept across to the right. With a vicious wound like that, she must have been dead before she hit the flags. This was clearly a deadly injury. No others had been inflicted; there was no need.

I was standing on tiptoe to peer as the Coroner climbed to his feet and grunted, bending to pick up the discarded dress. He held up the cloth to show that there were no stabs in the material, and no holes in the body other than that of her throat. Blood had stained the fabric. 'See here? The dress confirms the injury. There are no tears or cuts in the fabric. This one wound was enough to kill her. Did anyone see her or hear anything about the time she died? Was there a struggle, screaming, shouting or any other disturbance?'

There was a hush. No man there wanted to admit to being in the vicinity of the murder.

After a moment's silence, Sir Henry Bedingfield stepped forward. With his beard and bushy eyebrows, he reminded me of a small, wire-haired dog backed into a corner: anxious, irascible, and apt to snap.

'She was supposed to be with the Princess, but for some reason she was not in the chamber,' he growled, turning a ferocious stare upon the Princess.

'I asked who *did* see her, not who *should have* seen her,' the Coroner said testily.

'She was not at her duties,' Bedingfield said grumpily.

'Are you not responsible for all the staff of the palace? Yet you do not know where she was?'

Bedingfield's mouth worked like a man chewing his inner lip. 'I cannot have my eyes everywhere at all hours,' he said.

'So you are of no help to this inquest.'

Bedingfield retreated, shaking his head. 'This is too much for my Norfolk understanding.'

'Who found the body?' the Coroner said.

I found myself looking about the chamber, before realizing that people were staring at me. I reluctantly ducked my head, holding up my hand. 'I think it was me, Sir.'

'Think? *Think?* Consider again before you assert that. Was it you or not?'

'I did find the body, yes. If someone else found her before me, he didn't declare himself First Finder.'

'What is your name?'

'Jack Blackjack, Sir Richard,' I said with as much humility as I could manage.

'Is that your real name?' he said, peering doubtfully. 'Step forward so the jury can see you, then! Explain how you found this body. And speak up!'

I did as I was bid, moving into the space near the body and telling how I'd been at the end of the hall – I pointed – with three maids from the household, when we heard a strange noise, and how I went through to investigate. I didn't have any idea of murder at the time, but thought a hound had stolen a bone from a plate on a table, or some similar nefarious escapade. Instead, I took a tumble over the corpse on the floor at the side of the staircase.

'That means nothing!' a voice shouted. 'He could have seen her, stabbed her, and left her there. Why did he run so sharply when I found him?'

I turned a baleful glare in the direction of that voice. It was my uncouth comrade One-Eye.

'Who speaks there?' the Coroner demanded.

'Me! I am Matthew Huff, the warrener, Sir Richard.'

'You will stand there in silence, Matthew Huff the Warrener,' the Coroner said. 'If you do not, you will soon be Matthew Huff the Pilloried Man. Do you understand me?' Then, to me, 'You, fellow, continue.'

'I was seeing whether she was still breathing, when that man Huff ran in, made some accusation about me killing her, and called the guard.'

'He had an accomplice there, and I was knocked down!' Huff declared excitedly.

'I warned you already of the stocks, I think?' the Coroner said with poisonous politeness. He nodded to me to carry on.

When I shot a look at her, I saw that Lady Anne had blanched. There were two spots of red at her cheeks, and she stared at me rather like a child waiting for the first blow of the strap. I looked at the Coroner again. 'Sir Richard, Huff was foolish enough to turn his head from me. I hit him and he fell. I saw no reason to wait there since he had called up the guards already, especially since he had jumped to the ridiculous conclusion that I had something to do with the lady's murder, and I thought I could be assaulted. I left the room. I was already sure that the poor lady was dead. There was nothing to be done for her, I fear.'

'You should not have fled the scene. Did you not realize that it could lead to you being suspected?'

'I did. But I was more anxious that the Lady Elizabeth could be in danger,' I said. I looked at her. 'If her guards came running because of Huff's foolish cries, she could be left alone. I went to ensure that she was safe. After all, there was a murderer stalking the corridors of the palace.'

'You went to her?' the Coroner asked and looked at her.

The Lady Elizabeth's eyes were on me as I spoke. 'I went to her door. I didn't think to knock and alarm her, but stood outside the door in case of danger. Then, as things calmed, I made myself known to Sir Henry. He heard from Sal and Kitty that I was with them when the poor woman was slain.'

On Sir Henry's corroboration, my statement was accepted and written down by the clerk, and I was dismissed. When I glanced around, Lady Anne was smiling at me, still pale, but with a little more colour in her face. Huff glared with all the ferocity a one-eyed man could manage. Behind him, I saw my master and the Bear. The Bear was grinning fit to burst, from the look of him. When I looked, I saw my Friar Tuck standing some distance behind them still, a pensive look creasing his brow.

I realized that no matter what I had said before, John Blount and his Bear thought still that I was guilty. Perhaps that was good. They would be sure to keep me in my house and paid if they considered me so dangerous and competent.

On the other hand, there was someone else in the palace who had actually committed the murder. However, although I was unhappy with the thought of some fool wandering the place with a knife, I was reassured by the thought that the killer had achieved his aim. He wouldn't be keen to kill anyone else. One murder was easy to perform, but the more deaths he brought about, the more likely it was that someone would notice him and bring about his capture.

I was wrong to be so complacent.

While I was congratulating myself on escaping further comment, Sir Richard moved on to speak to others.

'When did she leave the Princess?' the Coroner asked, and stared at Lady Elizabeth. 'She was supposed to be a lady-in-waiting; I presume she did perform some useful duty there?'

There was a significant pause, and then Lady Elizabeth lifted a hand and beckoned. One of her manservants stepped forward and bent to her. She spoke quietly to him.

He nodded and looked up. 'My Lady says that the woman was not needed and was sent out to aid her master, Sir Henry Bedingfield.'

Bedingfield made snarling noises, looking like a chained, enraged terrier confronted with a suave cat just beyond reach. It was some moments before he could speak coherently. 'What? Pah! Lady Margery had duties to perform, on my soul! She was supposed to be with *you*!'

'I had no need of her.'

'What you want is—'

'You mean she was to be with me at all times?' Lady Elizabeth said sharply. 'You mean she was to be imposed on me, whether I wished her or no?'

'She had duties, ma'am.'

'I am sure she did. Perhaps those included informing you of all my private conversations, Sir Henry. But I am the daughter of a King. I have no desire to see all my confidences breached with your intelligencer.'

'That is not the point at issue!'

'Really? You say that I am to pay for servants I do not require or desire? You prevent me from the proper management of my estates and leave my peasants uncertain as to their future, and now you demand that I pay for a useless mouth for no purpose other than to allow you to spy on me, while refusing me the benefit of my own counsellor.'

'You have no need of others. *She* was there to serve you.'

'And I have said that I had no wish for her service. I will pay for you and your men, but I will not pay for an intimate spy.'

'So you had her killed?'

Lady Elizabeth turned slowly, her gaze passing over all the jury and witnesses in the room before it came to rest on Bedingfield. I could feel the strength of her indomitable spirit in that look. Some say that eyes see by sending out rays. If so, her spirit was in those two orbs. When they alighted on me for a moment, it felt as though they could ignite wood. I imagined her peering out over a forest, and wherever her eyes touched, the trees ignited as if touched by Greek fire. There was a fierce rage in her voice when she spoke. 'You accuse me? You dare to suggest that I caused her death? For what possible reason?'

'To stop her informing me about—'

'You admit she was a spy sent by you to keep a close eye on me? Is that the case, Sir Henry? I am desolate to think that a gentleman could think of such an act. You would set a *spy* on the Queen's own sister?'

'I would do my duty by you and your sister!'

'Would you set a spy to watch your own Queen? How fascinating. I shall be sure to mention that to her.'

Sir Henry was reduced to near apoplexy, his face the colour of a beetroot, making inarticulate noises deep in his beard. The Coroner gruffly cleared his throat, glancing towards the man with a raised eyebrow, but when it grew clear that Sir Henry was so angry that he was incapable of speech, the Coroner turned his attention back to the body, instructing the women to roll the corpse over and over before the witnesses.

I was still staring at the body. To my eye, there was a line about the corner of her neck, where the shoulder met the side beneath the ear, as though a man had drawn a mark in charcoal across it. It was only visible now because she had been washed so carefully. It was not obvious, but I was sure that there was a bruise's darkening. 'What's that on her neck?' I wondered and, without intending, I spoke just as the room was in silence.

There was a moment's pause. If I had farted, the Coroner could not have glared at me with more virulence. I felt my belly curl in fear. Lady Anne stared at me with all the joy of a hawk spotting a mouse; so too did other ladies and men in the chamber. For my part, I felt like the mouse.

'A bruise! She had something about her neck. Right there!'

There are times when I surprise myself. This was one. I was nearer than most, for the simple reason that when I tried to return to the large group of witnesses, no one gave way to let me past, so I was left before them and nearer the body than others.

One of the matrons stepped forward and rubbed at the mark with a fresh cloth. The line remained, quite stark against her pale flesh now it was clean. When she wore her gown, it was not visible because the low collar was enough to conceal it, but now she was naked, there was an injury apparent. The two women leaned down, and even the Coroner peered closer.

'It is a very slender mark,' one of the ladies said.

'A rope or ligature?' the Coroner asked.

'I think not. A thong, perhaps? Or a thin chain,' the woman said. 'A necklace.'

'Did it kill her?' the Coroner said.

'Nay. I think it was a simple necklace chain, and her murderer pulled it from her to steal it.'

'I see,' the Coroner said. He glanced at his clerk. 'Note that. She wore a necklace, and it was stolen. It must have been valuable, I presume?'

Lady Elizabeth spoke up again at this. 'I never saw her with anything more than a fine silver necklace chain. But it broke.' She looked to her ladies-in-waiting, and both concurred, but there was something in Lady Elizabeth's expression that caught my attention. Anger? Confusion? Sly deceit? Controlled glee? I couldn't make it out.

Sir Henry held out his hands in blank incomprehension. 'I never noticed. Why would I notice a woman's finery?'

'Her husband – where is he?' the Coroner demanded.

One voice broke through the hubbub. It was the sallow-faced man with the boy who had declared himself her husband. The same fellow who had risked a broken finger. 'It was a chain, Sir Richard. A plain, unadorned chain of silver, but she was proud of it because it was an excellent example of the smith's art. It was very fine, which is why it broke. After that she had another, silver again, with a crucifix.'

His finger appeared to have recovered from where the younger fellow had bent it. He left his place and took a pace forward.

'Your name?'

'I am Sir Walter Throcklehampton, Lady Margery's widower.'

I looked at him with interest. He had a grim, grumpy look about him, which should not have been surprising, but I had heard him the night before in the buttery. I know quite a few men who could be upset to lose their wives, but in his case it did not ring true.

The Coroner glanced sideways at his clerk's notes. 'Was it strong enough to hurt her? Could it have been used to strangle her?'

'No. Neither was expensive.'

'This second with a crucifix. Where is it now?'

'I don't know. Perhaps it was taken? But it was not of any great value.'

The Coroner frowned and nodded. 'Then it's of little importance. If it was too unimportant to be worth stealing, and did not kill her, it is of no relevance.'

There was more discussion of the murder and questioning of the three maids who had been with me to corroborate my story, then two servants were interrogated because they had discovered the body of One-Eye slumped next to that of Lady Margery. Finally, there was a short summing up, and the jury declared that they had no comments to add.

The Coroner stood then. 'I find that this woman, Lady Margery Throcklehampton, was murdered. She died because of a deliberate act by a man or men who cut her throat with a fine-bladed knife or dagger. The slash opened the veins and her blood was drained. I estimate that the blade was some seven to eight inches long, and must have been worth at least six shillings.'

'Six shillings!' I heard a man gasp. It would have made the knife one of the most expensive money could buy.

The jury quickly set to talking among themselves. One man, reluctantly accepting the position of foreman, put up his hand submissively.

'What?'

'Sir, the blade could have been only a cheap dagger. We think it would be worth only a quarter of that.'

'I set *deodand* at six shillings for the dagger,' the Coroner concluded, glaring about the room as if expecting dissent, 'and because the necklace was probably used to restrain the woman for a period, I will add another five shillings to the *deodand*.'

Nobody met his gaze, but from the angry muttering about the hall, it was plain enough that the people were not happy to hear that the Coroner had valued the weapon so highly, nor that he had added the cost of the necklace. It was the people here who would be paying the fine.

The Coroner stood, glaring about him, and motioned to his clerk. They both walked from the chamber, haughtily ignoring all the others about them as they passed out through the main doors.

I shook my head. The Coroner would be well advised to leave the palace urgently after testing the people here so harshly. I turned and would have followed the two from the room, but then I was restrained.

A hand grabbed my shoulder, and One-Eye rasped, 'That's the bastard! Take hold of his arm; don't let him flee again!'

Instantly, my other arm was also grabbed, and there was a rattle of old armour as a pair of castle guards took me by the elbows. They turned me around. I found myself confronted by One-Eye.

'Thought you'd escaped, did ye?' he spat. 'I haven't forgotten the bruise on my pate you gave me, you bastard!'

It was then that I saw his fist hurtling towards my face.

Now, I have been the recipient of a number of blows in my time. You could say that I have a connoisseur's interest in them. I can recall with a wince the buffet I received when I was laid out in a tavern's yard, and the occasion when I was struck by a bawd's pimp, as well as the time I was attacked in the street by a bailiff with a grudge, but none was quite as unpleasant as this. I could tell what was about to happen; I could see his fist approaching, but everything seemed to happen so *slowly*. He moved with the speed of a tadpole swimming through mud; I could see the vicious glee in his eye, and I knew it would hurt when that hand met my face, but with both arms gripped I was incapable of moving from his blow's path. Instead, I stood with the appalled confusion of a nun watching her first orgy, until there was a truly sickening crunch, and his fist smashed into my nose. I reeled, and then my legs went as soggy as a minute-old foal's, my knees knocked together, and I collapsed.

The last thing I remember was seeing Blount, his fist gripping a lead-filled leather cosh, clobbering the one-eyed man over the skull, and feeling genuine satisfaction as the fellow's good eye rolled up for the second time in as many days. But then the floor's paving seemed to open up and swallow me into a black pit that went on for ever and ever, and I knew no more.

The last time I woke from a blow like that, I was optimistic that life would improve. This time, I was unpleasantly certain that the same was too much to wish for. I could feel flags and rushes under my back, and I could hear the murmur of a lot of voices, and I was happy to remain there with my eyes closed and hope that people would leave me alone. With luck, they might decide to spend their time emulating Master Blount and attack the one-eyed bastard a little more. He deserved a good kicking, I reckoned.

If the Coroner and others were convinced that I had been severely injured, perhaps they would give me a decent bed and bring a physician. It was something to aspire to, certainly. For now, just in case of further harm coming to me, I kept my eyes shut and listened.

There were raised voices. It was two of my merry maids from the hall, Kitty and Meg. These two, God bless them both, were loudly decrying One-Eye and declaring that I could not have been the murderer. It was enough to make me breathe more easily. I had just decided that I could open my eyes with safety when I felt a hand on my brow.

It was soft, smooth, cool and delightful. I decided to remain there a little longer. Then I was pinched very hard on the flesh just above my elbow, and I stifled a curse and jerked upright, almost striking Lady Anne in the face. She stared down at me with her serious brown eyes, and if she had not just started to snigger, I'm a Yorkshireman.

I rubbed my upper arm, chewing over a few choice comments as I did so, but the sight of the chamber brought me to my senses.

One-Eye was sitting on a stool, his back to a pillar, holding a damp cloth to the side of his head. From the bucket at his side, I think he had been sick a few times already, and the sight gave a flutter of delight to my heart. What was less attractive was the sight of Blount a couple of yards away. He had a gash over his eye that was bleeding steadily. He stared at me grimly. My two maids were volubly declaring my innocence, while a sergeant held up his hands to stem the flow of invective and try to bring some order to the noise. When I looked about, I saw that Lady Elizabeth's seat was empty. She must have left the chamber as soon as the fighting broke out. She was the fortunate one. I wished I'd been quicker.

My head was swimming. You know how, when you glance over a fire in summertime, and the view at the other side moves and dances like a picture seen in roiling oil? That was how my vision was. I felt as sick as a youth after too much brandy, and I was unpleasantly aware that as soon as I was to lie down, the room would begin to swirl and dance about me. To counter this, I opened my eyes wide, trying to force the scene to steady itself.

'Are you well, Master Blackjack?' Lady Anne asked, and I'm still convinced that there was more than a touch of amusement in her tone.

'I think . . . I'm going to be sick,' I said.

Suddenly, I was alone. The crowds about me parted like the seas before the Israelites fleeing Egypt on hearing I might puke. I sniffed, and my bruised nose made me wince. It was enough to make me forget to throw up at that moment. Sparks and flares flashed before my eyes, and I thought I must collapse again. It lasted only a few moments while my head tried to explode, but then it was over. I had one brief moment of relative calm before the nausea returned, and I felt I might have to go to One-Eye's bucket. The idea of moving was even less appealing than the idea of what lay inside the bucket already. Those two thoughts were enough to persuade me to swallow down the bile and remain where I was, unmoving.

'How are you?' Lady Anne said again.

It was a good question. I did not think that any bones were broken, other than my nose, but then I glanced down and I was silent with horror. My new jack was covered in my blood. It would take an age to have that cleaned. My best London jack, the finest I had owned – ruined!

I would have risen to go and punch him, but the first movement made my nose feel as though it was about to be torn from its moorings. 'He's broken my nose!' I said. 'Will someone fetch me an ale? And put that cocksure little one-eyed snake in gaol for attacking me in the middle of a royal inquest!'

'That will not be necessary,' I heard the sergeant say. 'Although the Coroner may decide to make an example of the dull-witted pizzle and put him in the stocks for a day or two.'

That was a much more pleasant thought. Once he was safely in the stocks, I could lob a rock at him and see how he enjoyed being the target of *my* attentions.

A hand took me by the neck and helped me to a sitting position. Another friendly person thrust a large pot of ale into my hand, and I sank a good portion gratefully. It made me feel a little better almost immediately.

'What happened to *him*?' I said, indicating Blount.

'He knocked down the gaoler, so two men knocked *him* down,' Lady Anne said. 'The sergeant has ordered him held until my father decides what to do with him.'

'But your father cannot hold him. He's my master. He has urgent business with Princess Elizabeth.'

'Lady Elizabeth will have to make do with your aid while my father considers Master Blount's case.'

'All he did was defend me, his servant,' I protested.

The sergeant glanced in my direction. It was the same man who had arrived with the Coroner. 'He viciously attacked a man in the hall here, right before Lady Elizabeth. Using weapons before a lady like her means he will likely be punished. He should have left things to my men, rather than taking the law into his own hands.'

'I'd likely be still worse injured if he had! Why don't you arrest that little cock over there?' I said, pointing at One-Eye. 'Do you want to join him? Then hold your tongue! Otherwise, you will quickly learn how accommodating the cells are here!'

After that, the room was soon emptied, my master being led away by the sergeant and two of his men. One-Eye was prodded and poked by the steward, who used his staff of office with some pleasure, I thought, until the git shuffled to his feet and lurched from the door, carrying his bucket still. I was glad to hear a sudden retching just after he left the hall, and hoped he was bringing his guts up again.

The steward seemed to think about using the same tactics on me, but a look from Lady Anne was enough to end that idea. When Lady Anne demanded a refill of my pot, he sent a servant to find the bottler, and soon I was sitting on a stool and nursing a fresh ale. Lady Anne was at my side, and I was glad of her presence. My head was pounding unpleasantly once more.

Soon afterwards, Lady Anne was called away, and I was left alone. I finished my pot of ale, and as I set it beside me, I heard a noise. Looking up, I saw that the squire was peering around the door.

To my astonishment, the squire crossed to me, and now he caught me by the arm. 'Come with me!' he hissed, and I found myself being propelled from the room. Outside, I was hauled across the yard to a snug little chamber where the squire had a table and chair. It was a small room set into the palace's wall, and I could feel the cold as soon as I was thrust inside. He slammed the door behind him, standing with his back to it.

'What are you doing? What's this about?' I demanded as he wiped at his brow.

He glared at me. It was the sort of look that would wither a rose in a second. 'Sit down!'

I retreated until I encountered a stool. My head was still spinning, although the urge to vomit had passed. I sat.

'Well?' I said.

He gave me a very old-fashioned look. 'I am not an experienced man, but I can see when you are making eyes at a woman like Lady Anne, and when she is looking on you favourably, too.'

'Me?' I stared back at him with some astonishment. The idea that she might have felt anything for me other than annoyance had not crossed my mind.

He curled his lip. 'I'm not blind. She is a powerful woman, and you should beware if you trifle with her.'

'I wouldn't dream of it,' I snapped. My nose was so sore, and it felt like an inflated pig's bladder – it could have been used by Woodstock for their annual football match with the neighbouring villages.

'So you say! You should be wary.'

'I know. She's a violent woman.'

He picked up a rake, and his fists twisted at it as though he was seeking to break the shaft, or perhaps he was merely dreaming about twisting my throat. 'She is a lady, and her father is a good man.'

'What of it?' I said. 'There is nothing between us. Nothing whatever.'

'How does she know you? Have you tried to force yourself on her?'

'*Her?*' A memory of her face after using One-Eye's head as a drum sprang into my mind. The idea of forcing myself on her was so remote that for a second or two I could only mouth wordlessly.

'Well?'

'The woman petrifies me!'

'In bed or out?' he sneered.

'I wouldn't dare find out!'

His brows lowered and he shot a look at me. 'In truth? Then why does she look on you with such favour?'

'*Favour?*'

He glowered in a distinctly menacing way. I did not want to be beaten again. Instead, I decided that Lady Anne's secret was not mine to keep . . . so I could share it. I gabbled quickly, 'She rescued me from that gaoler with one eye, but that's all. That's why he dislikes me so much. He was knocked down by her when he was trying to hold me.'

'He has cause to dislike you even more now. And that man Blount – he's your master?'

'Yes. I saw him strike One-Eye as I fell. But then he was bested. How did that happen?' I asked.

He grinned. 'When the one-eyed shite knocked you down, Blount thought it was better to protect you, but the Coroner's men were not keen to see a brawl. They clubbed him and bore him to the ground. I had to pull one of them from your master, and stopped another from beating you as you lay.'

I supposed I should be grateful, and muttered my thanks.

'I have a duty to protect the weak against injustice,' he said. He seemed to come to a decision, and walked from the door, resting his backside on the table, eyeing me with apparent distaste. 'And the weak-minded.'

I didn't like that, but he stood between me and the door. 'Is that why Sir Walter poked you in the breast?'

A frown chased the smile away. 'That fool? He was demanding to know whether I had lain with his wife.'

'Did you?'

'I had no interest in her.'

'So, tell me,' I said.

'Tell you what?'

'What is your interest in this? Lady Anne is not a lady you aspire to, is she?'

He wiped a hand over his face and gazed at me. Suddenly, all his belligerence left him.

'Not her, no,' he said.

There are some fellows who can put on a show of bravado, some who can don a cloak of deceit with enormous ease; others find deception and mendacity do not come easily to them. For those, attempting to dissemble is always a challenge, and it is easy to tell when they lie.

The squire's head dropped a little. He looked at me from the corner of his eye with a melancholy air, like a hound whose disobedience has been noticed.

'Not Lady Anne, no. I could not aspire to her,' he said.

'I see.'

He shot me a glance. 'What do you see?'

'I have heard rumours . . .'

'Well?'

'That you were carrying on an affair with Lady Margery.'

His mouth gaped. '*Me*?'

'You weren't?'

'I liked her well enough, but an affair? With her? No!'

It was, of course, what he *would* say if he had killed the woman. 'Who do you think would have killed her?'

'I have no idea.'

'Why are you so worried about Lady Anne and me?' I asked. He looked away with every appearance of guilt. 'Her maid, Alys.'

'I don't know her.'

'She is a marvellous woman – so calm, so shrewd, so determined. I adore her.'

'I haven't seen her.'

'No. She's not here,' he said, and then the banks burst and the words came in a torrent. 'She and I are wed, but we cannot tell anyone yet. She did not have her mistress's permission to marry. We feared that Lady Anne would be mightily angered if she were to learn, so we tried to wait until there was a suitable moment, but that moment never seemed to come. And now Alys is hidden away . . .'

'Why?' I asked as the fellow trailed away in his narrative. I was confused, for he said nothing for some while, and I gazed at him. His attention appeared to be taken up with the fascinating pattern of straw on the floor. 'I said, why is she . . . Oh!'

The proof of the maid's behaviour, of course, would become highly visible in one manner. I could have kicked myself, I confess. The lad wiped at his face again, and would not meet my eye. Instead, he gazed over at the wall near my shoulder.

'We didn't think she would . . . when she missed her monthly . . . we didn't realize that it meant . . . and now the child is on the way, and I ought to be with her, but I'm stuck in here instead, and . . .'

'Where is she?'

'I cannot say.'

'Squire, you are married to her! Do you not think you can ask for time to go and ensure that she is well? Any woman would surely understand that she has need of your company at this moment. Lady Anne would certainly understand. Your wife needs you.'

'If I go, Lady Anne will know that we misled her.'

'If you *don't* go, your wife will think you don't love her!'

'What if Lady Anne decides my wife cannot return to her?'

I shrugged. 'Well? What of it? If she does, you must find your family a home, somewhere you can see them safely installed and where you can visit as often as you may.'

'Alys would be sad to lose her position. She loves her mistress.'

'Then she should have asked permission to marry sooner, rather than going behind her mistress's back.'

He nodded glumly.

'Anyway, why were you so keen on what I may be planning? The lady is not your mistress, after all.'

'I just thought that if you were intending something with Lady Anne, then I could earn her favour, let her know I knew her secret, keep her confidence. She might take Alys back with less reluctance, were she to realize that we could be of service to her.'

'You may be of more service if you help determine who it was who cut the throat of Lady Margery,' I said.

'You think so?'

I had been speaking without thinking, but now I considered my own impetuous comment and slowly nodded my head. 'As matters stand, Lady Anne's father is in a sore position. He must serve his Queen by holding the Princess prisoner, and he was to install Lady Margery in order to have a spy ready to warn, should the Princess conspire with others to the harm of the Queen. Not that she would, I am sure,' I added hastily. A man could never be sure who was listening to a conversation, even in a small room like this, and I didn't want to be denounced. 'However, it was a sensible precaution for Sir Henry to take. Now that his intelligencer has been killed, there will be many questions asked about his suitability for his role, and whether he was as assiduous as he should have been in finding the murderer.'

'As to that, surely he will uncover the man responsible.'

'Perhaps. But once the manor is open once more, and the Coroner leaves with his men, who can say what will happen? Why was the woman killed? Was it a planned murder? Was it to win someone else's favour, or the act of a madman?'

The squire looked up and I saw that I had hit the mark. 'To win someone's favour?'

'Who do you think could have killed her?'

'I don't know.'

'Where were you when she was killed?'

'I was in the palace's inner court. I had seen the seneschal and Lady Anne, and wanted to stay near the lady.'

'And?'

'There is not much more to say. They were talking, so I left them to their discussions. Then, when they walked off, I walked after them. Lady Anne turned into the building, and Sir Henry stood for a while. After some time he strode off towards the hall himself. I trailed behind him.'

'But you were alone?'

'Do you mean to accuse *me*?'

'No, Squire, but it would be easier if someone saw you. Was there anybody else at the inner court whom you saw who could have been involved?'

'No, I was at the passageway, but I saw Lady Anne come along the passage and out through the door to the chamber where Lady Margery was killed.'

'Was there anyone else?'

He shrugged. 'A large man, built like a cardinal,' he said, and I thought of my Friar Tuck. 'There was a slimmer fellow, too,' he said, and described Atwood to perfection.

'There was one other man out there,' the squire said slowly. He shot me a look.

'Who?'

'Your master, the fellow Blount. He was out there too.'

I laughed at first, but not heartily.

The idea that John Blount would have tried to kill the woman when he had already ordered me to do so was clearly so ridiculous that I almost pointed out the foolishness of the idea.

I was about to say, 'Why would he hire me and bring me

here to kill her if he was going to take the first opportunity to do it himself?' Luckily I only got as far as 'Why would . . .' I felt the air turn to acid in my throat, and the effort of changing my speech made the words catch. My response was choked off and soon turned into a prolonged coughing fit as I realized that I was about to confess to being Blount's paid, professional assassin. That was no way to enhance my position here.

However, the thought remained: Blount had been in the yard and the idea that he could have killed the lady and set me up came back to me. If a man wished to commit murder and escape punishment, it would be easy to blame another, especially if the gull had been set up to appear to be the ideal suspect. I had been brought here to kill Lady Margery, and she had died. Blount had been in the yard at about that time, according to the groom. Perhaps Blount had found her and decided to cut her throat while she was alone, thinking that any blame would attach solely to the obvious felon: me.

No. He had spent much time and money in recruiting me. Blount would not throw away that investment. Surely not. Not unless he had good reason, such as being accused of the murder himself. I had known many felons in my time and never yet had I found a man who would not willingly pass the blame on to an innocent, if it meant avoiding the rope himself.

'I think it hardly likely,' I managed at last without conviction. I wiped tears from my eyes and took a deep breath in an attempt to calm myself. It was not easy.

'I know. You find it difficult to think that your master could be guilty of such a crime,' the man said, oblivious to the real reason for my inner turmoil. 'Who else was there, however? You yourself were in the next room with three witnesses, so you were secure. The man with one eye was behind the chamber, so he said. If anyone had rushed out, they must have pushed past him; the only other exit was the door to the yard. I would have seen a man running out there. No one did.'

'You didn't see my master slip inside, though, did you?'

'Well, no . . . but that means little. How long would it take for him to slip inside while I was not watching, kill the woman and return to the yard? A matter of moments only.'

Later, as I left him behind in the room and walked out into the courtyard, where I stood staring at the door with blank incomprehension, I had to admit that he had a point. No one had come into the hall where I stood happily chaffing with the three maids. I would myself have seen anyone trying to escape that way. The killer could only have come past me, into the courtyard, or into the passage by the third door. Unless, of course, he had climbed the stairs. That was surely the route he must have taken, I thought.

Except I had my doubts. Perhaps Blount had seen the woman go into the little chamber, and sought to take advantage of what appeared to be a heaven-sent opportunity? As Squire George said, he could easily have gone in there, cut her throat, and then returned out to the yard. What would it have taken? Moments only, and he could have ambled in his unconcerned way over to the trough and washed his hands of any blood that had sprayed on him. With his fastidious approach to fashion, wearing only black, any excess blood would be all but invisible. And no one else had displayed any signs of blood, I thought. Surely a woman having her throat cut like that would smother anyone nearby in gore? I had seen men have their heads cut off during the rebellion earlier in the year, and all had erupted with great gouts of blood. I felt nauseous again, but I knew I was right. The stains over the floor and walls in the chamber were proof of the effusion of blood.

I swallowed. Perhaps Blount fancied taking on the task himself. He might not have trusted me. Or it was a spur-of-the-moment decision: he saw an opportunity and instantly took it. It was logical enough. However, I was left with a distinctly unpleasant thought: what if he had always intended to do this? Could he have come here with his carefully selected black clothing, intending to kill the woman, and only brought me along as a scapegoat in case things went badly wrong and he was forced to discard me?

Much as I respected Master Blount, I would not mistake my respect for him as in any way implying a reciprocal sense of loyalty. Although I had never given him cause to distrust me, the man was not beyond throwing me to the wolves, if he felt it necessary. He was one of those dangerous fellows who had beliefs. Personally I've always distrusted such folk as a matter of principle. Give me a man who has beliefs in one political character, or who believes in how he can make more bearable the lot of other people, and I will show you a man who has no scruples and will be prepared to kill in order to make another's life 'better'. Personally, I'm happy with my lot and would be much happier to be left alone to enjoy it.

Blount was not formed from the same base mould. Rather, he would be prepared to see me slain in order to help his ambitions for the Princess and the Kingdom.

Outside, I saw two guards. One seemed familiar, and I thought it could be one of the two who led Blount away after the fracas at the inquest. I walked to him and enquired as to where I might find my master, and was directed along the courtyard to a small doorway set into a wall.

I went inside to the buttery and filled a costrel with ale, then went to the door to the gaol. There I tapped, and was soon rewarded by the appearance of a stooped, wizened old tatterdemalion with greying hair and the look of a man who had spent so many years drinking ale that the colour had seeped into his bones. His face was pale brown, and his eyes seemed bulbous, as though, were he to sneeze, they might both shoot from their fixings. A drip dangled precariously from the very tip of his nose. It remained there all the time I spoke with him, wobbling and dancing, but never quite disentangling itself.

'The prisoner? Yes, he's here.'

'Can I speak to him?'

'The prisoner? No. He's to be held quiet.'

'He's my master. I wish to speak with him to—'

'The prisoner? No, he's got to be kept . . .'

'Two pennies?'

Suddenly, his hesitation was cured. My coins were snatched away as fast as an adder striking, and in a few moments I was standing at the door to the cell while the turnkey slowly pulled it wide.

I peered in, recoiling at the smell of foulness that came out. It stuck in my throat. Inside was a cold, dingy, malodorous chamber. As my eyes grew accustomed to the dark, I saw thick moss, heard the steady dripping of water, saw little glimmers reflected from the large stone blocks of the walls.

Then, in the farther side of the cell, I saw him.

Master Blount didn't look well.

My master had been badly beaten. He looked up blearily like a waking owl, but he was pleased to accept the ale when I held it out. As he did so, there was a rattle and clank from chains at his ankles that restricted his movement. He drank thirstily and muttered his gratitude. If he had planned to kill the woman and then knock me on the head to keep me quiet, there was no evidence of shame or embarrassment. Rather, as soon as the ale's level had reduced, he began to berate me for not bringing him comestibles.

'I've not had time to find you anything. I came as soon as I learned where you were being held,' I said.

'You had time to visit the buttery,' he said. 'What would it have taken for you to find a small loaf of bread and a sausage or two? I'm not here revelling in the comforts of a full trencher of meat and gravy, you know!'

'No, but—'

'And I'm only here because I tried to save you a hiding,' he snarled.

He was right there, and he had taken a good thrashing in my place, from the look of him. There was a cut over his right eye, and his hair was matted and thickened with blood from another injury. The fact that his knuckles were well bruised and scarred seemed to show that he had not taken the assaults on him meekly. Someone else was feeling battered after trying to hurt Master Blount.

'Are you still safe?' he asked.

'Yes, I'm fine,' I said.

'Good. You need to get me out of here, though, in case someone tries to put the blame for this murder on you.'

'How can they? I have witnesses.'

'Witnesses can be coerced, bribed or otherwise enticed to change their story. Your three maids depend for their livelihoods on the palace. It would take little to make them feel so threatened that they decided to throw in their lot with, say, Sir

Henry. After all, you managed it somehow, and one of them may be bright enough to realize the fact. Bedingfield may not intend or wish to bring about an injustice, but if he heard that you were employed as an assassin, he would surely respond.'

'Oh, Christ's wounds!' That was enough to make a cold fist of steel grip my bowels. I had not thought of that before. 'What should I do?' I demanded.

'First, stop bleating like a demented ewe! You need to speak with Bedingfield and persuade him that I am innocent.'

'There was one man saw you in the yard when the hue and cry was raised.'

'Excellent! Then go and let Bedingfield know.'

'The man thinks you could have killed Lady Margery,' I said.

He gazed at me without speaking for a few moments. It made the atmosphere in the room rather tense. 'If you hear others expressing a similar view, you may just have to use your knife on them too,' he said.

I said nothing to that. There was little I could say. Pointing out that I was not only terrified of the idea of being caught, but also that I was not used to killing people, seemed insensitive just now when he was depending on me as the key to his escape.

'I can't go round executing anyone who exhibits a sensible caution or suspicion,' I said.

'You can do all you can to get me out of here,' he growled. 'I don't want to be left here to rot for the night. I expect you to secure my release.'

'I will do my best,' I said, with as much haughtiness as I could muster.

Leaving him there, the chains clanking as he shuffled back to the wall with the costrel, I made my way out to the fresh air again. I felt a pang of sympathy for him. Yes, I know he had no particular liking for me, and that he would in all likelihood be willing to slit my throat for me, were he to learn that I was not the crazed murderer that he thought he had hired. Still, although out here there was an all-enveloping odour of horse muck, pig muck and all the other normal country smells, yet was it vastly preferable to the scent of fear, pain and death that I detected in that little cell. I didn't want to have to spend more than a few minutes in there, let alone an evening.

The thought of that was enough to make me shudder like a man with the ague. I determined there and then to do all I could to liberate him from the cell.

Bedingfield was sitting in his seat in the hall when I entered, the Coroner and his clerk beside him, and he looked up as I marched inside.

He didn't look happy.

Bedingfield was not made for great events. He was not the sort of character who would seek to be thrown into matters of national importance. Rather, he looked like the kind of fellow who would be happier rising early and setting off with his hounds in search of a deer, returning for a hearty meal, and then settling with friends to roister and celebrate life by pouring wine down his chest and quite missing his mouth. He had the complexion of a man who had spent many hours in the saddle for pleasure, rather than from necessity, but now he was pale and fretful, unlike the Coroner.

This was a very different character. His face was still fixed into that scowl of disapproval. Whether it was his piles or some other malady, I could not tell, but it certainly soured his nature. Whereas Bedingfield looked like a man restrained against his will, forced to sit indoors when he knew full well that outside there was a world of pleasure to be had from hunting and hawking, like a boy who must stay indoors with his tutor when the sun was shining and the world appeared fresh and new, the Coroner looked like a man who would avoid wandering outside in case his hosen were splashed with mud. He looked more at home indoors.

'Ah, our First Finder is back, eh?' the Coroner said, leaning back from the table with a quizzical expression on his face.

'Master Bedingfield, I was wondering whether I could speak with you?'

'Feel free to speak, Master . . .' the Coroner leaned over to his clerk and peered down at a scroll. 'Oh, Master Blackjack, is it? Aye. Speak out, then!'

'I was hoping,' I began, but then saw there was no point in

beating about the bush. Apart from anything else, it was highly unlikely that Bedingfield could give any response without referring to the Coroner. 'That is to say, I wanted to ask that my master, John Blount, be released from his cell. He only became involved in the fight because he saw me, his servant, being assaulted. Naturally, he tried to prevent the men from injuring me. He had the duty to protect me, as his servant. I would beg that you see your way to allowing him to be freed.'

'I'm not sure that it would serve a useful purpose,' the Coroner said.

'He is only bringing messages to the Lady Elizabeth, after all,' I said. 'He and I were charged to bring them and seek her views on matters that are—'

'Unimportant compared with the complete lack of decorum and good behaviour displayed by your master during my inquest. No. He remains.'

'But, Sir Henry . . .' I began.

Bedingfield shook his head. 'It will not do, Master Blackjack, really it won't. The fellow could have caused a riot in there. It is unacceptable. I dislike it, but there it is. It's all too much for my Norfolk understanding, I confess, but if the good Coroner declares this, I cannot argue.'

'Be grateful,' the 'good Coroner' said, 'that your own innocence was so clearly displayed today. I would not like to think that you could have been involved in the murder or in undermining my authority here.'

'I wouldn't dream of it,' I said.

'Good. When you found the body, was she still warm?'

'Eh?'

He repeated his question and I shrugged. 'I think so. The blood was still liquid, and she must have died only a moment before.'

'Why?'

'I heard her drop the plate.'

'Did you hear her fall?'

'Well, the plate—'

'That's a "no", then?'

I looked from him to Sir Henry, baffled. 'Er . . . I suppose so.'

'So she could have been killed at that moment, or perhaps earlier, couldn't she? And someone decided to roll a plate on the floor to give the impression that she had just fallen?'

'Why would someone do that?'

'Do you have anything between your ears? If a man were to commit murder, he could do so from sheer evil – stab and run. A man could also try to kill with malice aforethought, and intend to put the blame on to another. Or perhaps he might desire simply to kill and then go and fraternize with some young women to establish his innocence, while paying a servant to sling a plate down the staircase, for example. Or maybe the servant could have his master do that for *him*. Not many would dare to arrest a man of quality, after all, if he was representative of the Lady Elizabeth.'

I gaped. Suddenly, the floor began to rock beneath my feet, or so it felt. I blinked and stammered my innocence, but the Coroner waved a hand airily. 'Just wanted you to see how this could be, Master. I think it is worthwhile leaving the gates locked for a little longer, while I consider this case. After all, there is a murderer here in the palace, and it's important that we don't let the fellow kill anyone else. Nor that he should escape and hurt others.'

He peered at me and all amiability fled from his eyes as he growled, 'No: be he ever so young and good-looking!'

I left the room considerably deflated. It was like the time when I was a boy, running through the streets of Whitstable, at my heels a small dog. The mutt had adopted me that morning, and I had thrown sticks for it, chased it, had play-fights with it, and had decided to keep it. I ran through the town to my father's yard, and as I ran, the dog bowled along with excitement lighting his eyes. He was lean, with a long nose, like a miniature greyhound, and wore a coarse, pepper-and-salt coat. I had never owned a dog, and this was wonderful.

And then a man came past at a canter on his great horse, there was a squeak, and my new companion was a whining, crumpled mess. The man's horse slipped slightly, and he threw me a scowl of contempt before riding on, leaving me with the injured dog. It was too late to help him, but a passing tradesman took the body, shaking his head and making tutting noises, and then quickly did something with his hands. When he passed the body back to me, the dog's head flopped.

I don't know why, but there was something about that memory that came back to me now. To have been so full of hope, only to have it dashed in an instant, was not so much appalling or distressing as strangely enervating. I felt as if all the energy had been sucked from my body in that instant. I tottered out into the yard again and stood there, feeling the weak sun on my face, and wondering how much longer we would all be forced to remain in this damned palace.

Palace be damned! It was a prison now. It held all of us in its grip, and we were forced to remain here no matter what our own lives or interests demanded. I really hated that place.

'I am sorry about your master.'

I discovered that Bedingfield had joined me. He cast a glance back at the hall. 'I cannot say that I like that man,' he said. There was a weary note to his voice. He looked from the hall to the gatehouse, then back at the hall. 'There was a time when I was delighted to be asked to come here. That was in the days of the old King, of course. King Henry was a man whom you refused at your peril – not that I wished to. He was a hard man, firm, rigorous, but fair. You know he sent me here?'

'I had heard something of it.'

'Yes, he had me installed to hold our Queen's mother here, and the Queen too. Of course, that was many years ago. And it was difficult, very difficult.' He seemed to lose his thread, shaking his head and mumbling, gazing at the ground.

'My master is being held in quite intolerable conditions,' I ventured.

'Yes, well, the Coroner demanded that he should be held.'

'But could he not be held in decent accommodation? His chamber is over there,' I pointed, 'and you could have him held within the palace walls. At least then he would have the fresh air and decent food. In the gaol cell, he is suffering.'

'The Coroner said that he must be held securely.'

'Then order him to be moved to his chamber and held there.

Have a guard on his door to prevent his escape. There are enough guards and to spare!'

'I do not—'

'Of course,' I interrupted as a thought struck me, 'it would be most upsetting if the Queen were to hear that her own sister's messenger was being held in such demeaning conditions, but you could say that you were overruled in the matter. After all, what are you, a man instructed by the Queen, compared with a Coroner with his warrant? She would understand if you had accidentally caused a fresh rift between the Queen and Lady Elizabeth.'

'Me? Cause a rift?' The poor fellow turned his eyes upon mine. They looked like badly poached eggs.

'If Lady Elizabeth complains about the treatment meted out to her messenger, the Queen will want to know why it happened. She will look to who argued for my master's better treatment. She will enquire who it was who kept him locked away and I will be duty-bound to tell her.'

'I have no authority here,' Bedingfield said, half to himself. 'The Coroner orders it, and I—'

'*You* are the seneschal here; *you* are the man responsible for the running of the palace, for the smooth organization and protection of your charges. The Coroner doesn't have to worry about such affairs, does he?'

'The Coroner seems to suspect him.'

'He can suspect many. He almost accused me just now, even though I had three witnesses to say I was not involved.'

'You had nothing to do with the Lady Throcklehampton's death?'

His eyes were disconcertingly steady when he looked up at me.

I shook my head. 'I swear on my mother's grave and the Gospels: I had nothing to do with her death.'

Bedingfield threw another look back towards the hall. 'It's not as if there's even an accusation to suggest that your master was complicit in the murder. This Coroner wants only to make trouble for others. He forces me to become involved.'

'Where were you when the lady was killed?' I asked.

'Me?' he said, and stared at me as if I had lost my senses.

'I was in the solar. I had been hunting all morning and took a few moments of rest, as I always do,' he added sadly. I think it had just occurred to him that he had missed his opportunity for a doze today.

'You were alone, of course.'

'Yes, I was walking with my daughter and . . .' His eyes suddenly hardened and he glared at me. 'Do you mean to suggest that—'

'No, of course not. But others may ask. After all, why should you kill your own spy?'

'Yes. It would be ridiculous,' he said, but there was an edge to his voice.

'Did you see her before her death?'

'I had seen her earlier, yes, but there was nothing for her to communicate.'

'No one could have heard you shouting and arguing.'

'We didn't shout or—'

'Good, because were that to have happened, people might think you had reason to kill her. Perhaps she refused to spy any longer, or she—'

'Don't be ridiculous! Besides, there were witnesses with me,' he said.

'Who?'

'I was with my steward and my daughter and others at the inner parlour discussing meals.'

That was interesting, but since I knew his daughter had been near enough to rescue me, it was quite possible that Sir Henry could have had a hand in the killing. 'That is good,' I said.

'There can be no suspicion on me or my daughter,' he said.

In that he was right. But then who *was* guilty? Blount? Squire George? Or One-Eye and the knight, Sir Walter? They had been talking about the seal last evening, and One-Eye was told he'd be paid well for it. What seal, though?

'You said the Coroner makes trouble?' I said.

'He has little understanding,' Bedingfield said.

'It must be hard to hold a position of power like this,' I said helpfully. 'It must be exhausting. A man like the Coroner perhaps doesn't realize that you have so many conflicting calls on your time, and naturally you have the difficulty of keeping your prisoner in a happy condition. You cannot allow her to suffer any degrading treatment, naturally.'

'No, that would be shocking. She is a lady.'

'And half-sister to the Queen.'

'She has been declared illegitimate,' Bedingfield said, but there was an anxious glance my way as he spoke.

'Yes. And others were accused of that in the past, only to come to great power, as you yourself know,' I said. I had no need to remind him of the fact that he had been gaoler to Catherine of Aragon all those years ago. 'And there is the other matter, of course. It is difficult to maintain a place this size and a complement of soldiers quite as large as this. You must have good financial support to keep Lady Elizabeth in the style that she expects.'

He gulped at that. I knew as well as he did that the money to keep Woodstock running came mostly from Lady Elizabeth herself.

'Lady Elizabeth is most generous with her support,' he said. There was a plaintive tone in his voice, like a child who still seeks a sweetmeat after accidentally letting the hounds eat the dinner: *I did turn the spit as you asked, and cooked the meat to perfection. I deserve my reward for that, surely?*

'I think she will find it difficult to keep her support for the place with her most important messenger held in gaol. She will not be able to release funds, nor call for other monies to be sent, while my master is held in your gaol. It is very sad, but she will undoubtedly restrict her assistance.'

'Then she will learn what it is like to undergo hardship,' he said with a firmness that alarmed me.

'No, no! You would punish her for something she cannot control? You cut off her sole means of support and therefore decide to make her suffer more indignities? She will be most upset to hear that.'

I had not meant anything by that. I was pleading to have Master Blount freed, and no more, but as soon as I finished speaking, his face crumpled like an old parchment in a fire.

'Please! Master,' he said, 'you will speak for me, will you not?'

'How can I, when my master is held in your gaol?' I said innocently with my hands held out.

Thus was the arrangement struck.

I hold no great affection for the man, but I did hope for a mild expression of gratitude when Blount was released into my care. He stumbled from the cell, rubbing at chafed wrists and glaring about him with eyes slitted against the sun for the first moments, and then grunted one word at me: 'Ale.'

I took him to the buttery and drew off a quart and a half of ale, but as soon as I had, the Bear and his young, fair-haired companion arrived. They took Blount from me and helped him across the yard to his room by the gatehouse, leaving me behind. I felt I was superfluous to their needs. I entered the hall, sat on a bench and was drinking a pint, morosely telling myself that it was typical that I should rescue my master, but no one would thank me for it, when I became aware of a quiet step. Glancing behind up the hall, I saw One-Eye dart behind a pillar. It made me grunt in irritation. Still, if I were to be followed by anyone, I would much rather it were a clumsy, one-eyed fool like him than anyone else.

There were more steps, and I saw the giant I still thought of as Friar Tuck walk down the hall towards me. He meandered amiably enough, until he reached the pillar where One-Eye was hiding. There he stopped and frowned. 'What are you doing there, Master Matthew?'

I could hear hissing and muttering, and leaned forward as though that could help me discover what was being said.

'Me? What, am I disturbing you? I merely wondered what you might be doing there. Nothing, eh? Ah. Very well, then I shall leave you there. Eh? No, I won't mention that you're there, if you do not wish it.'

He shrugged, and began to whistle as he continued on his way down the hall. Near me, he bent his head in welcome. 'Master Jack, perhaps you have a few moments to talk about matters?' Taking my nod as agreement, he continued, 'I could happily take a cup of ale. Can I replenish yours as well?'

*   *   *

Truth be told, I was nothing loath. I felt that I had performed well that day, and all I sought was a little display of gratitude. Friar Tuck led the way through to the screens, and along into the buttery. He drew himself a large jug of ale and sat on a barrel, drinking pensively. Occasionally, his left hand would go to his right wrist and rub it contemplatively while staring into the middle distance. I might as well not have been there. Then his eyes fixed on me.

'Master Jack, you are an enigma to me. At first I was convinced that you were a murderer, but the more I see of you, the less I think it possible.'

'Who are you?'

'Me? I am called Jonathan Harvey. A good name. A fellow should always protect his good name. For without it, what are we? A name that has been sullied is no longer a pass to polite society. If you spoil your name, if you poison it, you ruin yourself, for ever.'

'What are you?'

'Ah, that is different. Once I was a priest, but now I am a seeker of trifles for others.'

'Oh?'

'You are no assassin, young man. You have a keen interest in women, ale and a quiet life without drama. That much I perceive. However, you are keenly interested in this murder. I wonder why that is?'

'I was accused of it, almost.'

'Yes. The one-eyed warrener is conspicuously stupid. You are plainly more interested in investigating women's hearts than their throats,' he said. 'So who do you think was responsible for the poor woman's death?'

'I have no idea,' I said.

'Bedingfield is not competent to murder a woman. I've known some few women-killers. Rarely does a man of sensibility like Bedingfield commit such an act. He has learned over the years that he should protect women. It goes with his chivalric education and his protectiveness towards his daughter. Women are to be revered in his world. Others can kill women, but they are different. The man with hatred in his heart and a drawn dagger will usually be caught. He will stab or punch, or throttle in a moment of lunacy, driven by his black heart.'

'What of these "others"?'

He looked at me and his eyes took on a distant look. 'There are some who will slay, but rarely for no reason – they kill for money, perhaps – but most are hard, violent, unthinking men, who hold rage in their hearts, who lose their temper swiftly and for little cause, who draw a knife because they dispute the price of a coupling, or because they think their woman is playing with another man's pizzle.'

'Is there a man like that in this household?'

'Is there indeed? There is *you*, Jack. You are clever, devious, cautious, unscrupulous, aren't you? That is the sort of fellow who could do this. Someone who intends not to be forced to pay the price for his crimes.'

I didn't like the way this fellow thought. 'What reason could I have for hurting her?'

'She was spying on your master's Princess. I know all about it, my friend. I am to help you.'

'Sir Thomas told you to come?'

'Of course! To watch your back. You are clever, but some distrust you for that reason. However, no matter what others say, I consider you an unlikely assassin. Such men kill, but do so with care to make sure that their offences do not come to entrap them. They may stab, but they will know where to go afterwards to effect an escape. You tumbled over the body as though to ensure you must be caught. This killer was more careful than that. He killed for another reason, not for simple anger, but for money, for profit, for power, or . . .'

He returned to his reverie. 'There is something about this death that I have missed. I needs must discover what the motive was for this death. You did not commit this crime. Perhaps it was a bitter husband, or lover.'

'You are trying to seek the murderer?'

'Someone has to, and that blockhead of a Coroner is too alarmed of the impact on his personal future to do more than go through the motions. Who do you think could be responsible?'

'I see. Well, if by "lover" you mean the squire, I do not

think so. He is frustrated because he is married, and his wife is about to give birth.'

'Truly? Then, if he speaks the truth, he can be discounted.'

'And the killer is still on the loose somewhere about this palace,' I said.

'Yes. What could his motives have been? Money, or to further some other whim? Perhaps it was in order to win the favour of Lady Elizabeth?'

'Could she have hired a professional?' I almost added 'like me' but I lacked both the courage and the dishonesty.

'We must hope not!' Harvey said with bluff heartiness. 'If that were so, and there was a professional murderer in the palace, who could tell who might be his next victim? It could even be *you*!'

I was still for a moment. For what seemed like an age, he eyed me, and my mouth fell open, thinking he was accusing me, but then he chuckled and I realized he was joking.

'Why, he may decide to remove you just because you have spoken too much, and the man might think you his competitor,' he said, and laughed. 'Ha ha!'

I tried to grin, but it's hard to look happy when your eyes are flitting all over in case a maddened fool could appear to stab you with a convenient weapon.

'Ha ha,' I said.

I had another ale.

Harvey finished his second pot and smacked his lips, eyeing me speculatively. 'Bedingfield's daughter might be useful. She goes all over the place, and she knows the way into the Princess's chambers, as well as all about her father's business.'

'Fine, you can go and question her, then,' I said as we entered.

'No, not me: *you*.'

'*Me*?' I said.

'Don't squeak. You can't have missed how she was making sheep's eyes at you during the inquest. I was relieved when she left the room. In God's name, she looked as though she was going to whip your codpiece off and demand your services there and then on the floor before the whole congregation!'

Now, you can call me a dishonest fellow or even fool, if you wish, but I swear that I had not the faintest notion that the woman looked upon me with any feelings other than mild revulsion. Admittedly, that itself was considerably better than the first moment I met her, when I had thought she would run me through. Mild revulsion was a great improvement on a stab wound, from my perspective, so, hearing him say that, I preened. 'You think so?'

'She was at your side and fondling your brow with the care of an ancient whore who thinks her last patron's expiring,' he said unfeelingly. This Harvey was a callous fellow after the mould of Blount. I think he did not have enough affection as a child.

'Nay, I think you see more than is before you,' I said. But I was intrigued to hear his conviction so soon after the squire had intimated the same.

'What designs have you with her?'

'Me? None!'

'Tell that to her father. You may think Bedingfield is an old fool who has just enough intellect to take himself to a pot before his hosen are beshitten, but that man has survived keeping Queen Mary's mother prisoner to become gaoler to Lady Elizabeth. The man who can remain on the better side of Queen Mary even after that is one to be wary of. If you try to get inside Lady Anne's skirts, you had best be prepared to fight him. And Bedingfield is an old man who has survived many fights because he has great prowess with sword and dagger. You should guard yourself against him . . . and his servants,' he added thoughtfully.

I suddenly felt sick again. This was terrible. The room began to spin about me as he told me of the perils of upsetting a Norfolk countryman. He spoke of stabbings, bludgeonings, decapitations and even one case of a man skinned alive.

Thomas Falkes would have been keen to hear more. These people were soulmates to him. They were barbarians, from all he told me – almost as bad as the Scottish. And all Bedingfield's men were from Norfolk.

I was glad when, after further warnings to be more cautious, Harvey walked from the chamber, whistling happily to himself.

*   *   *

I had a need of open air. My head was splitting again, and my belly was queasy.

There was a stool near the stables and I sat. I know some folks say that the smell of horses and shit is not settling to a stomach, but all I can say is that it smells cleaner than some odours I've experienced in London: the rotting fishes at the riverbank when the hauls have been cleaned and gutted; the smell at the shambles when the apprentices have voided the bowels of the pigs and bulls; the odour from the tanneries . . . all have their own repellent qualities. However, sitting here, near the stables, all I got was a waft or two of warm grass and the scent of damp fur. It was restful.

The thought of seeking out Lady Anne and asking her whether she knew who could be guilty of killing Lady Margery was unappealing. I kept seeing in my mind's eye the way she had knocked down One-Eye with such competence. She reminded me of an Amazon and brought to life all the horrible thoughts that Harvey's words had inspired. Still, he was right in saying that she had unrivalled access to the whole palace. She would be a most useful ally.

I stood and made my way unsteadily to the hall's front door, thinking I might as well try to find her and speak with her. If she had been walking about the palace with her father before the murder as Bedingfield had said, she might have seen someone. It was worth asking, anyway. I shoved the front door wide, resolved to seek her out; however, as the door swung against the wall, there was a loud squeak, and I feared that I must have crushed a maidservant behind it. I pulled the door towards me and peered round, to find myself confronted by two terrified eyes at about the level of my breast. It was the boy who had been howling the place down at the inquest.

'What were you doing there?'

'Hiding,' he said simply.

Well, as far as hiding places went, it was not the worst I have seen. 'But you would be seen by anyone walking down the screens passage.'

'But Father's outside. Don't tell him I'm here – please, sir!'

I peered at him. If his parent sought to make his backside glow like a firefly's, I saw no need to dispute his right. This lad had given me enough pain with his caterwauling. It was tempting to call his father immediately.

'Please, sir? He's so distressed since my mother's death, and he has beaten me so already.'

It's a strange thing. I have been raised by a father who saw little need to spare the birch, since my mother died long ago (so the old man tells me, although I always wondered whether she fled from his tempers and took up a new life in a fresh village). While a muling brat gets on my nerves, a boy who has been forced to attend his own mother's inquest, who has seen her stripped bare and rolled over and over for the jury to see her injuries, well . . . I suppose I felt a sympathy for him.

'What's your name, boy?'

'I am Gilbert Throcklehampton. My father is Sir Walter—'

'Yes, I know who he is. He was with you at the inquest.'

'Yes.'

'What will you do now? Stay here hiding?'

'His black mood will leave him soon, I think. It usually dies out after an hour of the clock.'

I studied the lad. 'How old are you?'

'Nine.'

'Come with me.'

I took him through to the buttery and plied him with wine. He held it well, I'll grant, but he was smiling, slurring and snoozing by the time I'd had my quart, and I was belching with the satisfaction of a full belly and the feeling that I'd done a good thing in releasing the lad from his fears.

He came from the far north originally, but now lived at Throcklehampton, in some manor near a town called Evesham, apparently. His mother had spent most of her time away from home, because she was a favourite of our Queen. I may have seen her in London, because the boy told me that she was there with Queen Mary when the rebels had tried to storm Whitehall Palace, where the Queen had fled when the rebels approached the city. I remembered those days with a shudder, which wasn't helped by young Gilbert telling me that all the guards must have been wondrously brave to defend the place against the foul men of Kent.

I didn't tell him that most of us were terrified, and those who weren't were so sodden in drink that they could scarce hold a sword straight. The memory came back to me of Sir John Gage, the Lord Chamberlain and Captain of the Guard, roaring drunk as he was, confronted by the first of the rebels. His face! He bolted, or tried to, falling flat on his face in the mud and horseshit of the roadway, and I and his servant had to haul him up and push him through the great gates to the palace. I'll never forget his great goggling eyes as he took in the sight of the approaching army. Mind you, I still have dreams in which I find myself in that road again, with the appalling horde of rebels running at me, while I fear feeling a knife at my back at every moment from my other enemy. But that's a different story.

His father had been growing more and more bitter in the last months, Gilbert told me. It was perhaps just the effect on the man of having his wife taken from him to dance attendance on the Princess, when she should have been at home with her son.

'Do you have brothers? Sisters?' I asked.

'No. I had two sisters, but they died,' he said matter-of-factly.

I nodded. I'd had a similar lonely childhood. It increased the bond between us. 'Me too,' I said. 'My mother died when I was young, too.'

'It's hard,' he said quietly.

'Your father has much to think of,' I said.

'*So do I!*'

His emphasis was so pronounced, it was quite shocking. I nodded quickly, 'Yes, yes, of course you do! I was only trying to say that he will perhaps come to cope with his grief again soon.'

Gilbert shrugged and looked doubtful. When I prompted him, he pulled a grimace. 'He was angry before mother died. He was always angry. This just made him worse. He hates me!'

I was tempted to gather the boy up and comfort him, but it would not have been seemly and he wouldn't appreciate my display, I was sure. I wouldn't have wanted a stranger to smother me, were I his age. But then, I wouldn't have wanted to talk about my father either.

'I doubt he hates you, Gilbert. He's just sad that he's lost his wife.'

The boy did not look convinced.

'You heard them talk of the necklace. You have not seen it, I suppose?'

'Not since she died, no.' He looked away suddenly, and I knew he was concealing something. It took only a little prompting to have him confess.

'My father said it was not valuable,' he said, 'but it was to her. The necklace was always about her neck because she bore a seal of her father's on it. She was proud of it. Then it was broken, and she wore a necklace of the Princess's instead, the one with the crucifix.'

I wasn't interested in the necklaces. 'Her father's seal?'

'Of the Nevilles, her family. It was important to her.' His eyes grew sad once more. 'I should have been with her. I could have saved her.'

'The seal was an old decoration, I was told.'

'Yes. My grandfather used it when he had to sign documents or seal messages. My mother was proud of it, and kept it after his death.'

'I see.' Except I didn't. Why someone would take a defunct piece of decoration like that was beyond me. Yet they had; someone had ripped it from her neck.

Another half pint of wine soothed him enough to set him snoring. I left him there, propped on a barrel with his head against a wall, and left the chamber.

I had made precisely three steps into the yard when a great ham-like hand descended on my shoulder, and I was thrust protesting into the wall, my ravaged nose thudding painfully into the rocks, and I swore loudly as the blood began to flow once more.

'Master Jack, I want to speak with you!' the one-eyed man hissed in my ear.

There have been times in my life when I've been thankful of rescue from unpleasant experiences. Lady Anne's intervention only recently was a good example of my being glad to welcome the interruption of an otherwise difficult interview, and I cast about now for any guards who might be able to rescue me, or Master Blount, Will, Harvey, or anyone. But before I could even gather a breath to scream for help, I felt the prick of his knife at my ribs. It was a highly effective means of silencing me. I have never enjoyed the feel of steel on my skin, and would be most reluctant to feel it *in* my flesh. He took hold of my jack and shoved me before him into the alley between kitchen and hall.

'What do you want with me?' I demanded, trying to stem the flow from my nose.

'You were there, and I don't believe you had nothing to do with Lady Throcklehampton's murder.'

'So go and tell the Coroner.'

'I prefer to talk it through with you here,' he said, and punched me again.

The pain was intense, as if a bolt of lightning had struck me full in the face.

'You've broken my nose, you craven apple-squire!' I said. The blood was running like a thick Bordeaux wine. I stuck my chin out, so the blood could not drench my jack, but that only tempted him to punch me again, this time below the ribs. I gasped, desperate to breathe in, while he irritably tried to evade the shower of bloody spray that I'd blown towards him. Not that it mattered. Whole and hale, I could have pushed past him and fled, but after that blow to my belly, there was no possibility of making an escape. I couldn't even stand up straight.

He had picked a good place in which to attack me. It was a narrow space here, with gravel and pebbles underfoot, and the angle of the walls meant that a man had to be right at the entrance to see far along the way. None of the guards at the gatehouse or the walls would be able to see anything in the darkness of that grim passage. Meanwhile, escape would be hindered by the trash and garbage lying all about. I stumbled on a pig's skull and a collection of ribs from a cow. Clearly, bones were casually tossed in here rather than being taken to the midden when it rained.

One-Eye had me by the shoulder, and now he pushed me back against the kitchen's wall. My head slammed back and I saw some sparkling stars ignite in the air close by. They whirled and danced before my eyes, red sparks in purple spheres, and I watched them with fascination for a while, bemused, until he jerked me again. 'Listen!'

'What?' I mumbled. A star seemed to land on my nose and I flapped with a hand until it disappeared. Then the others all twinkled out and I could concentrate once more.

The bridge of my nose, where he had broken it earlier, felt as though it had swollen to the size of my fist. The blood was trickling now, rather than pouring, but I could feel its viscous heat and tasted the iron in my mouth as I tried to breathe. Still, although I was bruised and beslubbered in blood, my anger was not diminished. He pulled at my shoulder, and I brought my arm up, knocking his away. But then I felt his knife's point again, and was persuaded to stop further attempts at escape.

'You know what I want,' he said.

'Eh?'

'It wasn't on her. Someone took it.'

'Took what?' I said. I could feel his knife twisting slightly. It felt as if he was going to shove it into my guts to emphasize his irritation. 'I don't know what you're talking about!'

'The signet! She always carried it, but it was taken before I could!'

'What? You were trying to rob her?'

I felt the knife press harder. This fellow would have no compunction about opening my belly there and then. It seemed to me that, with him and Thomas Falkes, too many people wanted to investigate my internals. I began to gabble.

'I didn't have time to take anything. You found me only a moment or two after I fell over her!'

'I want that seal,' he said, and pushed his knife further.

'What seal?' I felt my new jack's material part, and the point was in my flank now. I could imagine that the moisture I could feel was more of my blood. This fellow clearly meant to drain me dry. However, one thing I was certain of was, he did not know that the man who told him to find the seal had himself already taken it, according to the boy. So, why was Sir Walter demanding One-Eye should find it for him? Was the little brat lying to me?

'Well?' he said.

I thought quickly. 'If it's not on her, then it must have fallen from her where she lay.'

'I've looked. Nothing.'

The blade pressed deeper. 'Then it fell beneath the sideboard, perhaps?'

At last the vile pressure reduced. I could see doubts in his eye. 'Did you see no one else near the body?'

'Do you think I'd have stood here for you to prick holes in my body if I could direct you towards some other victim?'

He pushed me to the wall. 'I don't believe you.'

That was when he intended to stab me, I had no doubt. This time he could not miss his mark. I froze like a statue. It was terrifying. I felt as though every muscle had turned to marble, and I could only stare. Then my mouth began to move, and I chattered some fine nonsense, utterly incoherent, I daresay, searching for words that could save me from his evil blade.

So when I saw his eye narrow, and I was convinced this was his moment, that I had only a finger's snap before he thrust his knife into my guts, I reacted like a cornered rat. I kicked his shin, grabbed for the wrist holding his knife, pushing it away, whimpering with fear all the while, and tried to knee him in the cods – but sadly missed so small a target. He fell back with a grunt, his hand on his thigh, and while he swore foul oaths about my parents and lifestyle, I scrabbled desperately, trying to find a weapon of any sort, my hands rifling quickly through the filth. I found the pig's skull and snatched it up, bringing it down on his head with a satisfying crunch.

He roared with pain.

I fled. The passage in which I found myself was an alley, and alleys tend to lead somewhere. That meant there was a place to run *to*. I flung the skull at him and ran and ran as I have never run before. When I glanced over my shoulder, I saw he was recovering. His good eye narrowed into a glare, and he clambered to his feet, knife still gripped in his hand.

Running is easy. When I was a youngster, I learned to run from my father to avoid his beatings; when I grew, I learned to snatch a pie or apple and bolt from the market. If I claim it myself, I have the right to be proud of my ability to disappear with alacrity. I have been told that I have an impressive turn of speed for such a scrawny wretch, and that day I put every ounce of strength into my legs and fairly flew up the way. I did not pause to look behind me, but hurtled along, paying no heed to anything but the urgent need to be somewhere else. I heard him grunt once, and thought he must have turned an ankle on a loose stone, but didn't bother to turn and look. Instead, I made it round a corner, and found that in front of me was a wall, with a door on the left. I snatched at the handle as I reached it, flung it wide, and was in through it like a rat into a sewer. As soon as I was inside, I slammed the door with full force. There was a bellow of rage and pain, and I saw his hand, caught between the door and the frame. I barged into the door with my shoulder, putting the full weight of my body into it, and heard a cracking noise just before the knife fell to the floor. I put my foot on it and kicked it away, and as I did so, the hand was withdrawn. I pushed the door shut quickly. There was a bolt, and I shoved it across before setting my eye to a crack in the timbers.

I could see him, dancing angrily on the stones of the alleyway, his left hand gripping his right wrist, obviously in great pain, which gave me a degree of pleasure, and I smiled as I turned and stepped forward into the blasted knife again. This time it was held by the lovely Lady Anne.

And I learned very quickly that George might be an excellent squire, and Harvey might be a good spy, but neither had any ability when it came to reading a lady's mind, for the look she gave me had nothing of affection in it. In truth, I had to step back urgently to stop myself being paunched on the spot.

'What are you doing here?' she hissed with real malevolence.

Now, admittedly, I was not looking at my best. My nose was as bloated as an ancient cider-drinker's, I suspect, and I had a series of scrapes on my cheek where One-Eye had shoved me into the wall. My chest had been smothered in so much blood that anyone could have been forgiven for thinking that my throat had been cut; added to that, my nose was blocked, my eyes rheumy from ale, and I had a headache like the worst two-day drinking hangover I've experienced. All of which is probably why I curled my lip, grunted and said, 'If you're really going to use that, just get on with it, will you?'

To my relief, she did lower it slightly, peering at me with what Harvey might have considered sympathy, but which was more likely revulsion. Her eyes, I noticed, were red from weeping. She looked despondent. 'Are you well?' I asked. 'You look as though—'

'What business is it of yours?'

'None!'

She gave me a grim look, then seemed to relent. 'My father's very concerned. Since this woman, Lady Margery, is dead, it will reflect badly on him. I'm worried for him.'

'Oh, I see. But she was his spy, wasn't she?'

'That does not matter. She was a woman who found it easy to make enemies.'

I recalled the groom had said something similar. 'I've heard few liked her.'

'She was . . . difficult to get on with.' She peered closer. 'What's happened to you?'

'Our friend from the other day, whom you so usefully tapped on the head, just accused me of theft and wanted to investigate my guts, presumably to see whether I'd swallowed the thing he is looking for. Unless it's your standard Woodstock welcome here, since *you* seem to want to open me up as well.'

She reluctantly pushed the knife into her belt. 'I wasn't expecting you to burst through the door, that's all.'

'Well, he chased me down the alley, and this was the first door I found that was open,' I said, slightly petulantly. I was not happy to escape one knife-wielding lunatic only to run into another.

'I am sorry,' she said. She had the grace to look a little ashamed.

'Why did you want to attack me?' I said.

'You suddenly lurched through the door, slammed it on to someone's hand, then bolted it like that. What would you have thought? You could have been a murderer or cut-purse for all I knew.'

'Do I look like a damned cut-purse?'

'You look more like Morris dancers have been using your face for a stage,' she grinned.

'You are Lady Anne, aren't you?'

She looked suspicious, but then I explained I had seen her at the inquest, and she shrugged. Her shoulder moved most deliciously under her gown, I noticed. I longed to get better acquainted, as Harvey had suggested I might, but the look in her eye when she glanced at me told me that the likelihood was remote.

'Doesn't your father worry about you walking about down here on your own?'

She tilted her head to one side. 'You think I can't protect myself?'

'It's clearly dangerous with all these men about the place.'

'It's not entirely safe with the Queen's sister here, but there are as many men-at-arms here as there are to guard the Queen herself. I'm as safe here as I would be with the court in London or Oxford.'

'Do you think the Princess is in danger?' I wondered.

'No.'

I was bemused. Perhaps she didn't understand the nature of the politics. 'You see, if the Queen suspects her, it's quite likely that the Princess could be taken back to the Tower at any time.'

'She is safe here. My father will see to it that she is secure. At least . . . he will do his best.'

'What does that mean?'

She gave me a cold look. 'Only that he is a strong-willed man, and he's very determined . . . but we're from Norfolk, and we aren't really used to this sort of thing. Oh, Father was the guard for the Queen's mother for a while, when Henry was King, and no one dared to challenge him. But Queen Mary has already had Lady Jane Grey try to take the throne and declare Mary the usurper, and there has been a rebellion too. Who can tell what may happen here?'

I frowned.

She gave an exasperated – and exaggerated – sigh. 'Do you not understand? We aren't here to protect Princess Elizabeth from attack; we are here to protect the Queen. Elizabeth is a focus for all sorts of rebels, and some might come here to try to free the Princess.'

'Who do you think would attempt a thing like that? The rebels were all captured. The Queen had several hundred executed, and their heads are on spikes at London, their bodies hang in chains all over the—'

'And still more are prepared to take up the fight. Those who follow the true religion of . . .'

I clapped my hands over my ears. It was painful, but I had to stop her words. 'Enough! I don't want to hear any more! You should be more careful to whom you speak sedition!'

'Why? Would you report me?'

'After all the troubles with the Queen's choice of husband, any discussion about religion is likely to cause you problems, and there are many more men and women in here than only me for you to worry about!'

'But many would willingly give their lives to protect the Queen, as would I,' she said firmly.

She had a sort of noble pride as she spoke, and she extended her neck to raise her chin, but all I could think was that she looked like a woman preparing herself for the headsman's axe. I quashed the thought immediately. 'I would be glad to protect her too,' I said, 'but just now you are talking about betraying your father's duty. That can help no one. His task is to keep her here safe and well.'

'And he will; so will I. I will see her safe from all dangers, if God wills it.'

'Oh, good,' I said sarcastically. 'And that includes injuring poor gulls like me, I suppose?'

'It includes anything I deem necessary for her safety,' she said.

There was a hardness to her tone as she said that, and I had a shiver run down my spine at the thought of her attacking me – and no, it wasn't the sort of shiver that I'd get from one of Piers's tarts in the Cardinal's Hat, nor that which I enjoyed when Jen Falkes woke me up in my bed and . . . but there's no need to go into that sort of detail here. No, the only shiver I got from seeing Anne Bedingfield look at me in that speculative manner was a deeply unpleasant sensation that dribbled down my spine like chilled quicksilver.

She was eyeing me suspiciously now.

'What?' I said.

'You mentioned that Matthew wanted to open you up for something. What did you mean?'

'He's hunting for a seal, apparently. Sir Walter wants this thing. It's a seal that Lady Margery used to have on a necklace.' I didn't mention the second necklace the boy had spoken of. 'I suppose that's why she had a little bruise on her neck. Someone grabbed it and broke it. Afterwards she wore a crucifix. Although it wasn't on her body,' I added. Perhaps One-Eye <u>had</u> taken it?

There was no mistaking the look on her face. She was shocked or surprised. Perhaps she was alarmed too.

'What do you know of this?' I said.

'Nothing. But if that's so, what was this seal?'

'Her son said it was Lady Margery's father's. Apparently, he was a great magnate up near Scotland at the border.'

'But he's dead, so his seal is valueless.'

That was true enough. A man's seal was proof of his identity. Once he died, the seal's relevance died with him.

'Perhaps the thief thinks it has some other value. It's made of gold, or has an expensive stone in it?' I hazarded.

'Or it's a trifle, and Sir Walter merely wishes to find it again to learn who the murderer was,' she said. She had recovered, and there was more colour in her face again.

'Good. Well,' I said, and prepared to push past her.

'Wait!' she said, and put her hand on my breast to keep me in my place. Her – or rather One-Eye's – knife remained in her other hand, well out of my reach, and I wasn't going to test myself against this sturdy Norfolk wench. She'd have me on the floor and calling for my mother in a blink of an eye. Not only because she was a hardy maiden, but also because my head was ungently reminding me that I had already had a deeply unpleasant day, and really needed an opportunity to go and rest it.

'Well?'

'I would be glad of your observation to help me,' she said, and now her voice was more uncertain. Her chin fell a little and she looked up at me from those enormous eyes. It was like having a puppy gaze up at me. Yes, I know, I'm a fool, but it's difficult to reject a woman who looks at me as if I'm her very own Lancelot du Lac. My heart swelled at the sight.

'Well, of course,' I said.

'All I would ask is that you keep a look on the gatehouse where Princess Elizabeth is being held. We have to protect her.'

I eyed her without favour. 'I can never find you. Do you have a maid whom I can meet to pass on any news?'

'You will have to find me.'

'But didn't you have a maid? Her name was Alys?'

'She is unwell and left me some months ago. No, I have no maidservants just now. You will have to find me. That way is more secure, anyway. If there is something significant to report, it will be safer for you to find me, in case of spies.' She looked at me, very straight. 'We will be safer that way.'

Yes: *We*. I heard it too. As I stood outside, feeling the sun warming my face, I could not help but wonder how I had managed to become so enmeshed in this tangled web of politics and espionage. Only a few weeks ago I had been a contented foist, purloining people's purses and coins with a range of simple tricks and nimbleness; then I was ensnared by Blount and others, and now here I was, working for the man.

And I had been brought here to kill the woman who died.

Suddenly, that murder seemed even more troublesome to me. After all, One-Eye had been there so soon after the woman's death. The Coroner had the interesting idea that someone could have hurled the plate from the top of the stairs and run. That would mean someone had killed the woman a while before . . . and it also meant that my own innocence could be called into question again.

One-Eye and Sir Walter interested me. The boy had told me about the seal, but as Lady Anne had said, it was valueless if the owner was dead. What sort of seal could this be? Was it worth good money? One-Eye had tried to capture me once, and his intentions had been still more distinct just now in the alleyway. I shuddered to think what his next approach might be. The only good aspect was, with any luck, he would have a shattered wrist after I slammed the door on it, but I wasn't keen to test the matter. He had seriously believed that I had taken the opportunity to steal this thing. It was reasonable to assume that the seal had not been found, then.

The woman who had died was, so Blount had said, a spy in the household of Princess Elizabeth. That meant the Princess would have had no reason to like Lady Margery; she must have been aware that the woman was installed there to report on anything that was going on. So she had a good motive to have Lady Margery removed. But One-Eye was more likely. He wanted something that the lady possessed.

Others had the opportunity to kill her. Blount had wanted Lady Margery dead, and he had been near to the door. It would not surprise me if he met her in that passageway and decided to take advantage of the opportunity presenting itself as Harvey had hinted. From my own experience, Blount was not a man to be lightly set aside as of little consequence. He was a murderous fellow, well capable of taking a life if presented with a safe, easy chance encounter, and then fleeing to leave the blame on a poor innocent like me. Which would be easy enough, bearing in mind he brought me with the command that I should kill her myself.

I was not happy with this reflection. If I'd felt a little less battered, I would have gone to him and demanded to know the truth, but the fact was that I felt awful, and while I would have been happy to see Blount beaten, I was in no fit condition to take on the task myself. The thought of punching a man, with my nose so swollen and painful, was enough to induce waves of nausea once more. So, instead of seeking him out, I walked out to the courtyard, thinking to find a space where I could cogitate about matters. The main thing, I decided, was to remain in full view of as many people as possible and avoid the darker, quieter spaces where an assassin could put an end to my ruminations. Ironic that I was supposed to be the assassin, yet here I was, hiding from another, who was plainly more competent and less fearful of the sight of blood than I was myself.

'Keep back!'

The man-at-arms blocked my path with his spear. It was a

persuasive gesture. I peered over his shoulder. There were carts and sumptermen entering and leaving the gate, and I pointed. 'They are all coming and going; why can't I?'

'The Coroner told us to keep all the household in here,' the man said.

'I'm not from the household. I'm staying down at the town,' I explained.

'Tell the Coroner that.'

'Where is he?'

'In the town.'

'Then I will go to speak with him.'

The spear turned to point at me. 'You'll wait until he's back. You can't leave.'

I considered trying to make a run for it, but in my state I wouldn't be able to outrun a one-legged cripple, so instead I made my way to a bench and wrapped my arms about me, staring at the gates and glowering at the guards.

Where I was, I was concealed from the left by a buttress at the hall's outer wall; on the right, an open door hid me. I could see much of the courtyard from there, but I was inconspicuous. I could see the gates and the stables, but that was not in my mind. All I wanted to do was sit back with my eyes closed and feel the sun on my face, warming my legs and chest. I was exhausted and angry to be kept in here like some kind of prisoner. There were others here who deserved to be held, but I just felt it to be a fresh injustice heaped on my head.

The gatehouse which held Princess Elizabeth had a door that opened to the outer court, and as I watched, I saw a familiar figure stride from it. A portly gentleman, dressed in the most expensive of velvets and scarlets, with a merry cap upon his head, and a fashionable cloak trimmed with fur that would have looked good on a man twenty years his junior, and perhaps five stones lighter. For this was the Welshman, Sir Thomas Parry.

Parry had a ready charm, his eyes twinkling brightly as he spoke. His voice carried a poetic and musical delight, and I've seen him hold an entire tavern spellbound when he wanted to. He had a light step for a big man, and his belly and chest were so swollen he could have been inflated. I've heard that there are men who could charm women from their husbands' beds and still be favoured by the cuckold. This Parry was a man of that mould.

I watched him leave the door, passing a coin or similar token to the guard at the door, and then make his way to the gates. He nodded to the porter and sauntered on through. Outside, I saw a horse and waiting urchin. Another coin, another smile and nod, and Parry was mounted on a sturdy pony.

I rose to my feet. Thomas Parry was the man for whom Blount worked, and I was keen to speak with him. I hurried to go to him, but he had already spurred his beast and was trotting out through the gates. Increasing my speed, I was about to follow him when two polearms dropped and crossed before me. 'What?' I said.

'The Coroner has ordered . . .' said one guard. It was my friend from earlier.

'But you just let *him* go!'

'He has the right and authority. You, on the other hand, don't.'

'What right and authority does he have?'

'Sir Henry has given him permission to come and go, and since he wasn't here when Lady Margery was killed, the Coroner has agreed.'

'But I thought no one was allowed in since the murder?'

'He's the chief steward to the Queen's sister. Who's going to stop him seeing the Princess?'

The guard had a point. To try to stop a sister to the Queen from seeing her key adviser would take a brave man, or a very foolish one. It was the sort of task that was well above his rank, and any man like him would be cautious about exposing himself to the anger of a woman who was quite so well connected. However, it made me wonder why on earth my master felt the need to come here when Master Parry could come and go at will. Perhaps it was only to watch my back, I reasoned. I was not convinced.

I nodded, but not happily, and turned away. As I passed the narrow way between hall and kitchen, where One-Eye had tried to spit me on his knife, I saw something that made me pause. There was a small pile of trash at the entrance, and now, prodding it with a toe, I saw a familiar leather pack. It was my bag.

Pulling it free, I searched inside. All had been emptied, as though someone had upended it. There was nothing inside.

I wondered who could have done this. There was nothing of value in it, after all. What could someone have been hoping to find in a servant's bag?

It was pointless standing there with my empty pack in my hand, so I dropped it back on the rubbish heap and turned and went back to my bench, hoping that the guards would see my contempt for them in the way I held myself. I suspect that they didn't notice. Certainly, as soon as I made off, I heard them begin to chat in a desultory manner about the lunch they had eaten, the prospects for supper, the beers they would drink, and a certain maid with a saucy smile. I tried to pick up more about her, because she sounded an exceedingly friendly young woman, from what one guard was saying, but they stopped talking before they could mention her name, and I heard them declaring that the gate was closed.

When I glanced around, I saw that the fair man whom I had seen on the day of the murder was again trying to leave the place. Squire George of Carlisle stood before the guard, and if he was not so clearly a member of the wealthier class, I would have said he was pleading.

'I have to get out! This is intolerable.'

The guard shrugged. It wasn't his problem, he seemed to imply.

'Have you no cares for other people?' the squire demanded. 'I should . . .'

The two guards had grim faces now, and any bantering tones were gone as they stood carefully side by side. Their polearms lowered slightly, and one narrowed his eyes. 'We have cares only for our Queen and *her* officers,' he said. 'Now be off.'

'I am a *squire*!'

But his voice had a panicky, fretful tone to it. If I could hear that, so could these two. I sat on my bench and prepared to watch a good bout, which would make a pleasant change after all the injuries I had endured, but before any blows could be struck, the squire threw up his hands and made his way towards me.

'What, did you not find the entertainment to your liking?' he demanded.

'Do I look like someone who would take amusement from another's suffering?' I said.

He eyed my nose and features for a moment, peering closely with distaste. 'What happened to you?'

'I seem to be a target for men's fists.'

'Perhaps I should punch you too. It would work off some of my feelings towards those two,' he said, throwing a glower over his shoulder at the two guards. When he looked back at me, a grin was already twisting his features. 'I apologize. Those two put me further out of sorts.'

'I doubt whether punching me would work well. Perhaps you will be thrown into gaol for your assault and held there for a week or two until the next manor court. That wouldn't help you get out of here any faster, nor allow you to see Alys any sooner.'

'All my life is out there,' the fellow said. He slumped on to the bench beside me, and I'd swear that he had tears in his eyes. 'All I wish is to ensure that my wife is fit and healthy, that my son is well . . .'

From the look of his hose and the cut of his jack, tight-fitting and of good material, I'd say that this was a fellow worth getting to know. It was plain that he had money, and although I was earning a regular retainer, I was always happy to try my luck with a new gull who left his purse dangling too close to my light fingers. I shifted up a little as if conspiratori-ally, and my hand naturally fell to the small gap between us. His purse was so close, and I had already made sure that it was held by only two laces. A simple slip of my knife with its razor edge, and the purse would be mine. The knife was a small eating knife that I kept in a sheath on my left hip.

'Oh?' I said encouragingly. 'You have still not told Lady Anne about your wife?'

'How can I? It is impossible to find her alone to speak to. I want to let her know about Alys and our child, but Lady

Anne is so busy, and there are no moments to speak with her alone. Even in her chamber, her father is there, or Sir Walter, or another. And all I want to do is leave and be with Alys when our child is born.'

I tried not to pull a face. There are two places I never want to be: at the birth of a brat and at my own death, if possible. Still, some men do like to put themselves through troubles. This fellow was no different. The purse was at the back of my hand now. I could feel it. The coins gave it substance and weight. I licked my lips. 'Why worry? Go fetch a pot of wine and we can celebrate the boy's birth.'

'Wet his head?' the man said, and he shifted in his seat. I let go of my little knife hurriedly. 'How can I do that? It may be bad luck. If the child isn't born yet, it could mean that my woman will have a poor birth, perhaps even a stillbirth!'

'Apologies. I have no children. I didn't think,' I said, baring my teeth hopefully.

He grimaced. Perhaps trying to smile with all the damage done to my face was not so good an idea. 'I understand,' he said. 'But to drink now . . . it would be a terrible temptation to fate.'

'Then, perhaps just a pot of wine to calm your nerves,' I said. 'You need something to settle yourself.'

'How can I sit here drinking when poor Alys is out there, perhaps even now . . . even now . . .'

'Is this your first child?' I said.

'Yes.'

'And your wife is strong enough?'

'She . . . she is well enough, I think.'

There was a hesitation about him. I wondered at that as I tried to manoeuvre myself nearer to him on the bench. I got a splinter in my arse for my troubles.

'Do you have something worrying you?' I said. 'Apart from the woman and child, I mean.'

'Why do you say that?'

He turned to me and I was reminded that this youngster, when not bent with trouble, was a large fellow with the sort of physique that would make an oak tree whimper. Lancelot du Lac would take one look at this fellow and go hunting for an easier foe. In short, when the lad inflated his lungs, he made me feel as though he'd sucked all the ether from the courtyard. I felt light-headed again.

'I was only trying to help.'

'You can't help me,' he said, and as suddenly as he had risen in rage, he was sunken in gloom once more. 'I'm lost. I should be at Alys's side, but instead I'm locked away in this prison!'

I was confused. In trying to lighten his mood, all I had achieved, apparently, was to make him angry enough to want to hit me. I'd had enough for one day. Standing, I left him and made my way to the buttery again.

It was the one room where I felt secure just now.

There are some fellows who fill a man with a sense of good humour and content, and others who . . . I don't know . . . who just set the teeth on edge, I suppose. That squire was one such. I had no idea what could make a man so impatient, so angry and desperate to leave. Few would hanker after witnessing a woman going through the pains of childbirth, especially a woman whom they loved. His desire to be away was inexplicable. A birth was one thing, but murder was another. It wasn't as if *he* had to worry about One-Eye coming after him to open him from gizzard to gills. Pouring a jug of ale from the strong barrel, I shook my head. The squire had nothing to worry about. I had fears and concerns because of the murder of Lady Margery. It wasn't as though the squire had to worry about that, was it?

Yes, I nearly dropped the jug. For a second, my hands almost released it, nerveless as a corpse's, before I came to my senses again.

I'd suddenly thought that the young man could have been the murderer of Lady Margery. It was ridiculous, I know, but sometimes these flashes of inspiration can strike and make even the most level-headed man review matters. If the squire had been responsible for Lady Margery's death, he would obviously be in a great hurry to escape the manor. He would want to put as many miles between him and the scene of his crime as possible. In short, he would behave exactly as he had. And while he had told me that Blount was outside in the courtyard, so was *he*. Either of them could have slipped in through the door and murdered Lady Margery.

I thought about the squire's behaviour, how he had been so keen to run away, his desperation, his fears. Suddenly, his smiles took on a more sinister appearance. Perhaps there was still more reason for the squire to want to escape the palace. Not because he had a woman in the town over the marshes, but because he had been pushing his pork sword in another man's sheath.

I poured ale and drank deeply, and common sense returned. It felt as though my sanity had been teetering, like a heavy rock balanced on a smaller one, waiting to fall. But now reason was restored to her pedestal. The man would have needed a motive to commit such a murder. Men do not regularly kill their lovers, even when they are already married. For that, the squire would have wanted to see her dead. What could be the cause of that? A jealousy, a hatred, an unreasoning passion? It was hardly likely. Still, I decided I should mention it to Blount, and see what he . . .

But no. If I told him, he would know that I had not killed the woman as he had ordered. That was a pretty conundrum. There would be consequences, were he to realize that I was not the hound from hell that he had anticipated, and paid for. Because my entire livelihood and lifestyle depended on the money flowing still, regularly and reliably, so that I could afford the new clothes, the fine foods and wine, and the women. Confessing that Lady Margery was not dead by my hand might make him wonder whether his investment in me was worth the money.

I heard a snivelling sound and temporarily set my worries and troubles aside. It seemed to come from behind the barrels, and I had a vision of a large rat. There were enough of them around here. I'd seen one the size of a cat the other morning. I pulled my dagger from its sheath and crept slowly towards the barrels.

Yes, I had forgotten the brat. He was there, still partly asleep, his mouth hanging slackly. Anyone would think I'd filled him to the pate with the strongest wines in the buttery, but no, all

I'd given him was a few pots. Still, it took a fair amount of shaking to bestir him. At last his eyes gazed up at me blearily, and I asked him what he was doing on the floor.

'It was easier to lie here than fall here,' he said, with eminently reasonable logic.

'Do you think you should seek your father now?'

'I don't think he wants to see me. He wants to go and fight the other man.'

Which other man? I was going to ask, but the boy looked down and spoke so softly that it made me still my tongue.

'He was too friendly with my mother, I've heard. He said I was a bastard, in all likelihood, and the squire forced him to wear the cuckold's horns.'

It was enough to make me want to laugh aloud, to be honest. The idea that she could have been playing hide the sausage with the squire, I mean, just when I had persuaded myself that it was highly unlikely . . . It obviously wasn't funny that she was dead. And then I thought about the earnest expression of panic on the squire's face and I couldn't help but chuckle to myself. If I had ever mistaken a man's motives more, I could not think of the time. Then again, perhaps it was mere hogwash. Sir Walter was likely wrong. Why would the squire with a young wife throw himself at a woman like Lady Margery?

And then the humour was wiped from my face as I heard a quiet step behind me.

The lad's father did not bother to demand explanations, but stepped past me and cuffed his son about the head, staring at the boy as he began to weep.

I felt I had to speak. I said, 'What was that for?'

He turned to stare at me. 'You think you have the right to question a father's righteous chastisement of his own son?'

Well, if he was going to put it like that, of course I had no right whatsoever. However, that didn't stop me wanting to protect the little fellow. And then I reflected that this man could already have murdered his wife. I didn't wish to be his second victim. 'No, of course not,' I said hurriedly, stepping away to give him more space.

He slapped the boy again, making his head whip around. I

swear, if there were stones in his head, I would have heard them rattling like dice in a pot. The boy looked up at him then, and when I expected him to plead for mercy, instead I had a shiver of horror run down my knave's spine as he hissed, 'You think to beat me like you did Mother, and think I will endure like her? I will not! *I will not!*'

His father lifted his hand again, but before he could let his blow fall, the boy had darted between us and pelted out along the screens to the main courtyard.

That was when his father began to sob and collapsed on a barrel.

'What's the point? What is the point?' he wailed.

'Do you want me to try to catch him?' I said, my thumb over my shoulder, pointing in the direction the lad had fled.

'What then? He hates me enough already. He blames me for his mother's death. I had thought that this would bring him and me together, but her death has only enlarged the gulf between us. The divide separating us is as vast as the seas. He will do nothing that might please me. He loathes me.'

'I'm sure he doesn't. You're his father, after all.'

'Only in law; he's not my blood, and that seems to count for much with the brat,' the man snapped, and then hid his face in his hands. 'What will I do with him?'

'If you go and catch him, you could lock him in a room until he sees sense,' I hazarded.

'Beating him seems to achieve little,' he continued, as if I had not spoken. 'Perhaps I should just send him away. He could go to his uncle's house and there learn how to behave, learn the martial arts and courtesy. Because the foul piglet has little enough of manners so far!' Then his eyes clouded. 'With her dead, he'll be taken soon, no doubt.'

'When you say "Only in law", do you mean your wife had him before you married her?'

'What else could I mean, you fool?' he peered at me. 'Have you been fighting?'

'There are other reasons,' I said coolly, ignoring his other question.

'With a mouth like yours, I can see why someone might

decide to ride his horse over your face,' he said. 'Are you suggesting that my wife could have become pregnant with another man while I was married to her? I should add to the damage on your face, would it not make a mess of my clothing.'

'No, I was only thinking . . .' I shut up. I wasn't sure what else I could have been suggesting. 'I was very sorry to hear of your wife's death.'

'Why? Did you know her?'

'Me? No.'

'Then you cannot have been affected. Not as much as those who did know her and love her,' he said.

'No. Of course,' I said. 'You loved her, then?'

'She was my wife. And now, with her dead . . .'

'She was a wealthy woman, I heard.'

He glared at me. 'Yes, and with her dead, I have nothing. Nothing!' His eyes welled again, but now I knew it was self-pity I felt less sympathy.

'Where were you when she died?'

'Out in the yard there.' He pointed over his shoulder. 'We had argued about things again, and I went out to calm down.'

'Better than punching her, I suppose,' I said nastily, thinking of what Kitty had told the groom.

'Hold! You were the man who found her, weren't you? The gaoler said he found you over her, as though you had struck the blow.'

'No, no. I was with three ladies in the adjacent room. We heard a scuffle, and when we went out, there she was, dead, on the floor.'

'So you found her already dead?'

'Yes. And the gaoler was there shortly after. He must have heard something, I suppose.' I considered this for a moment. I had heard the noise, almost immediately I had been pushed towards the door by my three charming companions, and I found her. Except a moment or two later, there was One-Eye with his dagger. Yet that was not a part of the palace in which he would have been permitted or welcomed, surely.

'Did you not see anyone else out there?'

There was a sharpness to his tone.

I glanced at him, but he avoided my gaze. 'No,' I said.

'My poor Meg,' he said. 'She was always so devoted to me and the boy.'

'The gaoler said something about a jewel that was missing – a signet or seal,' I said.

'Did he?'

I was thinking new suspicious thoughts about old One-Eye. He had been there; he had time to grab a jewel after I had fled, surely. Then he could have made out that I had been the murderer, and gone and hidden it somewhere else. And if you are going to ask why he would have brought it up, well, someone was going to at some point. If it was that large and conspicuous, somebody was sure to ask what had become of it. Gilbert had said it had no value, but what would a boy like him know? One-Eye could have it, and be pretending to Sir Walter that it was lost purely to drive up its value. Or something.

'Was there something that she was habituated to wear?'

He shot me a look. 'Only her father's old signet ring, which she used to wear about her neck on a silver chain. She was very proud of her father, Sir Robert Neville. He was a reckless brute of a man, but he held the Scottish Marches against the clans from the north.'

'Was it a valuable ring?'

'No! When Sir Robert was alive, it was a very important bauble. He used it to seal his letters and other important documents. But its authority died with him, of course.'

'Didn't you think to ask where it was?'

He shot me a look. 'An old ring? Of no real value? Why would I want it? It wasn't even my family's, and there was no precious stone or gold fitting with it. Why would I worry about that?'

I left him there. He was lying, of course. I had heard him discuss it with One-Eye. But if it was of no intrinsic value, then she was surely not murdered for it. But why would he offer good money to One-Eye for it? Why was he so interested in it – it had been summarily dismissed during the inquest, after all.

There was little else to occupy me. Keeping a careful watch for One-Eye, I left the buttery and walked through the hall and out through the rear, where the door gave into what had once been a solar suite, but which was now a ramshackle affair of smaller chambers with tawdry decorations that should have been replaced during the reign of old Henry. Or his father.

It was through here that I had encountered Lady Margery's body. I had been here, in this side chamber, with the three pretty little maids, Sal, Kitty and Meg, trying to pick which would be best to warm my bed that evening, when we all heard the crash and clatter.

I found myself in the small corridor again. On my left was the door to the courtyard, while to my right was a flight of stairs leading up to the next floor. Beyond these a passage ran to another door, which gave on to a corridor that led off to more chambers. At the side of the staircase there was a sideboard with a display of pewterware. It was that which I had heard when the woman was killed.

She had collapsed and knocked pewter from the sideboard as she fell. Perhaps she had stretched out her arms and caught the plates in her death throes. They had rolled and clattered to the stone flags of the floor, causing the noise we had heard.

In the hallway, I stood and glanced about me. There was a large stain on the ground where she had lain, I saw, and knew it was her blood. No amount of scrubbing would clean that up. Not a nice sight. I've always hated the sight of blood. But since she fell there, if the necklace had broken, I thought, perhaps it had fallen away here, and the ring, too.

I was determined to look. But although I searched some little while, feeling under the sideboard, bending and peering, the only thing I could find was a single twisted piece of metal. It looked like a circle of silver, a 'C', where the two ends had once been connected, but which had been torn apart in a moment of violence. It could, I thought, have been a link in a tiny chain, perhaps a part of a thin necklace made to hold a crucifix and a signet ring.

I stood with the link in my hand. It was just a little circle of metal that had been twisted and broken, but it told of violence and murder, and the mere touch of it made my hackles rise.

I shuddered at the feel of it and almost dropped it again. I was thinking: with the mark on the woman's neck, it was plain enough that the necklace had been ripped from her by main force. Who would want to steal something that was of little value, something that had once been important as a seal but which now was irrelevant? I was reluctant to admit it, but I had a feeling that Master Blount would be able to make more sense of this than me. Walking to the door that led outside, I slipped into the yard.

His chamber was at the farther side of the court when I walked out. I had to pass by the end wall of the hall near the chapel, and turn left to walk past the gatehouse, and I was about to march to Blount's door when a hand fell on my shoulder. Turning rapidly, I found myself looking up into Harvey's face. His affable smile did not reassure me; it did not seem to meet his eyes. In any case, I've learned over the years that often those who smile most are those who are most ready to attack under an amiable cover.

'A friend would like to see you,' he said.

I was suddenly bustled into a doorway near the gatehouse, up some stairs, and into a comfortable, well-appointed parlour. There was a fire in the hearth, and wall hangings with fine needlework and bright colours, but none of them struck me at first. All I could see was the fine, pale features of the woman sitting on the chair.

Harvey gave me a shove between the shoulder blades as he sank to one knee. I copied him quickly.

'You are Master Jack?' she said.

'Yes, your Highness,' I managed. I was tongue-tied and concerned to be here with her.

'You are servant to John Blount?'

'Yes.'

'And you discovered the body of my good friend, Lady Margery Throcklehampton? You were the First Finder? Tell me, did you see the necklace about her neck? Her crucifix?'

I looked up. There was a distinct sound of sadness in her voice. She did not sound like a woman who had heard of an enemy dying, yet a spy was surely not an ally to her.

'No. When I found her, I would swear that it was not there. But when she was cut, the blood went everywhere. If she had a thin necklace, it would have been hidden, perhaps.'

Harvey's voice was a low rumble as he stood and wandered to a sideboard. A manservant reached it before him. Harvey smiled, aware he was not trusted. 'I do not think so.'

'Why so?' she said.

'A body will not bruise easily after death. If there was a bruise, she won that while alive. I would think the necklace was snatched from her, and that she died a little later.'

'How would you know this?'

'I was a priest, my Lady. I have seen many dead bodies before I buried them.'

'In that case, who could have taken it?' the Princess mused.

'The necklace or the seal?' I asked, and got a very sharp look indeed.

'What do you know of the seal?'

'Nothing. Only that others know of it.'

'I would forget what you have heard of the seal,' she said. 'But if you find it, tell me quickly. It may be perilous to keep it.'

Harvey deposited me in the yard once more, and I looked up at him. 'What was all that about?'

'She wants to know what happened; that is all.'

'But why should she care about a spy?' I wondered, and then I understood. 'It's not the woman; it's her seal she's worried about.'

Harvey shrugged, as if that was not something I need concern myself about. He left me and walked over towards the stables, and I was about to walk to John Blount's door when I saw something that made me hesitate, then surreptitiously sidle back to the doorway once more.

Crossing the yard in front of me were four men-at-arms, one with his sword ready, and as I watched, they marched to Master Blount's door and tried the door quietly. Finding that it was barred and bolted, their leader took to beating with his fist on the timbers. The sound echoed unpleasantly about the courtyard, and I saw several grooms pausing in their work to stare. Even the smith paused in his hammering to peer over.

'Open in the name of the Queen!' the commander bellowed, and in the subsequent silence, I found myself holding my breath. At a signal, two of the men started to pound on the door with the butts of their polearms, slamming them at the timbers with full force.

I slid further back until only one eye could peer around the corner, and was set to wondering what could have caused this pandemonium. Just when I thought that the guards would be forced to fetch axes, there was a cry from inside and the noise of bolts being shot. In a moment, Master Blount was in the doorway with a ferocious expression. 'Is it so urgent that you require a man to stop taking a shit? What is all this?'

'You're under arrest.'

'For what?'

'For plotting against Her Majesty, for planning to aid rebellion, for spreading sedition, and for murder.'

'Whom have I killed?'

'Lady Margery Throcklehampton.'

'I wasn't even in the building when she died!'

'Tell that to the Justice. You'll come with us.'

I moved away from the doorway and fell back against the wall, panting slightly.

There was no reason for me to feel any sympathy for Blount. He had been a useful ally at times, and a good conduit for money to keep me in bread and ale, but he was always so cynical, so suspicious, that he could never grow to be a confidant or friend. At best he was a miserable, intolerant acquaintance with the compassion of a wounded bear. He blundered through life, dealing out pain and injury to all who crossed his path, with barely a thought for those over whom he trampled. The man deserved neither sympathy nor aid. Yet I felt a twinge of guilt to see him in such straits.

I peered around the corner in time to see a man-at-arms slam a fist into Blount's belly. It was the sort of blow to make even me wince. If that had been me, I'd have been spewing in a second. Blount collapsed, body arched like a spitting cat's as he dropped to all fours. Then a boot caught his flank and he rolled, but even as I saw the wicked little blade appear in his hand – where did that come from? I'd have to remember that, if I ever tried to disarm the man: he grew weapons like the spines on a hedgehog's back – a boot slammed down on his wrist, a sword was at his throat, and the fight was done.

There was nothing more to see. I rested for a little longer, my back to the wall, listening as the guards pummelled Blount's body, and then laughed and made jokes at his expense, dragging him away from his chamber. I had little doubt that he would soon be returned to one of the foul gaol cells, and I didn't think his stay there would be comfortable or enjoyable.

'What are you watching?' a quiet voice said beside my ear.

You know when people say that they all but jumped from their skin after a sudden shock? I'd never truly known what that meant before that moment, but to hear that breathy voice so close to my right lughole was enough to make me leap like a faun startled by a hound. 'What the—'

Lady Anne made a most unladylike sound, partway between a snort and a whinny, and I glared at her. It served only to increase her amusement.

'You leap like the greatest tumbler in the Queen's Court,' she said, not even trying to conceal her smirk. 'If you were a lamb surprised by a fox, you could not be more shocked!'

I felt the blood rush to my face, but there was no unkindness in her eyes – only a kind of affectionate amusement, like a mother smiling at a dim child who strove to do his best. My voice was as hot as my cheeks. 'You surprised me, is all! Have you any idea what is happening to Master Blount?'

She set her head to one side and lifted an eyebrow. 'Has he died, that you thought me his ghost?'

'Perhaps not yet,' I said, 'but he soon will if nothing is done. He's accused of murder, treachery and I don't know what else besides. The guards have just taken him from his room and they're giving him a solid beating.'

'That is your master?' Her levity departed her at once on hearing that. 'Wait here. I'll be back in a little while.'

She slipped away along the side of the hall to the farther

corner and disappeared around it. I was left alone, and I need scarcely say that I was unhappy about the situation. I left my doorway and went over to the hall's wall, from where I could at least see if someone approached me. Then, seeing a guard standing and staring suspiciously, I sidled around the corner of the wall.

I wiped at my nose. It felt as though it was about to bleed again, and I winced. That was an end to my good looks, I felt sure. I know some men with their noses broken could show little effect afterwards, but I was equally certain that I would not be so lucky. In my case, my face was a large part of my success. I could persuade my gulls to trust me because my looks endeared me to them. They knew instantly, as soon as they saw my rugged, square features and open, faithful brown eyes, that they would be safe in my hands. That conviction would remain with them for exactly as long as it took for me to deprive them of their purses. But with a twisted, broken nose, I would look like little more than a brute who would waylay a nun if there was profit in it. My looks had been my treasure; they were responsible for my good fortune, such as it was. Without them, I was lost.

If I have a strength, it is that I always look on the favour-able balance of the scales. I am not prey to doubts and complaints. I prefer to look at the good that might come from a situation. However, this time I was flummoxed. If there was a positive aspect, I could not find it. My master arrested and held meant that my source of income was gone; without Blount, my house and board were lost.

Except that then I remembered that Sir Thomas Parry, Blount's master, was the man who held the purse-strings. Perhaps it would be better to seek his assistance. But no, he was not in the palace; I had seen him leave. And we were still held inside this hellhole, at the Coroner's pleasure. I peered around the wall. Yes, the gates were still locked. The guards, meanwhile, were enjoying themselves, kicking seven barrels of something out of Blount.

A hand touched my shoulder and I squeaked. It is a miracle that my bowels did not lighten my load considerably, but as it was, I turned with trepidation to expostulate with Lady Anne for startling me again, and found myself staring down the length of a long-bladed dagger.

'A good day to you, Jack,' Atwood said, smiling.

I felt a sense of déjà vu: just as when One-Eye had pricked my neck, I could scarce take my eyes from the blade. Occasionally, I have watched fighters performing their skills with the aid of rebated blades, when the edges are blunted so that they cannot harm anyone, and there's little excitement in it. When you go to watch a real duel at the bear pits, you can see the light glistening on the blades' edges. They look very different. The edge is almost a continuation of the blades' flats. That is a sign of real danger. A man can see the wicked gleam as the blade moves.

There was no rebating on this dagger. The blade was fire-blackened from its forging and quenching, with a straight back and a gleaming, wickedly angled section where the whetstone had ground away the metal to make a razor-sharp edge. It looked like a weapon that had been designed specifically for stabbing a man like me with the minimum of fuss or effort. I didn't like the look of that blade. It looked as though it didn't like me much, either.

'Hah!' I managed at last. 'Atwood!' I didn't feel this was sufficient somehow. 'How are you?'

'What are you doing here?' he asked.

'Me?'

His eyes bored into mine. If a man tells you that eyes are all soft and pliant like a boiled egg, all I can say is that Atwood had eyes that were made of the same stuff as his blasted dagger. It felt as if I had already been stabbed when they struck me, and I sank back against the wall.

He looked over my shoulder. 'Your master appears to be in a little spot of trouble.'

'He's been arrested. They accused him of killing Lady Margery!'

'Yes, well, it's easy to believe. He is a keen supporter of Lady Elizabeth, and the Queen thinks treachery is a terrible offence.'

'He's not guilty of treachery!'

'No? If the Queen or her Coroner decides he is, who are you to argue?'

That was indeed a thought. If Master Blount were to be accused, it would be very difficult for him to defend himself. It was hard to argue against your Queen or her representative. And then, of course, any companion of his would likewise be suspected.

Someone like me, for example.

If I could, I would have copied an empty sack and slumped to the ground, but the dagger prevented that. I didn't dare move for fear of impaling myself. Instead, I tried to think clearly. 'What are you doing here?'

He bared his teeth. 'The same as you, I'd imagine.'

I thought of the body of Lady Margery Throcklehampton. 'You're a bit late, then.'

'Yes,' he agreed, staring past me to the court. I could hear the men out there laughing and joking. It wasn't the sort of sound I enjoyed listening to. Then there were some shouts, the sound of a heavy object being dragged across the stones of the yard. It sounded a lot like a bag of cabbages being pulled along, but I knew it was Blount's body. With luck, he wasn't too badly injured. There was the noise of a door opening, and then silence.

'That's him done, then,' Atwood said. He turned his face back to me. 'So, Master Blackjack. What will we do with you, eh?'

'You said you were here for the same reason as me. All I want is to escape this place.'

'Yes, I can understand that,' he said. 'After all, things will get rather warm and dangerous now, I'd imagine.'

'I don't want to hang around for that.'

He frowned then. I'd forgotten that he was rather an idealistic fellow. He had wanted the rebellion to succeed, thinking, I suppose, that Queen Mary was an unmitigated disaster for the country. Some of us, me included, thought it a case of better the devil you know, but Atwood seemed to think the situation could be improved, and wanted to make things better all on his own. He was a firm believer in improving people's lives – sometimes by ending them.

'I remember your courage was always in rather short supply.'

'Mine? I was as brave as I could be, but the times were difficult!' I said heatedly. 'You had the fun of riding hither and thither, but I was stuck in London, guarding one gate after another, then helping the guards protect the Queen . . .'

'Yes, you suffered greatly,' he said with a snigger. 'And look at all the good you've achieved!'

I heard a door open. It was the one I had come through. There was the sound of nothing happening, and then the door shut again. I turned my head, but there was no one there. I had hoped that Lady Anne might have returned, but whoever had peered out had seen no reason to interrupt our conversation.

'Why do you want to hold me here?' I asked. 'You don't want to kill me. They'd assume you were responsible for the other murder as well, if you did that.'

'Not if I kill you and put you into Blount's room, for example,' he said coolly.

I confess that had not occurred to me. 'Oh.'

'Now, be silent and let me think,' he said.

'Why are you so determined to remove the Queen from her throne?' I said.

'Because she will take us back to the misery of the Roman Church. Now be silent!' he said.

'How did you get here, anyway? You pretended to be a carter, but someone must have spoken for you in order for you to get inside. And you were with the company of the Coroner, so he must think you're loyal to the Queen . . .' I said, and then I was stilled, for the knife's point was making his feelings on the matter of my continued speech rather plain.

'All I want is to get away from here and return to my home,' I said without thinking.

'Yes. Why don't we walk out of here?' Atwood said.

'You can. You're a carter,' I said bitterly. 'For men like me the gates are locked.'

'But now the Coroner's inquest is over, and you say Blount has been arrested for the lady's murder and attempts to rebel, so there is clearly no further need for the ban on poor servants and churls leaving,' he said. 'I think we should depart this place.'

'You think you can persuade the Coroner to let us go?' I said.

'I am sure of it,' he said. His dagger was withdrawn. 'I will be at the cart again shortly. You go there and wait. I'll be with you very soon.'

As he withdrew, I felt my entire body sag. That dagger had been so much a part of my vision that it seemed a surprise to look about me now and see that life continued. Stablemen and grooms cleaned and swept and shovelled and polished, while guards stood on the walkways high overhead, chatting with each other as they scanned the horizon for a view of brave but foolish men who would dare to try to assault such a strong palace, set in what was, mostly, a dangerous swamp.

I tried to saunter around the corner of the hall, but almost at once I found that my legs were reluctant to obey me. I stumbled and was close to falling. It was only by putting out a hand and grabbing the wall that I saved myself, and I stood there, panting slightly, my head whirling, and the blood pounding in my veins (and nose).

'Master Blackjack, come with me,' I heard, and saw Lady Anne had joined me. She wore a concerned expression, and I was grateful for that for an instant, before I realized that she was thinking more of my weakness attracting unwelcome attention from guards and servants, rather than displaying any sympathy for me. I tried to pull myself together, but still my legs shook and wobbled so badly that I was forced to lean fully against the wall. Still, at least now I was in plain sight of the gates, and Atwood would find it more difficult to hold a knife to my breast and threaten me with death. Not that the man would be too concerned about details such as being caught. He seemed to have an infallible certainty of success, no matter what he did, and even when he was shown to be on the losing side in a fight, he would still survive. It was a trait I desired to emulate.

That was when he came swaggering from the hall, pulling on thick peasant's two-fingered gloves. He threw a look in my direction, giving me an unreadable glance, as if I was of no more moment than a peasant at the side of his road, and made his way to his cart, where he spent an unconscionable age fetching his pony, rubbing her down, harnessing her and setting her between the shafts, the while whistling tunelessly and all but oblivious to me, as it seemed.

Soon he had the beast prepared, and stood at its head, leading it towards the gates with a click of his tongue and gentle murmurings. He stood a moment at the gates, holding out a parchment. One guard looked at it, at him, and at it again, but the second guard took it, read it slowly – I could see his lips moving – and then bellowed to the porter to open the gates. The order to hold all in the palace was rescinded.

Atwood turned and glanced at me. I smiled and stared back. If he thought I was going to join him after he had held a knife to my throat, he was mistaken. I waited until the cart was gone and had rattled its way halfway along the causeway before I levered myself away from the wall. Atwood shot a look at me over his shoulder once more, but seeing I was not following him, he urged his pony to a greater pace and appeared to set me from his mind. I stood a moment, urging my legs to stop wobbling, and then began to walk to the gate.

'What are you doing?' Lady Anne said.

'I'm just going into town. I want to make sure all my belongings are safe at the inn,' I lied, and, taking a deep breath, walked to the gates. For a moment, I had the horrible feeling that someone was going to stop me, but then I passed beneath the gatehouse and out beyond into the flat, wet countryside.

It was horrible. Never have I longed so much for the comforts, the welcome stench and shouting noisiness of London, but it was infinitely better than being locked inside that appalling palace with the reek of death about it.

As I entered the inn, Thomas Parry was sitting at a great trestle with his back to a wall, a clerk sitting to his right, scribbling furiously. From his post, Parry could see everyone who entered the place before the door had a chance to close. There was a roaring fire in the hearth, and he looked a little warm in his heavy jack and cap, but the gleams of the flames set off his chins and made his eyes glitter like jewels. There was a line of men waiting to speak with him, some supplicants with their hats in hands. All looked anxious except one who stared at me. I ignored his unsettling gaze.

'You decided to try to avoid your rents, didn't you?' Parry was saying to a tall, older man. 'The Princess is not turned moon-struck just because she's being kept here.'

'I didn't think she was, Master, but—'

'But like all the others who suddenly discovered that their Lady was being held here, you thought that you could hold on to your due taxes and rents, rather than paying what you owed, because she might be kept locked up for an age. You thought that you would be able to avoid paying, didn't you?' Parry said, with a world-weary tone. He leaned back in his seat, his hands on the table, palms uppermost, like a trickster about to pull a coin from a man's ear. 'I am not a fool, either.'

'No, Master, but . . .'

Parry leaned forward, and there was a dangerous light in his eyes. 'You will pay all the rents and customary fees due by the end of the week, or you will be evicted from your farm. I will not aid those tenants of her manors who try to hold on to money owed to her. And consider this: she is soon likely to be released, and when she is, she will hold to account all those who were tardy in providing the funds she needs. You do not wish to be one of those who is held to account?'

'No, Master, I—'

But Parry waved his hand dismissively, looking over to his clerk. They had a brief conversation, and then Parry was looking up at me expectantly. He beckoned.

I didn't have a drink of any sort to calm my stomach, and my last ales with Sir Walter seemed a very long time ago now. I regretted the lack as he peered up at me with a frown on his face. He took in my nose and my badly stained and ruined jack, and could scarce control his shock. 'What happened to you?'

While I explained, Parry clapped his hands and a well-presented herald brought a pewter tray with a jug and a cup. Parry sent him away to fetch a second for me, listening all the while as I spoke of the inquest, the uncouth Coroner, the attack on me, Blount's attempt to save me, his arrest, and lastly the fresh assault on Blount himself and the reopening of the gates.

'What of the Princess? How did she look?'

'She is fine. Only bored with the Coroner's inquest, I think.' I did not mention the seal.

'Yes, she told me she detests being held against her will,' Parry said. He glanced at a sheet of parchment his clerk passed him and nodded.

I took the cup proffered by the herald, who gave me the impression he would have spat in it, had he not been so near his master, and sipped the wine. It was very good.

'Come, sit next to me,' Parry said, and his herald disappeared to fetch me a three-legged stool, setting it down with a disdainful glance at me. Parry leaned towards me, his eyes still fixed on the rest of the people in the room. He spoke in a faint whisper so quiet I had to lean closer.

'I understand that the Lady Margery has died? Very sad.'

'Yes, she was—'

'I don't need any details. You have done well.' He pressed a soft leather bag into my hands. It had the delightful heft and feel of a purse filled with good coins, and I felt my mouth begin to spread into a broad grin. 'There will be a need for more work soon, but for now you should take your rest for a day or two.'

My grin disappeared. He thought me guilty of the murder of Lady Margery, too. I just hoped his idea of 'more work' wouldn't mean I would be expected to actually kill someone else in the near future.

DAY THREE

I had an enjoyable time at the inn. It was perpetually filling and emptying with new faces. All those who were responsible for the Princess Elizabeth's estates were coming for orders, to confirm progress on previous commands, to bring money, or just to gather or disseminate news. The landlord of the place was hurrying about with a fixed grin on his face that threatened to separate the top of his skull. He had not seen so much business in many a long year.

There was much news to relay. Up and down the country there was a rising annoyance with the way that the Queen was riding roughshod over the interests of others. The reasonable religious reforms of her father and brother were being dropped, according to many, and the sober priests who had been installed in the name of the English Church were being removed. There were rumours that the monasteries could be brought back, and people feared that great taxes would be levied to pay for the replacement of roofs, decorations and ornaments that had been stripped out on the orders of King Henry. Although the Queen was still head of the English Church, it was well enough known that she favoured the return of the Pope as spiritual leader, and many Englishmen were unhappy that the Roman faith might return.

However, it was not until later the next day, when Parry called me to his chamber, that I realized how serious matters had become.

'Sit, Master Blackjack,' he invited as I walked in. There was a clerk at his side, and two men-at-arms in the Princess's livery stood at the door, but when Parry waved his hand, they went to stand outside. 'Have you heard the rumours?'

'Of the Church, you mean?' I said. 'I know many are up in arms at the thought that the Catholics might demand the return of monasteries and manors.'

'No, it was the Princess I was thinking of,' he said. He took his seat near the fire. 'You can ignore Paul here. He has been my clerk for many years. But we have received very alarming news. It seems that there is no evidence to have my Lady Elizabeth executed for treason. Although the torturers went about their business with their customary zeal and determination, they could not force any of the rebels to implicate Elizabeth in any of their plans. The rebel chief, Wyatt himself, must have suffered a great deal at their hands while he was imprisoned in the Tower, before he was executed.'

'That's good, then,' I said. 'She is safe.'

'No. She is not to be murdered on a pretext, but that does not make her safe. Now she is at risk from others who would see her removed. Some would have her disinherited, so that she would be forced to beg or endure constant hardship. Others would see her murdered in a counterfeit of execution, wanting her assassinated.'

Perhaps it was my pain, but this was washing over me without my being able to comprehend the full meaning. 'Who would dare?'

He looked at me. 'The Spanish, because they are determined to remove a potential difficulty; factions in parliament who want to see Mary reign without the embarrassment of a half-sister who is clearly head and shoulders above her in intellect and learning; Bishop Gardiner, in his position as Lord Chancellor, would prefer to see the Queen rule without the threat of another rebellion. In God's name, we have seen poor Lady Jane Grey try to take the throne from Queen Mary already, and then Wyatt raised his banner in support of her or Elizabeth, and Gardiner will not want to see another threat. He is a good man: he seeks to placate all sides, but he knows that this troublesome realm will not rest easy while Mary has a rival.'

I nodded. 'I am glad all such matters are above me!'

He cast me a look that seemed to me to carry a weight of meaning. 'It is not your primary task, but I have a new role for you. Master Blount was intended to keep a close eye on the Princess. In his absence, you must take on his duties.'

'What? But I—'

'I appreciate that it is not what we hired you for, but we

have no option but to protect Princess Elizabeth as best we can, and you do at least have full access to the palace. It is more than I have.'

'I can't, though!'

'Why not?'

That was a difficult one. Again, I found myself in the troublesome position of not being able to speak of my personal reservations about ending other men's lives. Parry eyed me for a moment, and then nodded as if the matter was agreed.

'You will need to have help. There is a man who is reliable, who can take messages to the Princess when you need, and he can arrange to bring news to me here when necessary. He is already known to you.'

He clearly meant Harvey.

'I can't do this! Bedingfield will be certain to suspect something, and—'

'Bedingfield doesn't have the wits of a harvest mouse. He demands much, but he cannot force our hands, and he knows it. He insisted that I should not be permitted to visit the Princess, but then he realized that it would mean he must pay for her staff and guards. So he agreed that she should pay, but the consequence of that was that I have to be on hand to help with the finances. As it is, he knows that he is on difficult ground. The Princess is paying for herself, her servants, and also his own men. He cannot afford to pay for them himself. His "Norfolk understanding" does not stretch to comprehending how to resolve matters.'

'What if his men decide to attack me? Even now they could have beaten the truth out of Blount, and be preparing to arrest me! They may think that I killed Lady Margery, and that I plan to harm another!'

Parry shook his head. 'You will be safe enough. You have one function only, and that is to guard and protect the Princess. Do that, without fear of consequences. Serve the Lady as best you can. You will be secure. Is there anything else?'

I was about to leave when I recalled the link. I had placed it carefully in my scrip, and now I fumbled about deep inside to bring out the small silver circlet. I held it up.

'What is this?' he asked.

'I don't know whether it's important, but when Lady Margery died, it's said she had a signet of her father's about her neck on a silver chain, but it's disappeared. Then she bore another chain, with a crucifix, but she wore nothing when she was dead. When I looked at the floor near where she was killed, I found this, as if the chain had been pulled away. Or the crucifix.'

Parry looked at the link with bafflement and little interest, then up at me. 'What of this? Her father's been dead these five years past. His signet cannot endorse anything now.'

'I know that, but someone has stolen it.'

'So what? The woman was robbed. If you happen,' he said, and cocked an eye at me, 'if you happen to come across this crucifix or the signet ring, I would dispose of it in London, where there are many men who will accept a ring and melt it down without asking embarrassing questions.'

I was already trudging back towards the palace before I stopped in the road and nearly went back, so outraged did I feel. The man assumed *I* had stolen the ring after murdering the woman! At least he had no interest in it.

The walk to the palace from the Bull took me past a number of small dwellings, and it was while I was passing these that I heard the sound of a man in great distress. His cries of grief would have been audible in the palace a half mile away, I should think, and I was about to walk on, but something about the sound was familiar. I turned and followed the sounds to a peasant's hovel. It was a cruck-built house, with wattle and daub walls, but the daub was poorly painted, and great lumps were falling away. The door was little more than a series of planks that could be propped in the doorway, with neither hinge nor lock. It reminded me of so many poor houses near my home in Kent when I was a lad. I had no desire to see inside a shabby dwelling like that and was about to leave when the sound came once more. It was, I was sure, the young squire from the palace.

I leaned around the doorway. Inside, lying on a low palliasse on the floor, was a pretty maiden. She could only have been twenty, no more. Her skin was the pale of the moon on a winter's evening, and she had lustrous dark hair, but today it was unnaturally spread about her and her hands were placed on her breast, crossing at the wrist.

She was not breathing.

The squire was kneeling beside the palliasse, and a middle-aged old maid stood beside him while he bawled. He had his face hidden in one hand, while with the other he reached out to clutch the hand of the girl on the palliasse. I would have slipped back and continued to the palace, but as soon as I glanced in, the woman behind him saw me and nudged the squire. 'This a friend of yours?'

He looked up. His pale eyes were red-rimmed and filled with a kind of savage grief. 'What do you want? Are you here to gloat or laugh?'

'I'm sorry,' I said. There was no need to ask what had happened. The clothes balled up in a bloody mess and the basket with more lying at the foot of the bed told the rest of the story.

The midwife gathered up some herbs and made her way past me to the door. 'Someone needs to stay with him this night,' she said quietly. She was older, at least thirty years or so, but had a firm conviction in her low tone. 'Your friend needs a companion.'

'Wait!' I said, but she ignored me and bustled out.

Which left me there, staring down at the two of them. I was not sure how to begin a conversation, and he was in no mood for chatter, so I left him to it, pulled up a stool and sat with my back to the wall. I could see through the doorway to the causeway leading up to the palace from here, and I idly picked up some little pebbles and pieces of gravel from the corner of the floor, throwing them one at a time at a couple of stones just over the threshold. I was not very accurate, but at least it was a distraction from the man's moaning.

'I loved her so much. I never wanted any other woman,' he said.

'Oh?' I said, trying to sound interested.

'She was so kind and gentle. I loved her from the first moment I saw her.'

'I see.'

He was going to grow maudlin, I thought. It was tempting to get him to drink some ale, so that I could have an excuse to join him, but I didn't relish the idea of sitting all night with him, listening to his miserable complaints and then trying to get him back to his own bed, while probably avoiding his fists. If I knew anything, it was that men like him would get violent when they grew drunk while mourning the loss of a loved one. I didn't want another buffet about my head. I'd had enough of them since arriving at Woodstock.

'We were so happy when I was told to come here, too. She was already here with Lady Anne, and we had hoped to plan our future, and . . . and then . . . we hoped to remain here . . . that Lady Anne would understand.'

My ears pricked. There was a significant pause there, or I was a Dutchman. 'Whom do you serve here?'

'I am here to watch over Princess Elizabeth,' he said.

'For whom?'

'I am a loyal subject of the Queen.'

That could mean anything or nothing. He could mean that he would do nothing against Queen Mary, or he could mean that he was scared to be thought of as disloyal, in which case asserting his credentials was important. However, his wife had been maid to Lady Anne, who was fervently Royalist and supported the Queen. If the squire was to get anywhere, he must surely have supported the Queen, too.

'You saw Lady Margery. Did you know anything about a seal she used to wear?' I asked. 'I have heard it was a value-less trinket of her father's.'

The squire nodded. 'It was. She showed it to me once. A small ring with her father's arms graven on to a small stone. It was nothing valuable, just a cheap stone in a cheap setting.'

'What use could that be to anyone?' I wondered.

He shrugged, staring down at his wife's body. 'A seal is only of use when a man lives. It's the proof of his intentions, his signature. But when he is dead, its value dies with it. Death ends all.'

He was maudlin again. Not that it mattered to me. I had to return to the palace before the gates were locked. I rose to my feet. 'I have to get back. What will you do?'

He explained that he must sit here and hold vigil for the woman. That was fine by me. Personally, I was more interested in getting away from him than listening to his doleful tones. I bid him farewell, and was about to walk from the room when I heard steps – many steps.

I leaned forward to get a view of the road back to the village, and saw a party of men clad in hardened leather, two with steel caps on their heads, all of them armed with swords. They were an impressive sight, especially with their commander at the fore. He looked a particularly warlike warrior.

Slipping back into the room, I flattened my back against the wall.

It was that damned Atwood again.

The men continued, muttering to each other as they set off along the causeway towards the palace. I counted them as they passed by. Three-and-twenty all told, I thought.

'Squire, did you see them?' I hissed when they were a safe distance from the hovel.

Squire George looked over at me. 'See what?'

'A party of men marching off towards the palace. Are there more soldiers expected?'

'I don't know.'

'Do you know of a man called Atwood? This high, good-looking, in a way? Sort of scrawny, but in a way you wouldn't want to test?'

'No, I don't know!'

I described Atwood even so, and he eventually nodded. It was one of the men he had seen near the chamber where Lady Margery was killed.

'Now, why don't you go and ask in the tavern or the inn? There are men there who would like to make conversation with you!' he said. 'Leave me alone with my grief!'

I could see his point. I wasn't really helping him, no matter what the midwife had hoped. I glanced at the door, at him, and the woman's body, and finally summoned up the courage to ease myself outside, where I stood awhile, breathing shallowly and listening carefully. There was a raucous noise from further up the road, where Atwood and his merry men were making enough din to raise the devil. It was still daylight, and I thought I could get up to the inn as Squire George had so refreshingly suggested, but that would mean stumbling into the figure of Sir Thomas Parry once more, and that was not to be borne. He would be certain to have questions, such as why I had returned so swiftly, who were the men who so alarmed me that I allowed myself to be diverted from my duties, and what were they up to?

It was deeply alarming for a poor fellow like me. I stood there indecisively for a long while, my eyes flitting from the causeway ahead and then back to the inn, over and over again until I grew quite dizzy. I had no idea what was my best course of action. I could remain here in the town, hiding in a stable or barn, perhaps, but that would be the end of my regular income. Blount and Parry would not maintain my lifestyle if there was any doubt about my loyalty and commitment, and they would know instantly if I did not return to the palace. Then again, there was the temptation to find out what I could about these ruffians. Perhaps they were threatening the palace. I could discover what they were up to, perhaps, and report back to Blount or Parry, and prove to them how useful I could be. It was worth an attempt, I thought.

I do not pretend to be brave. I am not. I have the heart of the most craven cur in the country when it comes to being attacked by men of the calibre of Atwood, and yet this appeared to me to be little more dangerous than a walk in the woods. Yes, there was always the risk that I might be seen, but if I was, I was at least young and relatively fleet of foot. I saw no reason to fear an assault. Besides, what would they do with someone like me? I was known to be a man of little merit or significance, only a servant to Blount, and even Atwood couldn't know that I was Blount's hired assassin.

The causeway was a secure path through the marshes. It was a track that rose a yard or more over the wetlands, with a great curved top. Ruts and muddy puddles abounded, and grasses grew at the edges and the middle. I walked along swiftly enough, making little noise. Every now and again I paused and listened. Each time I could hear the men ahead of me, even though the road curved like a snake in the grass, and occasional trees blocked the view ahead. There were odd bursts of laughter, as though these were no more than students on a ramble to find another alehouse, but I did not relent in my careful movements. I wanted to make sure that I learned what I needed to without running the risk of discovery.

After a half mile or so, there were some bushes, and I sidled up to them, listening intently. I peered through the leaves, and could see nothing, so continued to raise my head, and there, up ahead, a good two hundred yards away, I saw the men. I nodded to myself and hurried along the road, but I had only got a matter of three paces when something snagged my foot, and I went down like a stooping hawk.

I fought to get back to my feet and was about to run back to the concealment of the bushes when I looked up and found myself confronted by a smiling brute with three front teeth and the odour of a long-dead badger. Those were the good aspects of what I saw.

On the other side of the coin, in his hand he gripped a halberd with a long blade at the tip.

For once, this man didn't bother to point the blade at my throat or chest, but then he didn't have to. He would have swung that thing at me before I would be able to get to my feet.

I remained where I was and essayed a smile. He shook his head and called to his companions. 'Look what I've got here!'

Atwood smiled down at me, arms akimbo. 'So, Master Blackjack, we meet again!' he said, and began to laugh.

You can hear a man's soul through his laughter, I was once told. He cannot hide his actual nature when he laughs. If there is simple pleasure, you will hear it; if there is anger, you will hear that too. In Atwood, I had feared to detect something – lunacy or a desire to see me slowly roasted over a hot fire, perhaps – but instead I heard only genuine happiness. It was a relief.

'I had thought you were not going to come with me, Jack!' he said, and, leaning down, offered me his hand. 'I had thought you were so angry after our last escapades together that you would never try to rejoin me.'

'I don't know why you would think that,' I said, although in my mind was the time in London when he had been close to slitting me from groin to gizzard. Still, he'd perhaps forgotten that. And the other time at London Bridge . . . although I was happy to allow bygones to be gone. I patted myself down. There were generous splashes of mud on my hosen and jack from rolling on the ground, and I took in the sight of my besmottered clothing with irritation and dismay. This jack had been my best with its charming, light colour, and now it was liberally stained with my blood and with mud from the roadway. It looked shabbier than a peasant's third-hand cotte. I felt very undignified, and very unlike a Londoner. And the worst of it was, my spare shirt and hosen had been in my pack. They had been discarded when my bag had been upended in the pile of trash, I assumed. Certain it was that I would never see them again. So I was forced to wear my filthy jack and shirt and torn and stained hosen.

'It'll soon dry and clean off,' Atwood said. 'What were you doing here?'

'He was following us, just as you thought,' my friend the giant with the halberd said. 'He was skipping along like a spy, and peeping out between the branches of the bushes to keep an eye on you. Shame he didn't count, eh?'

I could have taken a dislike to the man. 'I was returning to the palace, and didn't want to walk through the middle of a large group of men such as this,' I said firmly, and truthfully. 'A man will walk warily when he meets a gathering of warlike fellows.'

'Fair enough! So, Jack, my old friend, how are you? It was hard to speak in the palace itself, but I left you deep in conversation with Bedingfield's daughter. She would tempt an angel down from heaven, that wench! You look well enough but for your nose, by God's pains! Look at the quality of your clothes, Jack! Granted, they've seen better days, but they're much better than the average draw-latch or dipper could hope to win. You have been fortunate!'

'Well, a man shifts for himself as best as he can,' I said.

'And Master Blount pays you well?'

'He is a good—' Too late I realized I had slipped into his

trap. When we had met before, this fellow and Blount were on very different sides of the table. Where one supported the rebels with Lady Jane Grey, Blount was for the Princess. Personally, I was for myself and no one else, but that was not the kind of statement I felt comfortable making in front of these men, all too many of whom were fingering weapons and glancing at me in the way that children would peer at saplings before cutting them down to make temporary bows. It was not a pleasant feeling.

'I know. Master Blount is a good man in a hard world,' Atwood said. 'And he has his own path to tread.'

'I doubt he'll go far. He was captured and taken to be questioned, you remember?' I said. 'He will tell all, no doubt.'

'No, he wouldn't speak. To do so would endanger all he holds dear.'

'Perhaps,' I said, although I couldn't imagine what a man would hold more dear than his own flesh and bones.

'But what are you doing following us? You must have known we would see you before long. You know me well enough to know I am a cautious commander. I take no risks.'

'I didn't know who was with this group. I had been to the town, and was on my way back to the palace.'

'What drew you to the town? I hoped you were following me as I had suggested.'

'Well, I would have done anyway, but I had other business.'

'What sort of business?'

'My own business.'

His smile broadened and I saw him nod to the giant. Suddenly, my arms were gripped by the elbows, and I could only squeak with alarm as I saw Atwood draw his knife once more. The blackened blade with the shining edge approached my throat again.

'Tell me, Jack, what other business did you have?'

'I was there to see Master Thomas Parry,' I said quickly. After all, a fellow can be badly injured by a lunatic with a knife, and I see no point in submitting to torture unnecessarily.

'Thomas Parry? Princess Elizabeth's steward and coun-sellor? The man who looks after her finances? What were you doing with him?'

'He is the man Blount works for. I went to tell him what had happened to my master.'

'And what did he say?'

'That I should guard the Lady Elizabeth to the best of my ability.'

He chuckled at that, and the knife moved towards my throat. I leaned back and he chuckled again. It touched my neck near my main vein, and the touch made me whimper. It was like a snake's kiss.

'And what will you do?'

'I . . . I don't know!'

'I do, Master Blackjack! You will do as you were told,' he said, and suddenly I was released, and his knife was hidden in its sheath once more. 'You will hurry to the palace ahead of us, and you will learn all you can, and in the morning you will see me out by the bakery where my cart was kept, and you will tell me of anything of interest that relates to the Princess Elizabeth's safety.'

'Why should I?'

'Because, you poor fool, we both serve the same master now,' Atwood said pityingly.

DAY FOUR

I made it to the gates before dusk and the curfew, although my feet felt like lead and my world felt as though it was slipping from me.

All the way, I was thinking about his words to me. He wanted me to spy on Princess Elizabeth for him – that was plain. So now I was stuck between the commands of Thomas Parry to protect her, and the demands of Atwood that I should betray her to him. For that was, I was certain, the result of his order. I could not believe that he too served Sir Thomas Parry. Harvey was there for Parry, too. He had told me so, and Sir Thomas had mentioned that there was an accomplice. No, it was more likely Atwood was there for his own advantage. He was trying to pull the wool over my eyes. Yet I had to wonder: Atwood had been a keen rebel against the Queen; he felt Queen Mary to be dangerous because of her faith. Perhaps he had thrown in his lot with Parry after all?

Not for the first time, I felt the horror of being a spy. To be thrust into great events, running the risk constantly of being discovered and slain, to live with the fear of a rope about the neck or a knife at the throat, and never any peace or security – that was a true, living hell. I just had to hope that I could survive long enough to discover an escape of some sort.

I entered the gatehouse and glanced upwards to the chamber where the Princess was being held. Then I was in the yard, and with nowhere else to go, I turned and strolled to the chamber where Master Blount had been sleeping.

His bed looked inviting, and I sat on it. I was not ready for sleep yet. I perched there on the edge of the palliasse and toyed with a thread on my muddy and ruined jack. In the space of a couple of days I had endured attacks, had my nose broken, been captured and held at knifepoint, watched my master being beaten and hustled away, and then commanded to risk my life to protect the Princess by both Thomas Parry and blasted Dick Atwood.

I had lost count of the number of times someone had tried to injure or kill me. Out of interest, I began to enumerate them, ticking them off on my fingers as I went. I could do with a cup of strong ale, or even a small wine, I thought. I remember that distinctly, and I was about to get up and fetch something when suddenly I was aware that I was lying full length on the bed and the room was filled with daylight. All about me I could hear the noises of a manor at work and the sun was streaming in through the windows. Somehow I must have dozed off.

Opening the door and looking up at the sky, I guessed it was still too early to break my fast. Like so many old-fashioned homes, Woodstock still had only two meals a day and the first would be in the hour before noon. Still, there were delicious wafts of baking bread and cooking meats emanating from bakery and kitchens, promising a wholesome meal before long.

I pulled the door to behind me and made my way across the yard, but before I could get far, I heard the rumble of wheels, and turned to see Dick Atwood riding in, kneeling on the boards of his cart. He smiled cheerfully and lifted his whip in acknowledgement when he saw me, and I gave him a sour nod in return. I didn't want to make a scene, but nor did I want his welcome. Behind him there was a series of wagons with provisions of different types. The thought gave rise to a sour discontent in my belly, and I decided to turn away and fetch a thin ale, both to settle my stomach and also to swill my mouth. It tasted foul.

I waited until the horses and carters were past, and then made my way across the courtyard, but before I could take a third pace, my shoulder was taken in a ham-like grip, and a deep voice rumbled beside me.

'It may be early but in this Godless manor, I daresay it matters little. There must be a quart of ale to break our fast.'

It was Harvey. My Friar Tuck was smiling broadly for the guards, except now there was no sign of amiable pleasantness in his eyes, only a stony determination.

* * *

For all that his face was wreathed in smiles, there was a decidedly piercing quality to the look he gave me. I was given the conflicting impressions that he was an affable buffoon and sharp, shrewd politician, expert in dissembling. Even now, I'm not certain which he was.

'Why does everyone want me to jump from my skin?' I demanded. My heart was pounding painfully, and appeared to have migrated to the base of my throat.

Harvey held up his hand and made the sign of the cross over me, with a grin that could have fitted any pirate eyeing a Spanish treasure-ship.

'My son,' he announced, 'I am in dire need of refreshment. Let us repair to the buttery, where we can partake of a small beer. For our health, you understand?'

'It's over there,' I said, pointing.

He leaned down a little. 'Let us pretend that I am a little confused about the direction, and at the same time we can pretend I won't happily rip off your arm and beat you senseless with the bloody end unless you hurry and lead me there, shall we?'

'I'll take you there, Master,' I said.

I led him away from the gates and into the hall, where I bade him sit while I gathered our drinks. I filled myself a pot first, sank it, and then refilled my pot before filling a jug with wine. There were goblets on the sideboard, I had seen.

By the time I returned, Jonathan Harvey was sitting in the midst of a sea of wagging tails. Like any gentleman, Sir Henry Bedingfield was a keen huntsman and kept many hounds of different sizes. Some had lost their tails, and many bore scars from attacks by wild boars or other fierce creatures, but all appeared to share an adoration of Harvey.

'There is little as delightful as a good hound, is there? A cat is an independent beast, with no interest in men as long as it gets its meals regularly. Provide a cat with food and lodging, and it will take all it can. Sometimes it will deign to sit in your lap, if it wants. It is a servant without loyalty. Like a thief, it will push its way into your home and demand attention, and in return should destroy all the rats in the yard, but rarely will it trouble itself. Meanwhile, a dog is a noble creature. Loyal, kind, always ready to do a man's will, always determined to protect his lord's house and table, always keen to help hunt and provide food for the household, and whenever a man wants affection, the hound is there, ready and eager. A true, honourable beast.'

'I've always liked cats,' I said, sipping at my ale.

'That explains much. You have been seduced by the feline's wiles.'

I had no idea what he was talking about, and moodily sipped again.

'You see, my friend, the cat is a dishonest creature. It will demand from its owner, whereas the hound will provide all in the hope that his loyalty will be noticed and rewarded. Much like good men.'

'Meaning bad men are more like cats, I suppose?'

'No. Often they are like dogs that are owned by a poor master. They think that being kicked and punished for no reason is all they deserve, and still try to curry favour with loyalty and honour. They are misguided in their loyalties; that is all. That is why it is important to know who serves whom.'

'What is your business?'

'Mine? The same as yours and Master John Blount's, of course. To see to it that the Princess is safe. We serve the same purpose.'

'How do you know of my master?'

He peered at me over the rim of his cup. 'Many know of Master John Blount. He is a legend in certain circles.'

'You speak of him as a comrade.'

'He and I have worked together before. We both serve Sir Thomas Parry.'

'Apparently, you are not alone.'

'What do you mean?'

I explained about Atwood. 'But you are the man Parry had told me to expect, aren't you?'

'He told you so. I wasn't going to speak, for I was not sure he had warned you of me,' he frowned. 'He was supposed to keep my presence secret.'

'You say the Princess must be kept safe . . . Why shouldn't she be safe enough here?'

'My friend, you must have heard some of the reports?'

'I know that the Queen wanted to seek out all those who had put her life and throne in jeopardy, but Lady Jane Grey and Wyatt paid for their crimes, and neither could tell of any offences committed by Lady Elizabeth, because surely if they had, she would be in the Tower now, and that not for long. She'd have been taken to the field, like Lady Jane, and parted from her head.'

'Aye, my friend, you are right there. But the trouble is that whereas the Princess may well be innocent of fomenting trouble, there are many others who see her as a prime candidate for replacing her sister on the throne.'

'But if she refuses . . .'

'She is a young woman. Were she to be ensnared, she might become amorously inclined. A man with a good leg, a dancer, a man of high fashion – one such as that might win her over.'

'There are all too few men like that about here,' I said. I looked down at my jack. The mud had dried now, and I spent a few moments ineffectually trying to knock the worst of it from me. I succeeded only in spreading it further. It was a mournful sight.

Harvey gave a guffaw. 'Panic not! There are maids here who can help you clean that. You seem to have made them friends very quickly. I saw you disappearing into the hall that first day with three of them! And while I am sure you are an eminently suitable fellow, there are others among our acquaintances who would be better suited – in every sense of the word. I merely chose to mention an example of their behaviour. This is the sort of nefarious effort that her enemies might try. They will wish to entrap her. They will send likely men to speak with her and, by drawing her out, find a means of persuading her to their ends. They are devious, these Catholics from Rome.'

'It must have been one of them who killed Lady Margery, then,' I said.

'Undoubtedly. A shrewd, cunning fellow, no doubt.'

'So you want me to guard her by killing anyone who goes close to her and appears to be a handsome sort of man?'

He cocked an eyebrow and peered at me seriously for a

moment. 'I want you to protect her by all means if you see her in danger, just as would one of these hounds, were they in your boots. You have a duty to serve your master, and he wants Princess Elizabeth guarded.'

'But I'm not even allowed to see her! I saw her once, briefly, during the Coroner's inquest, and with you, but you know she is guarded closely now in her chambers.'

'They will be allowing her out to walk about the courtyard before long. And she may be out sooner than that, if our plans go well.'

'What plans? You mean to rescue her from this place?'

The big priest smiled broadly and tapped the side of his nose. 'A secret kept is a secret safe,' he said.

A little later, we were evicted from the hall as servants arrived to set out the trestle tables for the first meal of the day. There was a large household under Bedingfield's command, with the men-at-arms garrisoning the place, as well as all the manservants going about their business. While the Princess remained in her chambers over the gatehouse, Bedingfield held court over the rest of the buildings and all the men who were installed here to maintain her dignity and Bedingfield's position as her gaoler.

It was a peculiar situation. I wandered outside with Harvey, and he regaled me with stories of his life. He had, so he said, been an enthusiastic servant of the Church, working at a small chapel in Devon until the end of King Edward's reign. Then, with the arrival of the young Queen, he had been taken by the conviction that there would soon be fights between those who wanted to return to the old Catholic faith and those who sought to retain the new English Church.

'I like the new Church. I was ever a poor scholar, and Latin strikes me as the most foolish language a man could design. Who would speak with a language which holds no word such as "the"? Besides, how can I be expected to translate every sentence from Latin into plain English that a Dartmoor marsh-dodger can understand? The peasants down there find it hard enough to comprehend English. I used to have to pick them up by the scruff of the neck and explain my more troublesome sermons with my fists.'

Glancing at his fists, I was sure that his methods would have been most persuasive.

'What led you to join Sir Thomas Parry?'

'It seemed better to me to seek to serve the lady who was more plainly with the English Church than the Catholic,' he shrugged. 'All know that the Lady Elizabeth is her father's daughter, whereas this Queen of ours is more Spanish. She is a chip from her mother's rock, I fear.'

So Elizabeth was still loyal to her father's new Church. That was certainly the way that I had heard matters. Many men who had become convinced of the merits of the new ways were enthusiastic supporters of the Lady Elizabeth since her stand against returning to the Catholic Church, even when her sister tried to force her. There were stories that she was even now reluctantly attending Catholic Mass under pain of her sister's displeasure. Yet most of us believed that she was not honestly engaged.

We were sitting on the bench where I had sat the previous day, and the carts began to move towards the gates, their wares all unloaded. The leading cart was at the gates already, and I saw the porters and guards moving to pull back the bars at the gates and haul at the ponderous timbers to open them wide. The carts began rattling their way through. I saw Atwood on one out by the bakery. He was looking at me in a fixed, stern manner. If Harvey was not at my side, he would surely have come and remonstrated with me for not going to meet him as he had planned. He nodded to me pensively, cracked the reins, and was on his way.

It was then that it happened. I saw Atwood's cart make its way beneath the stone arch, and another cart was lining up to make its way through, when there was a sudden flash of dark and white, and a cry, and Harvey and I stood quickly, while a horse whinnied and shied from the small figure it had knocked down.

From where I was, I could see the little huddled figure clearly. It was the boy, Gilbert. Even as I turned, I saw his stepfather in the doorway. He looked stricken.

I ran with Harvey to the body, and I allowed the giant to pick him up carefully. He was stronger than me. There was a raised

stone path beside the gatehouse that gave way to the steps
leading to the upper walkway, and here Harvey set down the
body gently.

Gilbert was shaking. His eyes wide and staring into the distance,
his brow was furrowed. A horseshoe had cut a long gash in his
skull, and his left arm looked broken. His breath came in little
pantings. It was like looking at an injured spaniel. I was distressed
to see the energetic little boy brought to this terrible, low pass. I
put a hand to his forehead, but he paid me no attention. I might
have touched a statue for all the effect it had.

But then there was a sudden rustling and commotion of
a different sort. The porter bellowed, and guards and others
ran to the gates, slamming them closed, while more guards
appeared, all with weapons.

Harvey held up his hands and bellowed at the top of his
voice, 'Hold! This child was run down by a carter; that is all!'

'Is he dead?' a man called, his voice brittle as though ready
to burst into tears. I thought it was Sir Walter Throcklehampton,
but I wasn't sure. In the midst of the forest of halberds and
lances, I couldn't see.

Harvey shook his head. 'No, the boy will be fine, I am sure.
But he will need a good physician. Is there anyone in the
palace who has experience of bone-mending? I fear his arm
is snapped, and he has a bad injury to his head.'

'Yes. Bring him up here,' a voice called. It was female and
very well bred.

'No! You cannot do that!'

'You think he might be a messenger? Or do you think this
boy is an assassin? Be not foolish, man. He is injured; he
has wounds and needs care. In the chamber we have three
ladies who can help him. Master Priest, please bring him up
here.'

It was only then that I dared to look up, and found myself
staring again into the pale, patrician face of the Queen's sister:
Princess Elizabeth.

This was better than the last chamber in which she inter-
viewed us.

I could wax lyrical about the chamber into which we were

brought. A marvellous blue barrel ceiling, with gold fleurs-de-lis and gilded ornaments. I saw roses and shields high overhead. Tapestries lined the walls and made the place feel warmer than it actually was. Some areas of wall were white-washed, and they had magnificent pictures painted on them, of red and gold and green and vivid blue. A great sideboard took up one end wall, and on it were plates and goblets and glasses of such beauty they took my breath away. Any one of those plates would have been worth a year's salary to me when I was a mere dipper in London. The glassware was worth almost as much, for it was faultless, and I saw the light gleam through one from the fire in the hearth. It was perfection.

There were chairs, four of them, just to show the wealth of the lady who lived here. And a table, on which were set papers, reeds and inks. There was a bible on one corner, and a small altar on which stood a cross and a rosary.

I could not have imagined a more cosy, warm, regal chamber in the whole of Christendom.

The boy was taken across to a long bench that had a stuffed cushion on its length. He was set down, and Harvey and I stood beside him, both of us more than a little overwhelmed by our surroundings. Two ladies-in-waiting came and examined the lad, one with a bowl and cloth, with which she began to wipe at his brow and clean away the worst of the blood and muck. The second came to Lady Elizabeth.

'Who is this?' Lady Elizabeth asked. She shushed and shooed away the superfluous lady-in-waiting, who fluttered about her like an ageing butterfly, begging her Highness to come away from the nasty, smelly little brute. I thought she was talking about Gilbert, but then I wondered if she meant me.

Harvey knelt and bent his head, and a moment later so did I. I was forgetting my manners. Lose your manners before a Royal, and you'll likely lose your head later. I said, 'His name is Gilbert, your Highness. He is the son of the poor lady who was murdered, Lady Throcklehampton. His father – well, stepfather – was in the yard just now. He saw the boy fall.'

'Yet he did nothing – neither ran to the boy nor attempted to help you,' the Princess murmured. She beckoned another woman. 'See what we can do to help this boy. There must be a bone-mender in the palace or over at the town. It is his left arm, see? It is bent very unnaturally. I would have this boy looked after. I should not wish to see him suffer.'

While the woman began to rush about, no doubt organizing warm water and the like, the Princess came to me and Harvey. 'I saw it happen. You were quick to go to him. I admire that.'

She passed me a small leather purse. It had a pleasing weight to it. Two purses in as many days. Life here was not so bad after all.

'Now,' she said, 'do you have any news for me?'

'I have seen Sir Thomas Parry. We are both to guard you,' I said.

'Ah?' She had a way of inflecting her words and exclamations with a slight interrogation, as though asking a fellow to elaborate. It made her rather daunting.

'Master Thomas Blount was to do that, but the Coroner has accused him of crimes and has him held in a cell.'

'Sir Henry Bedingfield has assured me I am safe here,' the Princess said. 'What do you think?'

'Me?' I squeaked.

'You have an honest face, even if you do appear to have been used as a punchbag by the Masters of Defence,' she commented. 'Come, Master, what is your opinion?'

She walked to the side of the table on which the boy lay, sat on a comfortable-looking chair and gazed at us expectantly.

There was a small smile playing on her lips. I was impressed to see that she maintained her calm manner, even though she must know that, as a prisoner here, her life was worth little. If the Spaniards or the Queen's Council decided that she was dangerous, her life could be snuffed out as quickly as a candle. Yet she had the composure of a saint, sitting there with her red-gold hair reflecting the candle light, giving a healthy glow to her pale complexion. She was, I confess, bewitching and beguiling at the same moment. Oh, and terrifying. She was still a Tudor.

'I am sure you have a greater understanding of the situation than a poor yeoman of London, my Lady,' I said.

Harvey gave me a look of contempt. 'The Lady requires

honesty, not platitudes,' he rumbled. 'My Lady, the fact is that the Coroner has brought a strong force with him. These new men outnumber Sir Henry Bedingfield's, and they are more keen and experienced. Your life is not safe while these men are free to make themselves comfortable here.'

'I see. I thank you for your honesty, Master Harvey.'

'However, you do have some men with you here, I believe?'

'I have three manservants.'

'How many doors are there to this gatehouse?'

'Two only. One at either side of the gatehouse.'

'But it would be possible to remove you to a strong chamber up the stairs? Could we not create a secure place for you to go in the event of a sudden alarm? A room with one door that may be bolted and locked?'

'I think my bedchamber would serve the purpose well.'

'Perhaps we could keep the boy here, with my friend Jack and me to guard him, but if there is an alert, we could go with you to that room and help guard your person. I shall go and see how best to defend it, with your leave.' He beamed as though this was the best possible situation. He looked delighted.

I was not; I would have protested, but the pair of them were more than happy with this ludicrous scheme, and were already discussing how best to delay any sudden irruption of men into the gatehouse. From the look of Harvey, I gained the strong impression that any foe entering against his wishes had best be well prepared. Before long, he left to fetch more foodstuffs in case of a siege, but it was only a short time before he was back harrying the servants once more.

For my part, I hoped I did not look too alarmed. My urgent desire just then was to leave this room, go down to the yard, and thence flee as fast as my legs could carry me all the way to London.

It was not to be.

We were to remain in the chamber for a day. The child was calm and said nothing in the first hours. His arm was splinted and bandaged, and he lay back looking feverish. I sat near him, and the Lady Elizabeth soon had her manservants and ladies-in-waiting hurried about, taking food stores, blankets, some benches and other items up to her bedchamber so that not only would it become a stronger defensive location, but we could also remain up there for a number of days. Harvey returned some while later, and if anything his smile was yet more broad than before.

The courtyard outside grew noisier as we prepared. I was aware of men hurrying about, although from inside we could not tell what was the cause of their urgency. Meanwhile, the ladies-in-waiting stationed themselves near their mistress as though to protect her from us. It was almost intolerable to be viewed as interlopers and potential ravishers, when all I wanted was escape!

I sat moodily at a window seat, gazing down into the court for much of the afternoon. It was late, and I could see guards gathering, drinking near the door to the hall, some looking up at the windows of the gatehouse as though they wanted to catch a glimpse of the Princess. I paid them little heed, still sunk in my own gloomy reflections, until a figure joined me. It was the Lady Elizabeth.

'They don't look so dangerous from here, do they?' she said.

'My Lady,' I said, flustered, and tried to rise and let her sit. She refused, but one of her men brought her chair over and she sat in it composedly.

'You know, I have spent much of my life in a strange limbo,' she said. 'At first my life seemed full of joy and promise. I was the King's own Princess, and he fawned over me and my mother. It seemed so natural. And then, suddenly, I was cut off. My mother was not in favour, and the King had her . . .' She broke off a moment, sniffed delicately, and continued, 'After that, of course, life changed. I found that I had no new clothes, and soon outgrew my old ones. My position was troublesome. And then Edward was born, and my brother came to join Mary and me. We had an enjoyable childhood, I think.'

'It must have been difficult, too,' I said.

'I believe that all have their own crosses to bear to their individual Calvary. My sister is very kind, you see. The only area of life which we dispute is that of our religion. She adheres to her mother's tradition, while I believe that my father and brother had a different vision. I tend towards the latter, although I am content to take my sister's instruction.'

She had a disarming manner, when speaking to a man, of turning her head so that she brought the strength of both of her eyes to bear. 'You know this boy?'

'Yes, my Lady.'

'It seems you are adept at discovering the dead and injured,' she said, and laughed to see my shock, clapping her hands in delight. 'Do not be afraid! I make no comment about your character – only your misfortune! This boy was helped by you and should be grateful, while Lady Margery's death was no fault of yours, was it? In truth, I am sorry for her. Her instructions were to control me and my household, no matter what. She was told to manage every aspect of our lives, and refused to allow me even to correspond with my friends. It was intolerable.'

'You still wrote to Sir Thomas, surely?'

'Yes.' She looked away.

A quick inspiration struck me: I recalled my meeting with Blount in his London home. It seemed so long ago now, yet it was little more than a week. He had mentioned that Lady Margery had taken the Princess's seal so that all correspondence must pass before her, so that she could report it to Bedingfield.

'I had heard that your own seal was taken?' I said.

The Princess looked at me very straight. 'You know that? Yes. She took it. That was why I was keen to learn about it when we last met. I had thought Lady Margery still held it on the necklace about her neck.'

'Why would you think that?' I said. I was thinking about the coincidence of Lady Margery carrying two seals about her neck. Yet no one had mentioned the second. That was curious. They had seen and commented on the one signet, as they had about the crucifix, but no one had seen a second seal.

'I had seen it. When I needed a letter validated, I would ask her for my seal, and she brought it forth.' Her eyes clouded.

'You are worried?'

'It is my seal. If it is taken by my enemies, who can tell what they will not do with it?'

'Still, it must be a relief that Lady Margery is dead.'

'A *relief*? She was my friend!'

Before I could speak on hearing this astonishing comment, there was an almighty crash below us.

We both shot to our feet, and I was staring about me like a peasant who sees his first cannonade when Harvey blundered into the room. He bellowed, 'To the chamber!' and held the door wide for the Princess and her ladies to ascend to the chamber, only waiting until the last had passed through the door before slipping through the door himself.

I was about to follow when the boy Gilbert moaned and rose to one elbow. 'What's happening?'

'We're being attacked, I think,' I said, and was halfway through the door when I saw the lad attempt to climb to his feet. He swung his legs over the edge and slid from his bench, whimpering as his splinted arm caught an edge and was jarred, but that was nothing compared with the noise he made as his feet hit the floor and he toppled.

'Quiet! Don't make so much noise!' I hissed, but it was no good. The lad was wailing and sobbing like a paid mourner, and I could do nothing to silence him. Instead, I hurried through the door to the main stair just as the first of the men were coming through it. I bleated pathetically, reversed at speed and grabbed the boy, picking him up in my arms. At least I was mostly protected that way, I thought, and then stood, irresolutely.

The men entered, swords ready drawn, and I haughtily gave them a quick look up and down like a captain assessing a troop's quality on the parade ground. 'Let me through, please. This fellow is in bad need of a physician.'

'Who is he?'

'Gilbert, the son of Sir Walter Throcklehampton. I have to take him to his father.'

To my astonishment, a look of respect appeared in the eyes of the men before me, and their sword-points were lowered some inches, so that I didn't run the risk of disembowelment, only of castration. Taking this as tacit agreement, I took my burden down the stairs and into the yard, all the while aware of the hairs on the back of my neck rising and waving as if in preparation for a knife or sword blade.

There was none. I reached the court without injury, and there I stood gazing about me like the village's idiot, wondering what on earth I should do now.

There were plenty of shouts and the odd curse as I stared about me. Gilbert groaned and I hissed at him to keep quiet. 'If they notice us, we could be in trouble,' I said.

'What do you mean?'

'Just keep quiet and I'll carry you away from all this,' I said.

'Don't you understand?' he said. 'This is my father's doing!'

'What!'

He was lucky I didn't drop him. The idea that his father could have been involved in this was a huge surprise, I don't know why. By that stage, nothing should have shocked me. I mean, in recent days I had fallen over a body, been beaten up, rescued, watched my master being imprisoned, and I don't know what else. Yet to learn that the widower of Lady Margery was in fact himself a traitor was somehow more of a bolt from the blue than I had expected.

I took a deep breath. 'So he is a rebel? He wants to see Lady Elizabeth on the throne instead of our Queen?'

'No. He wants people to think that the Princess is plotting to take Queen Mary's throne, so that he can denounce her and be rewarded.'

I considered this while walking towards the stables. If the Princess was right and Lady Margery carried both seals, that would explain why Sir Walter was still searching for a seal. He wanted the Princess's. The boy winced and sucked in his breath in pain a couple of times, but I was as careful with him as I could be. Inside, there was a bench where the grooms would sit and polish their harnesses, I imagine. I put the boy down on this and squatted at his feet. He was dreadfully pale, but at least he hadn't thrown up all over me yet.

'Did your mother know all this?'

'I expect so.'

'But you aren't happy about it?'

He looked at me very straight then. 'My mother disapproved very much, and so do I, but what could we say or do against him?'

I smiled at his innocence. 'I know it must be hard, Gilbert. But, you see, your mother was installed in there purely to keep a close watch on Lady Elizabeth. She was an intelligencer for the enemies of the Lady, who sought to watch her every move and gather evidence of her misbehaviour.'

He did not return my smile. 'She was forced to go there by my father. She hated spying on the Lady Elizabeth.'

'I think she would have been able to make herself less unpopular, if she wanted to help the Princess.'

'My father wanted her to incriminate Lady Elizabeth. He wanted her to use the Princess's seal to write a letter, but she wouldn't do it. That was why they argued so much.'

'They argued?'

Just then there were more shouts from the gatehouse and the sound of wood thudding, as though being beaten by a heavy hammer. The noise reverberated through the wall of the stable, as though the stables were complaining about the violence being done to the chamber nearby. Gilbert winced, and I looked up as a fine dust sprinkled down on us through the rafters above. Making a quick decision, I picked him up again – he was beginning to feel heavy by this time – and carried him to the door, but there I hesitated at the sight. Out in the courtyard, Sir Walter and the Coroner stood conferring in a corner, while Sir Henry Bedingfield stood quietly nearby, his face fretful as he watched the desecration of the Princess's quarters. In his eyes I thought I saw the panic of a man who has always attempted to do the right thing, and who now is forced to collude with others who hold to a different set of beliefs.

There were some men gathered near Sir Henry, but they were held under the watchful gaze of six of the Coroner's men. All were familiar. I could see a couple of the men who had been on the gates in recent days, and one who was a steward, and three grooms. They looked grumpy at being held at spear-point.

'Don't take me to him,' Gilbert pleaded in a low voice. He was staring at Sir Walter. I turned and strolled back into the stables before we were noticed. Dust was still filtering through the rafters with each knock above, but that was less concerning to me just now. All I could think of was Sir Walter and the look on Sir Henry's face.

'You said that Sir Walter and your mother argued a lot,' I said, making him as comfortable as I could on the bench.

'Mother felt that it was beneath her dignity to spy. She disapproved of the new religion, but she thought if God wanted England to return to the Catholic faith, He would make it happen.'

'How long were they married?'

'Sir Walter married her four years ago. After my father died.'

'Ah yes, I heard of him. He was a Neville, wasn't he?'

'No. My grandfather was a Neville. My father was a Percy. He was a brave man,' Gilbert said, lifting his chin with pride. 'But he died, and when he did, the borders became more dangerous, and my mother brought me down to London for safety. Then Sir Walter met her, and the marriage was proposed.'

'You don't like him, do you?'

'No. He is unkind, and only ever thinks of money.'

'I have heard that the Princess's seal was also on your mother's necklace.'

'I don't think so. She only ever had the one.'

'And that was your grandsire's.'

'Yes.'

'So what happened to the second seal, then? The Princess was adamant that it was about your mother's throat.'

And I didn't add the comment, but I was aware of the little mark about his mother's dead neck where a necklace could have been pulled away. Someone must have thought that the Princess's seal was still there.

There was a sudden crash, then a roar of glee, and the thundering changed from sledgehammer blows against timbers to the regular pounding of booted feet on the floorboards. The fine dust settled on us, and no more seemed to be falling now. I was just congratulating myself on escaping a nasty-looking fight when there came a rumble and shouts.

I went back to the doorway and was just in time to see my friend Harvey being bustled from the gatehouse. He was pushed hard at the top of the steps; with his hands bound at his back, he could do nothing to protect himself, while the men-at-arms behind him laughed to see him slam to the ground. He rolled over and came up on his arse, legs stuck out in front of him, apparently taking a careful note of all the people who were watching. After him came two of Princess Elizabeth's manservants, and then, with little shrieks of alarm, three ladies-in-waiting, before Elizabeth herself appeared.

She looked queenly, I have to admit. With her head held high, she walked out from her rooms with her nose in the air and glanced about her as though there was no one in the courtyard but her. She looked down at Harvey, and murmured something, but before Harvey could answer, a boot caught the side of his head and he went over again. This time he didn't rise so swiftly. I felt sick on his behalf.

'What is the meaning of this?'

The Coroner stepped forward with Sir Walter at his side. 'This gives me no pleasure, my Lady. However, it has been said that you conspired to see Lady Margery Throcklehampton murdered, and you paid a man to ensure that the foul act was carried out.'

'Who suggests that I was in any way responsible for poor Lady Margery's death?' Lady Elizabeth demanded.

'We have your captain held in the cell now,' Sir Walter said. 'It was only a matter of time before he confessed.'

'I have no idea—'

Sir Walter tried to speak, but the Coroner jumped in first. 'Lady Elizabeth, you don't realize how much we have already gleaned. Your man Blount is talking already. He could not cope with the various . . . implements at the castle's disposal. He has told us that he was ordered to kill Lady Margery because she was a spy in your household and had seen a letter you sent under your own seal.'

'This is outrageous! My seal was taken by Lady Margery.'

'So you deny having the Lady killed so you could write this.'

Lady Elizabeth looked at it and her face seemed to stiffen, like a dying man's just before his last breath when all turns to softness and relaxation. 'That is not a letter I recognize,' she said.

'You deny your signature, your seal, the mark of your office?'

'It is false! I have not had my seal in days, and any man can copy a signature,' she said.

The Coroner opened the letter and waved it. 'This letter clearly states that you want to have a force of men here. You instruct Sir Thomas Parry to gather men loyal to you to come and free you from your captivity, and to organize an army to march on London and the Queen.'

'That is a lie! I have never written that and—'

'Lady Elizabeth, I—'

'Do *not* presume to interrupt me, Coroner!' Lady Elizabeth spat, and if they could have, her eyes would have flashed lightning at the man. As it was, I felt her words like a kick in the ballocks. He would have been a better man than me, had he continued to speak. She continued with a loud, clear declaration: 'I may look like a weak and feeble woman, but I am not so foolish as to plot to harm my beloved sister! I am content with my lot here in Woodstock, and will remain here until it pleases my sister to release me. Until that day, I will stay. However, you may be assured that the foul mistreatment of my staff and my belongings will be noted. Even now your agents rifle through my clothes and letters, seeking I know not what. It is my belief that they seek to pillage and loot, and perhaps even one or more might deposit incriminatory material in my room.'

'They are only there to aid you, my Lady,' the Coroner said smoothly. 'They hope to recover your mislaid seal. Perhaps it will be discovered up there.'

'Really? And then you can, of course, accuse me of the crime of writing *that*,' Lady Elizabeth said, indicating the paper with a flick of her finger. 'Except I neither wrote, nor dictated, nor sealed that letter. You must try to do better.'

'We have the letter, and when we find your seal, my Lady, we shall have all the proof we need.'

'Sir Walter,' Lady Elizabeth said, 'I am very disappointed to find you involved in this treasonous fiction. I respected your wife.'

'She was a good Catholic woman. Your heretical views were enough to make her wish to help bring you down,' Sir Walter

said. He sounded like a man who was holding his anger at
bay with enormous difficulty.

'Really? She always seemed most accommodating to me,'
Lady Elizabeth said.

She said no more. Instead, she stood in the court and
surveyed the area with every appearance of patience. Upstairs,
the men lumbered about, and I heard heavy furniture being
moved, planks being levered aside, clumping boots and occasional thuds as items of value were unceremoniously deposited
on the floor. Through it all, the Princess stood like one who
can endure any indignity, until at last she glanced up at the
sky and spoke quietly to one of her ladies-in-waiting. At once,
her manservants formed an honour guard before her, one
helping Harvey to stand. He looked confused and wobbly on
his feet, but apart from that he was well enough.

'Where are you going?' the Coroner snapped. He was
growing testy with the lack of food and drink.

'You may stand here in the cool, if you wish. I am going
to Mass, as my sister the Queen wishes,' Elizabeth informed
him. 'I will not break her firm injunction.'

'You will remain here, my Lady,' the Coroner said.

'I will go to the chapel now, and if you attempt to prevent
me, you will have to answer for all your actions. I can assure
you, Coroner, that even if you were to install incriminating
items in my chambers, and find a written confession of mine
signed in my own blood, yet would you suffer all the indignities my sister could conceive of, were you to prevent me
making my peace with my Maker!'

She held his gaze with a haughty rage, and then she and
her companions crossed the yard to the chapel, and I saw them
stand aside for her as she entered, dipping her fingers in the
stoup of Holy Water at the door and crossing herself, before
the others in her party did the same.

I wished I was in there with her. I would feel much safer
in the presence of a strong-willed lady like her.

It was enough to spark an idea.

I did not dare leave the stable. It was in plain view of all the
men in the courtyard. I did glance quickly out, and I was almost

certain I saw Bedingfield's eye upon me, but I must have been mistaken because he made no sign of seeing me, but instead turned and stared at something over to the left. In fact, he was so engrossed in whatever it was he had spotted that the Coroner noted his stare, and he and Sir Walter both followed his gaze with some annoyance, wondering what he had seen.

It was enough for me. I peered along the stalls and saw that there was light at the farther end of the stable. I made my way along the cobbled floor until I found a second entrance at that end. It was much nearer to the chapel, and I hurried back to collect the boy, whom I was beginning to view as a personal mascot of safety, and thence back to the second door.

It was a good twenty yards along from the gatehouse, and the Coroner and others were turned mostly away from me. I took a deep breath and trotted out, the boy in my arms still. The chapel's door was only a matter of feet away now, and I bent double as I went, hoping to remain unseen. All would have been well, too, had there not been a pebble.

You know how it is. A man can hurtle along at speed, and if he's careful, even stony or tussocky ground is safe enough. However, I was carrying the boy. I could not see what was in front of me. Suddenly, my ankle twisted and I was thrown to the dirt. Poor Gilbert gave a shriek that could have been heard in Oxford as his bad arm was jarred, and I would have given a loud cry too, had the pain that suddenly shot up both legs not been so entirely unmanning. I am a strong fellow, and I have courage that would be the equal of any, but the agony I felt there was so acute that I thought my heart must stop. It went from the knees up into my groin and thence my belly, and I was forced to arch my back like a spitting cat and try not to puke.

I motioned to Gilbert to get inside the chapel, and even as he climbed to his feet and slipped to the door, I heard the march of booted feet. Soon I could see three pairs of them just by my ear.

This, I felt, would not end well.

'So you decided to visit me?' Blount said in that sneering way he had.

I was on my back, and from the smell of the place, my nice new jack would never be the same. 'I wanted to see how you were, Master,' I said in as sardonic a manner as I could accomplish.

My hands were bound, although only with ropes, not fetters. Rolling, I could get to my knees, but that was enough to make me whimper. Both felt as though they had been clubbed to submission by an expert. It must have been as I fell, I thought. Both knees had struck the ground at the same time, with the full force of my weight and Gilbert's behind them. My head was still very painful, and my nose felt freshly clogged. I snorted and hawked and spat a few times, and after bringing up great gobbets of clotted blood, I found I could breathe again. My head felt as if it was going to explode with every snort, though, and after the third attempt I decided that remaining partially blocked was preferable for now.

'Good of you to come,' Blount said loudly. 'Of course, it would have been better had you brought some ale and bread. It's not ideal down here. Perhaps you could have brought me a blanket, too? I think it will grow cooler tonight.'

'What happened to me?' I mumbled. My lips felt as though someone had swung me by the feet and slammed my face against a wall.

'Oh, as far as that goes, I think you were caught outside and beaten up by a few of the Coroner's men before they brought you down here. You were most entertaining, from what they were saying. You made for good sport. I suppose if you're a man-at-arms in a Godforsaken spot like this, you get your pleasures wherever you may.'

'It feels like I've been run over by the whole of the Queen's army!'

'You look like it too.'

'What have they done to you?'

Blount shrugged. I could make him out quite clearly. He had started out as a darker smudge against the blackness of the walls, but as my eyes cleared, I saw that he was sitting with his back to the wall. His long hair was lying about his shoulders in disarray, and his left eye was bloated. I felt sure that it would be black, blue and purple by the time I saw it in daylight. It felt good to know that he had shared a few of my tribulations.

'They enjoyed themselves with butts of pikes, boots and fists until they found it tedious, and then they kicked me some more. The usual.'

'And you told them about Lady Margery?'

He said nothing, but from the little hiss of warning, I gathered that someone could be listening. A little later he said carefully, 'I told them nothing but the truth, Jack. That we are here to deliver and take away messages for the Princess from Sir Thomas Parry. We have done nothing else, have we? The murderer of Lady Margery will have our suffering on his soul for all eternity.'

'Good. I hope the bastard lies in the deepest and hottest pit in hell. In that case, the whole story they spun was deceit. I thought I was just being kept in the dark. They accused the Princess of trying to organize an army to depose the Queen.'

'They actually said that?' Blount asked.

'She told them it was nonsense. You told me that she lost her seal to Lady Margery, so I don't understand why they are turning her chamber upside down.'

'You don't? What if Elizabeth arranged to have Lady Margery slain? Perhaps the seal was returned to her, and she could correspond again?'

'She thinks it must have been stolen. Now the Coroner and Sir Walter are searching her quarters high and low to find it. They have a letter that purports to be from her, but she denies writing it, even though it has her seal on it.'

Blount was silent for a while. Then, 'She has no seal, so the letter is a forgery. Sir Thomas Parry must be told. He must be warned. This could grow.'

'Grow?'

Blount's head, I could see, was turned from me. His posture reminded me of a hunter listening for the breathing of a deer. His eyes, I thought, were fixed on a point behind me, near the door.

He spoke clearly. 'Use your brain, man! Sir Walter and the Coroner are setting their faces against the Princess. They will try to make it appear as though she has been plotting, and they may succeed for a period. With the lies that spread as rumours of her plotting with Wyatt and his rebels, it would take only a tiny spark for gossip to be spread about her again. And that must generate much smoke before the true culprits are uncovered. But before that happens, many will be killed. Old and young alike will be arrested and disappear; families of honour who have committed no offences will find themselves under suspicion and will lose all; women will be torn from their fathers and mothers. I fear that the consequences for the kingdom must be dire, and then a natural reaction must set in. Since the Princess was definitely not engaged in any such activity, the Queen will demand to know who was responsible for such a misdeed as persuading her to punish her sister. She only has one sibling now that her brother, King Edward, is dead. The person who cast doubt in her mind about her last remaining sibling will earn her everlasting detestation. Not only Sir Walter and the Coroner, but Sir Henry would all fall under suspicion if that were to happen. An old man like Bedingfield would not be able to cope with much in the way of interrogation and torture.'

'You think that even he would be arrested?'

'Oh, yes. And he would die in a cell like this.'

I looked aside. 'Oh.' It occurred to me that Bedingfield was not the only man likely to suffer pain and death over this affair. First, all those whom the Coroner and Sir Walter had accused of any involvement would likely suffer a similarly unpleasant end.

There was a quiet sound like the last gasp of a dying wren, and then a soft click. I turned, for the sound came from behind me. 'Hello?'

'There is no one there,' said Blount, and there was an enormity of relief in his voice. 'Not now. With luck, I said the right things. All we can do is wait.'

I had no idea of the passage of time. There was so little light down there in that hideous dungeon that the only means of telling how much time had elapsed was by listening to the trickle and plop of drips falling from the walls. For a while I attempted to count them, as if that could give me an indication, but when I began to reach the high two-hundreds each time I found myself gabbling the numbers in my head to fit them between drops, and soon had to give up. I could not enunciate the numbers effectively enough.

It was not only the passage of time that caused me trouble. I spent a considerable amount of the time available contemplating my likely end, and could barely conceal the whimper that rose from my breast every time I thought of the tortures I had heard spoken of in taverns and alehouses. They involved lots of mechanical devices, such as pulleys and screws and racks. I didn't want to think of any of them, not here in the dungeon. But there were worse tools available to the denizens of such chambers: fires, knives, brands, pincers, pliers . . . the list was endless. I had heard much of the judicial armoury available to those who sought to enforce the law, or deter those who wished to withhold their secrets from their benign rulers.

There was no odour of charcoal or burned wood, so I was hopeful that at least while in here I should be safe enough, but that did not hold true for anywhere else. Surely, if the Queen were to suspect Princess Elizabeth of complicity in a plot against her, all those who were implicated would soon find themselves transported to the nearest location where they could be questioned. I knew what that would likely mean: a short journey to London, to the Tower. It wasn't set there as a decoration: the Tower was the symbol of royal power and authority, the place where those who had been guilty of any infraction were sent to atone. It was the place where poor Lady Jane Grey had been held and, only a matter of days after the collapse of Wyatt's rebellion, had been executed. The true cruelty of killing a girl of only seventeen or eighteen lay in the decision to execute her husband, Guildford, first, so that she could see him being taken away on the wagon, and brought back a little later, decapitated, just before she was herself led away to the scaffold.

It was a thought to make me shudder. Such barbarous treatment of a young woman did not tend to instil confidence in the treatment that would be meted out to me.

'Silence!' Blount said, and in that damp, dark, foul chamber, his shout carried like the roar of a gun. It jerked me away

from my panicky thoughts, and suddenly I saw clearly what
I must do. The door was locked and barred, but my hands
were bound only with rope. The walls were of a rough,
unsmoothed stone, and if I were to rub my rope against them,
they must cause the rope to fray and break. Soon, with luck,
I might be able to free myself. Then, when the gaoler came
back, I could attack him and run from this hideous cell . . .
or, first, take his keys, perhaps, and release Blount, for he was
more capable than I with his hands, and then make our way
to the courtyard, where we could steal a horse and ride off to
freedom at Woodstock, warn Parry, and make good our escape
while ensuring that the Princess was freed.

'What are you doing?' Blount asked while I stood at a wall,
rubbing my rope.

'I'm only bound with fibres. If I can wear them away, I may
be able to free myself.'

'Good!'

There was a degree of amusement in his tone that I did
not like, but just now it didn't matter to me. I was rubbing
hard. The fibres grew warmer, my skin was scraped and
bloodied, but I continued. I think I knew that when the door
reopened, I would not be able to win a fight with the gaoler,
who was fed and comfortable, while I was frozen and enfee-
bled by terror, but it did at least keep me occupied.

A cord came loose and fell away. Panting slightly, I grinned
to myself in the dark. I could not see the cord, but it was the
first proof of my theory.

'Working, is it?' Blount asked.

'Yes, the first has gone!'

I set to again, and on the third scrape, missed my mark.
The stone tore a strip of flesh an inch long, two inches wide,
from the base of my wrist, and I was close to sobbing with
the pain of it. I sucked at my wrist and cast a glower at Blount,
who appeared to be enjoying my discomfort.

All at once I was defeated. I knew it couldn't work, and this
was merely the proof. I set my back to the wall and allowed
myself to slide down until my arse was on the floor. I could
have wept, but I didn't want to before Blount. Instead, I
reminded myself of happier times, of Jen with her glorious

breasts bouncing over me, of the wenches at Piers's brothel, of the three maids here, Sal, Kitty and Meg, and how I had been trying to pick my favourite – or the one most available – on the day Lady Margery died. And I saw again her body, no matter how hard I tried to block it, and that thought brought another, more hideous scene yet to my mind: my own body lying broken, bloodied and ruined, with my head beside it in a basket.

I was about to sob for the pity of it when suddenly there was a soft rattle and slither, and then a chink of daylight entered, and I had to close my eyes against the glare. How long had I been incarcerated? A day? Two days? My eyes were so blinded that I could have been there for a week. If my appetite had not been so effectively destroyed by my fears for my future, I would have had a hunger as fierce as a lion's.

'Oh! Thank God!' I said fervently, recognizing the face at the door. 'How long have we been held here?'

'Hello, Will,' Blount said. 'You took your time.'

'Scarce a half hour since Master Blackjack was brought here. We came as swiftly as we may,' Will smiled.

It is a strange thing to be held prisoner and suddenly to be released. While you are held bound, there are a number of concerns going through your mind – what will happen to me, what will other people be doing, why does injustice happen, where should I go to urinate, will I be fed again? – and then all is resolved. There is light and life and the potential of laughter. The doors are opened, a large man bearing a large knife enters, and he releases you from your bonds, and suddenly the world looks a happier place. There is a hope of life to come beyond the confines of the cell's walls. Of course, your hands are suddenly full of pins and needles, and your legs refuse to behave, but apart from that, the world looks good.

I took Will's hand as he offered it, and then we made our way to the doorway. There was a passage beyond, and after a short flight of stairs at last we were exposed to the sunlight. There, Will glanced at me with concern, and I realized that after my most recent tribulations I was hardly looking at my best. My jack was, to be generous, ruined, what with tears, muddy stains and blood marring the perfection of the surface. My hosen were little better, with rips and more blood. My knees were very sore, but then again, little of my body wasn't. I sneezed, and it felt as though the whole of the front of my face was about to fly away.

'Shut up!' Will hissed.

'What?' I said. I was genuinely confused. Perhaps it was the beating I'd taken, but I'd forgotten all about the men in the courtyard and the danger from the soldiery. He turned and glowered at me, and I shrugged. Which was when I tripped over the body in the passageway.

No one had mentioned to me that Will had slugged the gaoler as he entered the cells, and how was I to know to expect a slumped figure on the ground at my feet? I was still staring at Will as my left foot caught the man's hip, and I felt as though I hung in the air for a full minute while my body tried to decide whether to float there or to slam to the ground like a man thrown in a wrestling match. The moment passed, and as I tried to bring my right foot to solid ground again, it too became entangled in the body, and suddenly I was falling. I could see Will's desperate attempt to grab me, and then I was clattering to the stone flags with a loud wail, both shins resting on the gaoler's lap, both knees striking the floor with all my weight behind them.

My knees had hurt before, but it was as nothing compared with this fresh buffet. Their existing swelling seemed to increase the sensation I felt from a tepid, general anguish to an exquisite pain that was so agonizing it was almost intolerable. If I say that it was so bad that I couldn't scream because the breath caught in my throat, you'll get a bland simulation of the way it felt.

Perhaps Will was happy that there was no screaming. He let out his breath with a great *whoosh* of relief. And that was when the gaoler's body moved. Beside him there was a collection of polearms, all resting against the wall. As he slid sideways, he slumped against all these, his skull leaning towards them as though attracted like a magnet to steel. For an instant I thought we were safe. His temple hit the first ash pole, and gradually his leaning head rose, until his cheek was settled against it like a drunk taking a snooze, his head coming up to the vertical, and Will visibly relaxed. He reached down for a second time to help me up. I could hardly think, my knees hurt so much, and it took a moment for me to realize that he was holding out his hand. I took it gratefully, lifting my legs from the gaoler, and as I did so, he slid a little further. There was a small scraping sound, then a rasp, and Will let go of my hand, his eyes wide, as he tried to grab all the weapons in a bear-hug.

He failed. The arms slid, some of them rattling, others slithering, until they hit the ground in a discordant clatter.

The noise seemed to go on for a long time. Will and I stared at each other dumbly, appalled. Ahead of us, when I turned, Master Blount stood with his eyes narrowed in a wince of horror. In front of him was another figure. I peered and was rewarded with the sight of Lady Anne.

She drew the door shut behind her, shooting home two rusted bolts, and swore in a most unladylike fashion. She sounded more like a whore from the quayside who learned her language from the sailors. Be that as it may, I took her general gist: *They're coming! Run!*

We pelted back along the passageway. A short way along, the passage divided, with one route leading off to the cells' corridor on the right. There was a strong door leading left. It was locked, and Lady Anne opened this with a key from her bodice, before pushing it wide. There was a short flight of stairs beyond. I glanced at her, and she thrust the key away on its chain with her chin held high, as though expecting me to make a comment about her selection of a storage space. An idea came to me, but this was not the time. What she stored down there, she was welcome to just now; I had other things on my mind, such as staying alive. Will and Master Blount hurried through, Blount hobbling slightly, and Lady Anne slammed and relocked this door, then took us up the short staircase, along a passageway, turning into a room and out through a door at the other side of it into the open air, then up a convenient ladder which she pulled up after us, and thence across to another door.

She opened it and waved us all inside.

It was a large chamber, with two maidservants doing whatever maids do. One, Kitty, gave a little scream as we ran past, and dropped a large armful of linen. Then we were in a long, bare, wood-lined corridor, down more steps, along a passageway, and ended up in a large chamber. Here Lady Anne, who hardly panted at all, for all that her face now wore a deliciously healthy glow, stopped and motioned about the room. 'You will be safe in here,' she said, glaring at me as she spoke.

'What are you doing helping us?' I demanded, once I had caught my breath and tottered my way to a stool.

It was a big room, this, with a ceiling that was high overhead. There was no fire in the grate, but we were not going to be upset about that, not when we compared it with the damp cold of the prison cell where we had been installed for so long. It was richly decorated, with a series of paintings on the limewashed walls, and tapestries hanging over any of the draughtier areas. The panelled walls were carved into fabulous shapes, with roses and shields picked out in bright colours, and overall, even without the fire, I gained a firm impression of bright colour and a warm, comfortable atmosphere.

I gazed at her as Lady Anne stood in the middle of this beauty, and I came to the conclusion that she was embarrassed. 'Why did you rescue us?' I said.

Suddenly, her face crumpled. She looked as though she had aged fifteen years while I spoke. She sank to a stool and put her face in her hands.

'She had little choice,' Blount said. He walked to her and stood before her, with his back to me. 'This brave lady has saved us, Jack, and that's all we need to know.'

'I overheard you speaking in the prison,' she said, and she peered over Blount's shoulder at me as though begging my forgiveness. 'I couldn't help it, I swear!'

'What?' I said, baffled. She seemed to be speaking in riddles, and I was in no mood for such games. I was sore, bruised, bloodied and anxious, so perhaps my tone was a little more peremptory than it should have been when I said, 'Speak up, woman! You're not some snivelling maiden of four and ten years – you're a grown lady! Speak plainly!'

'I did it!' she said clearly, and then burst into tears.

Blount turned to me with a face as black as a cauldron's base. 'You spoke bravely, Jack! Oh, yes! Why don't you beat her, too?'

'She said she did it? Did what?' I said, still confused.

'I took the Princess's seal. I wanted to remove her. She believes in this new heretical belief, and she will persuade her sister the Queen to give up her Catholic faith if we are not careful!'

'You took her seal? You stole it from Lady Margery? What did you do with it?'

She stood and flung her arms wide. 'I thought it would help us all. I wrote a letter as though it was from the Lady Elizabeth, asking for her vassals to be called to her aid, and I sealed it,' Lady Anne said, sobbing. She put her face into her hands, but I thought I saw her eye glancing up at me between her fingers. It made me suspicious.

'And because of you, we've been incarcerated in the dungeon!' I said. I was not content with her tale, or her manner. 'You tell us that you willingly spread the rumour so that the Princess would be taken? Didn't you think what that could mean for the likes of me? For us?' I added quickly.

'I didn't think about the consequences for others such as you! I am so sorry!'

I found my brows rising on hearing her confession. It would make sense. The silly woman had taken the Princess's seal, made up a dangerous letter, and made sure that it would be discovered by someone. 'You did that? Made up a letter as though it came from Princess Elizabeth?'

'It was an easy enough thing to do. I wrote it carefully, in the style she uses, and signed it with a fair copy of her signature. I need not even declare where it was found. I told my father that I had discovered it, but that I couldn't tell him who gave it to me. That way, he thought I had the ear of one of the maidservants or a lady-in-waiting. He needed little else. But I couldn't persuade him to act. He said that the fact the letter had been intercepted was enough for now, but I had to make certain that the letter was seen, so I told Sir Walter, and he spoke with the Coroner.'

'How long have you had the seal?' Blount said.

'Some days.'

'And where is it now?'

Her head held high, she shot me a defiant look. 'I threw it away,' she said. Her look dared me to call her a liar.

There were steps approaching the main door. Blount stepped forward, thrusting Lady Anne behind him. I remained where I was. My legs would not permit me to move quickly in their present condition.

As the door opened, we saw Sir Henry Bedingfield outlined in the doorframe. He was so surprised that he did not so much as pause, but continued marching in, his speed gradually slowing until he came to a halt near his daughter like a ship losing her wind. 'What . . . what is this? Anne, what are you doing here with these felons?'

'Father, you must listen to me,' she said, and crossed the floor to him. Clinging to his robes, she sobbed a bit, and gradually confessed all that she had told us. 'Father, I wrote that letter. I sealed it, and threw away the seal afterwards. It was all me.'

'Dear God in Heaven,' he whispered, and now I saw what people mean when they say that they have seen a broken man.

His face paled – indeed, the colour fled from his ruddy cheeks so swiftly that Blount and I feared that he might fall. Both of us hurried forward, and while Blount took him by the shoulder, I pulled a chair forward for him. Bedingfield half sat, half fell into the seat, staring up at his daughter. She was weeping prolifically, and now she arranged her skirts and placed herself at his feet. No mean feat with the petticoats and other feminine aspects of her dress. She looked as though she would never be able to rise again, as though she had erupted from the floor itself, and was fixed there by her dress.

'I am so sorry, Father. But at least this means we can escape this horrible place and return home.'

'No! I will not see that Lady executed because of a lie you have fabricated!' he said firmly. 'You cannot suggest such a thing, child.'

I was bemused. 'What would you do?'

'I must go and confess that I have learned that the Princess's story was true, that her seal was lost, and that someone fabricated the letter.'

'You cannot, Father! I will be punished for this,' Lady Anne said brokenly.

'No, I will take the responsibility for it,' Sir Henry said, his hand idly stroking her head like a man petting a favoured hound.

'You cannot,' Blount said. 'If you do, the deceit will soon become plain. First, Sir Walter and his friend the Coroner will be questioned. They will soon tell all they can. Then the questioners will go to you to learn what you know as well. There is no escape from such people. You know that. And you have the added difficulty that you are known to the Queen, don't you? She would perhaps look with more kindness on others, but in your case she will remember you were gaoler to her mother. The fact that you have been devoted to her service will not measure in her estimation.'

'I was one of the few in Norfolk who rallied to the Queen in the first days of her reign,' Sir Henry said, but his voice told how unconvinced he was.

'You were one of the very few who rallied, yes,' Blount said. 'You were one of the men who ignored the proposal of installing Lady Jane Grey on the throne and instead threw your lot behind Mary. She has been grateful to you for that. But she has a long memory, as a Queen must, and she knew that this was a test for you. A reward, yes, a position which others would see as a proof of her faith in you; however, it was a double-edged proof, for it also gave you the means of your own destruction. She knew you could be won over by Elizabeth, a woman of wily skill and intelligence.'

'That is true enough. I never claimed to be well versed in my learning,' the older man said.

'So, if this letter is shown to be a forgery, if the seal is rediscovered out here, that would spell danger for you and your family, Sir Henry,' Blount said.

'I shall have to take it and admit my crime, you mean?' Lady Anne said. She hid her face in her father's lap.

'No, child, you must not,' her father said gently. 'That would lead to your ruin, and I could not bear that.'

'There could be another way,' Blount said. He was pensive, and shot a glance over his shoulder at Will. Will, I saw, understood as much as me. His face held the same bafflement as was reflected in mine.

'There could?' Sir Henry said, and there was a quickening hope in his tone. His daughter turned to stare at Blount, too.

'We cannot allow Lady Elizabeth to suffer for what was a foolish act, not one that was intended to be malicious, but which will nonetheless cause great suffering to her and possibly to her servants. However, if it were to look as though someone else had concocted the whole story, we might be able to rescue something.'

'Put the blame on to another?' Sir Henry said with a slight frown.

'One who cannot be harmed by the revelation,' Blount said. 'Someone who was known to bear a seal about her throat: Lady Margery.'

'Her!' Sir Henry sank back in his seat.

'She cannot be hurt by the revelation, and it will mean that the entire issue is already solved to the satisfaction of all,' Blount said. 'Where is this letter now?'

'I believe that the Coroner has it,' Sir Henry said.

'All to the good. We shall win it back from him. If he wishes to know why, we can explain that it must harm the interest of his ally, Sir Walter Throcklehampton. He will not wish to see Sir Walter harmed by association with his wife.'

'I suppose so,' Sir Henry said, but he said it reluctantly.

Blount nodded. Then he looked over at Will. 'You stay here with Sir Henry. Jack, you come with me.'

'Me?'

But my present injuries were apparently no hindrance to my winning still more.

We left the hall by a door that led along a passageway and thence to a door that gave on to a stone staircase in the open air in the inner courtyard.

I hadn't been here before and I looked about me with interest.

Many of the buildings out here were plainly newer than those in the front of the palace. It made me realize how large the place was, looking about me now. The facades rose to the sky, their chimneys as tall as great pines. When it was new, it must have been an impressive home.

There was not much time to appreciate the place. Blount led me in through a doorway and through a number of chambers and passageways until we emerged into the sunshine once more at the side of the chapel. He looked about him, grunted with satisfaction, and drew me towards a door in the side. We entered and I found myself in a square, but tall nave. It was full of religious displays, and reeked of incense. A priest stood near the altar, and Blount hurried along the nave.

The man turned as we approached, and I was surprised to see that it was Harvey. No wonder he had reminded me of a St Paul's canon, I thought, as he nodded to Blount.

The two spoke quickly.

'Where is she?'

'The Princess has been permitted to return to her chamber,' Harvey said. 'I went to tell her. She has her ladies-in-waiting with her, but only one manservant. The others were injured.'

'Could we find another one or two to guard her? I don't like to think that she could be in danger,' Blount said.

'It would be too difficult. Who could we install in there?'

'We have more men,' Blount said.

Harvey pulled a grimace. 'If you say so.'

'At least they are hardy fellows. Not the sort who would show any feebleness or lack of courage.'

'True enough.'

'What of the Princess? Is she bearing her tribulations?'

'Well enough. But she was unimpressed by the assault on her and her rooms. They were badly broken apart, I hear.'

'Then the Coroner must be made to realize that he will have to pay for all the damage personally,' Blount said grimly. 'But for now we have other matters to resolve. The letter that the Coroner has must be liberated. Do you know where he keeps it?'

'He gave it to Sir Walter, I think. He probably still has it on his person.'

Harvey nodded. 'Would he keep it on him or place it some-where safe?'

Blount grinned and shook his head.

'*What*,' I said, slowly and distinctly, 'are you talking about?'

'Sir Walter is not a trusting fellow. Men of his character think everybody else thinks and behaves as they do. From what I've heard, he was not married to his wife long before he began to fondle each of the maidservants at his own home. His wife and he did not marry for love, of course, but even so his behaviour was distinctly demeaning to a woman of Lady Margery's birth. He is lucky that she does not have a father or brother to defend her.'

'She would have killed him, if she had divined his actions,' Harvey said, chortling.

'Be that as it may,' Blount said, 'I have no doubt that he would think others would behave as he would. He needs money, now that his wife is dead. And he may have the seal and the letter. The letter he will keep concealed. A wise man would hide the seal securely too.'

'But Lady Anne just told us she threw the seal away,' I protested.

'Yes, and she was brave to do that. She was trying to protect someone, no doubt. Perhaps she knows who is guilty, or thinks she does, and confessed for that reason.'

'You don't believe her?'

He looked at me. 'Does she strike you as a robust, bold, adventurous maid? She's a young countrywoman, Jack.'

I could not easily tell him how I first met her when she was clobbering One-Eye over the head.

'So, Jack, we must find this letter as soon as we may. I think here we need your surreptitious skills.'

I shrugged. I was more than a little bemused by the turn of events. It seemed to me that there was nothing this palace could throw at me that I could anticipate beforehand and prepare for. What was one little case of breaking and entering?

'Very well,' I said.

Fortunately, the knight had gone to the hall with the Coroner, so there was plenty of time to ransack his room. First, I asked

Sal where the man's room actually was, since neither Blount nor Harvey seemed to have any idea.

My plan was easy enough. I would march into the man's room and search through his belongings, and hopefully find the paper. It seemed a straightforward idea. So once Sal had told me where to go, I sidled my way past guards and grumpy-looking servants in the screens, trying to look unimportant and insignificant, until I reached the inner passageway to the knight's room. It was dimly lit and gloomy, with big splodges on the walls where the damp was entering, and a drip was assiduously making a puddle in the middle of the floor. In only a million years or so, there would be enough water to fill a bucket, but the drip wasn't letting that get to it. I hurried along, splashing in the puddle, and felt guilty. After all, that was thousands of drips that I had just consigned to splattering the walls and my hosen.

The door loomed. I didn't stop to think, but glanced up and down the corridor, slipped the latch and entered, closing the door behind me gently. I conducted a simple search of the room. There was a large chest in one corner, a smaller one beside it, and a table with papers looked hopeful too. I went to that first, thinking that I might find something useful, but the papers were only leases or tenancy agreements, and most did not even have a seal to validate them, so I shoved them to one side.

When I studied the larger of the two chests, I discovered that it had a simple enough lock. I soon had that unfastened, and threw open the lid. I should have guessed: it was not the knight's, but his dead wife's. I closed the lid after a brief rifle through, but there was nothing of interest (or value), so I turned my attention to the smaller chest. This was only about two feet by three and two deep. I had a quick look and was about to close that lid too, when I saw something in the corner. Half concealed by some linen was a small purse of soft leather. I drew it out, and was surprised to feel something inside; not coins, but similar. I untied the strings and pulled the neck open, and found myself looking at a ring with a circular stone set into a clasp, and there was an image engraved deeply into it: a seal. It looked quite masculine for all its size. I stood there considering, and while I did so, I had a sudden insight. It was not so much a flash of inspiration as a series of knuckle-bones that happened to fall into a logical sequence. For so long I had been thinking about the death of Lady Margery without thinking about why she was dead, nor why Lady Elizabeth had been robbed of her seal, and so much else.

For a good minute I stood there, eyebrows raised, as if the mere exercise of cogitation would drive all these links from my mind, let alone any movement of my hands or fingers. And then there was a rattle and click, and I heard an intake of breath, then the sound of a bolt being driven home.

Sir Walter walked to his bed and rested one booted foot on it. 'So, Master Blackjack, perhaps you are ready to explain to me what you are doing here in my room without my permission?' he said calmly.

I am not sure that I have ever racked my brains more swiftly.

'Sir Walter, what do you have to say about *this*?' I asked, turning and holding out the seal.

'It was my wife's. What of it?'

'It was on her necklace, was it not?' I asked loftily, like a pleader in court.

'She was wont to carry it about with her. It was a memento of her father. He was a Neville from the Northern March. Those Scottish borders have been the ruin of many a good nobleman, but her father kept the peace for a long while.'

'But it disappeared from her throat after she was killed.'

'No.'

I was flummoxed by that. 'Eh?'

'She lost it two days before she died. I know, because I took it.'

'*Two* days?'

'Do you always repeat everything said to you? Yes, I took it. She refused to let me have it, so in the end I snatched it from her. I suspect that is where she won the mark on her throat.'

'Why didn't she just wear it on her finger?' I wondered.

'Look at it! It's a man's ring. It was too big for her,' he said contemptuously.

'Well, why did you take it?'

He stood abruptly. 'Do you have any idea how difficult it is to establish yourself at court? Especially when you have a reputation for being loyal to the last incumbent? It is not easy. I thought that by marrying Margery I would soon have a better position, but no! Apparently, I was seen as a scheming person who would even use my own wife in my pursuit of advancement. As if the tight-hosed, pizzle-pulling politicians at the Queen's Court wouldn't sell their own mothers to get better positions! I was relatively mildly behaved compared to most.'

'You hated your wife.'

'No, I didn't. She was perfectly acceptable to me. However, I did find her intolerant and difficult to deal with. I was forced to use a belt to her on occasion, when she was most reluctant to do as I wished. Several times I was forced to go and enjoy myself with the maids. Have you seen the young girl Sal? She has a most satisfying figure. I have lain with her several times.'

'With . . .' I was dumbfounded. I had been so certain that she adored me, and here was this old charlatan making it clear that I was a fool. I felt as though I had been cuckolded. I could have taken her and given her a . . . well, a cuddle, probably. She was no worse than any of the tarts in the Cardinal's Hat, and I was happy to enjoy myself with them. I suppose she was no worse than me myself.

'When Margery discovered what I had been doing, she made it clear that as far as she was concerned, if I wanted to have my way with the staff, she would not try to enjoy herself in the marital bed. I could use her, by all means, but she would not . . . um . . . facilitate matters for me. So I have been stuck in a loveless marriage, and tempted by the wonderful young flesh all about.'

'You admit you killed your wife?' I said.

He moved as fast as a surprised adder. There was the merest hiss of steel, and suddenly I had a blade at my throat.

'You accuse me?' he snarled.

You can believe me or not, but after One-Eye's attention, then Atwood's and Lady Anne's, I was heartily sick of being threatened with various types of metalware at my throat. I took his sword's blade in my hand and moved it aside irritably. 'No, I don't accuse you of anything. I thought you just said that you removed her because you had a "loveless marriage". If that's not what you mean, by all means explain what you did intend, but don't think to scare me with a sword. I don't scare that easily.'

He took his weapon away with a look of faint surprise on his face and held it low, although he didn't resheath it. 'No, I did not murder my wife. I was in the outer chamber, and walking into the room, I saw her body. There was someone at the top of the stairs – not that I saw him at that moment. All I saw was Margery, poor woman. You saw her, too. Lying there, with the blood pumping from her torn neck. She was moving – just. I saw her eyelids flutter, but even as I went to her, the breath rattled in her, and she was gone. The blood . . . dear heaven, so much blood,' he added, and rested his forehead on the tips of his fingers. 'She did not have the seal then. I had taken it before, as she well knew.'

So the boy had told the truth about that. 'Why? What did you want the seal *for*?'

He sighed and dropped his arse to the bed. 'When Margery's father died, he left many tenants who paid very little on their parcels of land. I wanted to increase the revenues from the fields and towns under his control, so I wanted the seal in order to have new arrangements drawn up.'

'You would defraud the tenants and make them pay you more?'

'Yes, that or kick them from my lands.' No shame there, I noticed.

'So you took the seal.'

'On the table there you will see the documents I have had drawn up. All they needed was the seal, but it's irrelevant now. Even if I had the wax fitted to the pages, it's too late.'

'Why?'

He sneered a little at that. 'You have no brain at all, do you? Her lands came to me for her life. If we had offspring, her lands would pass to the child. Since she died without issue, the lands and all go to her boy. Her sister's family will have him as their ward. I get nothing.'

'Surely as her husband . . .' I began.

'Nothing,' he said flatly. 'She had to be alive for these documents to hold water. Now she is dead, it matters not one whit. If I try to amend the documents, so what? There is no point. It benefits me nothing.'

'So you did not kill her?'

He gave me a long, cold look. 'No.'

'The seal! When you found her body, did she still have the Princess's seal?'

He shrugged. 'I don't think so. I broke her necklace two days before and I didn't look for the new one.'

'So someone else took it from her and killed her.' My head was hurting now with the effort of thinking it all through.

'Perhaps. And now, Master Thief, who sent you in here to spy on me?'

'I was here because I thought you might have killed her.'

'What if I did? She was my wife.'

It's not considered the sporting attitude, but there was at least justification in his words. Although a woman killing her husband was obviously considered a perversion of the natural laws, and thus a treason, a man who beat or perhaps even killed his wife was only keeping her in check. Cutting her throat might be considered extreme, but a rich man would probably escape punishment. No man should actually *want* to kill his spouse. That involved destroying a part of his family's wealth. It would be irrational.

Perhaps this man was irrational, I thought. But if he was, he showed little sign of lunacy. Rather, he displayed a calculating, callous disregard for all others.

'But that matters little,' he said now, and stood. He was actually quite a large man when he loomed over a fellow. 'Again I ask you, who sent you here to spy on me?'

And suddenly I realized that I didn't have an easy answer to that. I stood and backed away, and he smiled, which was deeply unsettling in the circumstances. 'Um,' I said.

Then there was a tremendous crash from outside. A cheering came from the gatehouse, and then a loud roaring, a screaming, a thunderous clamour of pounding hoofs and feet, and the clatter of weapons.

'God's ballocks! We're being attacked!' Sir Walter said, aghast.

* * *

He and I stared at each other for a long moment. His eyes were wide with shock, but I saw something else: he was thinking to himself how easy it would be to remove me. I could be safely stabbed under cover of an assault, and no one would be any the wiser. Perhaps it was my new role as an assassin that made me think in this way, but whether it was or not, I could see the thought running through his mind as clearly as if it was printed in letters two inches high on a sheet on his breast.

I smiled. He smiled back. I walked to the door and shot the bolt open. He was holding his sword now, and I quickly pulled the door wide, expecting him at any moment to lunge and spear me with his blade, but he remained where he was. Perhaps I had guessed wrong, and he was going to wait until I was out and leave me to be skewered, while he locked the door and stayed hidden safely inside.

In my hand I still held the seal from the chest. For safe-keeping, I shoved it on to my left forefinger now, and sidled out. As soon as I was in the corridor, I started to pelt off towards the noise. I felt certain I would be safer in among all the noise and danger of battle than remaining there in the room with Sir Walter.

But he followed me. I had not expected that. Behind me I could hear his steps, steadily closing up; I increased my own pace until I was running at full tilt, and although I was going as fast as I could, he was close behind me. When I came to the door at the end of the corridor, I was panting with fear, expecting to feel steel in my back, but instead he passed by me, reached the door and was through it in an instant. I stood panting and stared out at the melee.

The Coroner's men had been surprised by the assault. From the scene of discarded carts and pack horses, it looked as if a travelling party of merchants had entered with a gang of his ruffians and surprised the garrison. Atwood's men, I realized. Now the court was filled with men fighting, apart from the growing number who were dead or who had retired from the fight. I felt a wave of nausea as I took in the sight of a forearm and hand lying on the ground. A man was staggering away, feebly clutching at the stump of his sword hand, but then a man took his shoulder and pommelled him over the head until he collapsed.

I watched with horror, and then saw two more men running. The man in front was One-Eye, and as I watched, the man chasing him hacked with his sword and One-Eye went down. His killer was one of the Coroner's men, whom I recognized as being from the men who had guarded the gates. He had his mouth open like a roaring lion, and when he saw me, I knew he was about to set about me. He came pelting at me, and I gave an involuntary jerk with my sword, and the damn fool ran on to the blade. It slipped in under his breast bone, and I felt the weapon twitch in my hand. I averted my face as his own expression hardened and then . . . well, it seemed to shear, like a steel coulter when the plough's put under too much strain and the metal snaps. The left remained fixed, but the right side about his eye became engorged with blood, seeming to swell and move with him, and his eyebrow rose, his eyes both narrowing. I held on to my sword with both hands. He mouthed something, and even as I tried to pull my blade free, Harvey appeared behind him and struck him twice more on his head with a small hatchet. The man's eyes rolled and he slid away from me, releasing my sword.

Harvey ran off to another fellow, snatching up a sword as he went, and I was left for a moment.

It was a peculiar sensation, like when you've drunk too much wine after ale, and the world seems somehow clearer than ever, but feels as if you are viewing it in a dream. This scene had that sort of quality. I looked up and saw two of the Coroner's men at the walkway overhead: one slumped with his back to the curtain, feebly holding a fist to a wound in his thigh that oozed thick blood; nearby, another was sprawled, arms dangling over the court, and a thin drizzle of blood dripping from him.

Following the drops, my eyes returned to ground level. Here it was mayhem. Men were writhing about on the ground in pairs or threes, each struggling to throttle or stab another, each holding on to the other's hands to keep their weapons away while their opponents strove to push their own blades into them. Men bellowed and screamed and shrieked and died. I saw the

gatekeeper kick his man in the cods, and make a wild slash
with his knife, but his blow went awry, and another man pinked
him in the breast with a long blade. The keeper fell back, but
then gave a loud cry and ran forward, the sword remaining in
him high on the left shoulder. I saw it appear behind him as
he ran down the blade and hacked at the swordsman's throat
until a sudden gout of blood showed he had succeeded. The
man fell with a horrible gurgling, and the gatekeeper glared
about him as he tried to pull the sword free. He was bleeding
badly, and another man ran at him, but his blade clattered on
the hilt of the sword in the gatekeeper's breast and went wide,
and the keeper stabbed him in the belly, twisting the blade
viciously and grinning all the while like a demon.

I looked away. Squire George was just coming out of a
doorway near the gatehouse, and as a pair of the Coroner's
men-at-arms went past him, hurrying to the fight, the squire
grabbed the nearer one by the neck and threw him over
his thigh to slam on the ground, winded. The squire took his
weapon and raised it immediately to the second man, but he
took one look at George's face and decided that there were
few easier ways to suffer pain and death than by accepting
the challenge. He took to his heels. The last I saw of him, he
was slipping out through the gate and making his way towards
Woodstock.

It was a good choice. Squire George strode to the thickest
part of the fight.

Nearer the hall's main door were Sir Walter and the Coroner,
the pair of them pressing back two others, pushing them with
vigour, until one fell and Sir Walter finished him with a lunge
at the heart. Then he and the Coroner took on the last man
together. He could not survive their dual onslaught and was
soon brought down.

I slid myself along the wall, desperate to avoid danger
in this madness. I sidled cautiously towards a buttress, and
that was when I saw Atwood. It hadn't occurred to me before,
but these fighters were those I had seen with him when he
caught me walking from the inn that evening.

He was standing now with Thomas Parry and Blount, and
the three were making quick work of a group of the Coroner's

men. Harvey was with them, using the hatchet in his left hand, the sword in his right. I saw him dispatch one man, and then he and Atwood were encircling the Coroner and Sir Walter with Blount and Parry. More men were joining them. Squire George hurried up behind the Coroner and began to assail him from behind, until one of the Coroner's men attacked him, and he was distracted enough to divert his assault. As he did so, the Coroner and Sir Walter were forced back, and gradually they were moved to the middle of the main courtyard, with men moving towards them on all sides.

When the ring of blades about them had become as thick as the prickles on a hedgehog's back, the Coroner finally accepted defeat and threw down his weapon with a bad grace. Sir Walter was made of sterner stuff and tried to fight on, but a pair of spears were found and he was forced to retreat, with men attacking him on all sides. Finally, a man with a shield managed to get close enough to grab his sword hand, and then he was beaten with fists until he was knocked to the ground.

Meanwhile, I slipped over to where a Coroner's man lay. I kicked him hard, so that my action fighting could be witnessed. I still had blood besmearing my blade, and I dare say I looked a fierce, savage brute at that time, with fresh blood on my filthy jack and a scowl like the devil's on my face. The broken nose and other injuries would only have added to my brutal visage.

All I wanted just then was to run away and pretend I'd never met Blount or Parry, or heard about seals. I glanced around, and no one paid me any attention. I took a step towards the gate, shuffled another yard or so, and it was closer: a huge, welcoming, yawning space through which I could lurch and be free of this place forever. But I couldn't go. Bedingfield would try to protect his daughter. He might try to put the blame onto the Princess, and I couldn't allow that.

Instead, I looked over to the doorway behind which Princess Elizabeth was sitting, no doubt, and sighed, before making my way back to the others.

'Sir Thomas? Master Blount? We have some matters to discuss, gentlemen.'

* * *

'Is this going to take long?' Sir Walter said.

We were gathered in the palace's main hall. The Princess with her servants sat a little away on a corner of the dais. Sir Henry and his daughter were standing near me, while Sir Walter and Master John stood behind them. Squire George was leaning against a pillar, watching events with suspicion and jealousy. Sir Thomas Parry had taken his seat in the place of honour, and was accepting a cup of wine from Kitty and eyeing the people in the hall with a benevolent eye, now that the battle was successfully concluded.

The majority of the injured and captured were installed in an undercroft, where the maids were running ragged under the instruction of a couple of clerks and Harvey, being commanded to fetch more linen for bandages, more honey and egg white, and all the other paraphernalia of the physician's toolbox. I was glad Harvey was out of the way for a while. It gave me a little more time to get my head around the various issues.

'I hope not,' Sir Thomas said. His usually amiable features were fixed on me with a shrewd cunning. I didn't want to upset him. But then I didn't want to upset anyone. All I ever wanted was an easy life.

I bowed to the figure on the great seat at the dais. 'Lady Elizabeth, Lady Anne, Sir Thomas, Sir Henry, Sir Walter, Coroner, Squire George, I think I can help all of us here.'

'Get on with it,' Sir Walter growled. He had a large strip of cloth about his head like a turban, and one eye was swelling nicely. I had no reason to like Sir Walter, and he was the least important man in the room, so I gave him a curt nod and continued.

'I don't like this place. I didn't from the first moment I came here. But I spent too much time thinking it was the atmosphere or the damp or the rotten timbers. I hadn't realized that the problem was the various factions within the walls. The Princess Elizabeth,' I bowed again, 'is held here against her will, and without the support even of more than a few friends. Sir Henry Bedingfield is here to represent Her Majesty the Queen, by holding Lady Elizabeth here. He has the sorry duty, unwillingly, of keeping her bolted away from rebels who might seek to use her as their figurehead. It is not a pleasant task, of course, but he does it to the best of his ability.'

'I have to obey my Queen,' Bedingfield muttered. His daughter laid a comforting hand on his forearm.

'Quite so, Sir Henry. And although you found it distasteful, you agreed to remove the Princess's favourite lady-in-waiting, and replaced her with Lady Margery. She took to her duties with great skill. Everyone thought she was a devoted spy, but some few knew that her family was very friendly with the Boleyns. She grew up as a companion of Princess Elizabeth. She would not betray her friend. However, her husband has his own reasons for being here. Sir Walter did not arrive because he sought to help his wife in her tasks. He came here in order to further his own interests. When he married Lady Margery, it was not a marriage of love. They wed because both families could see advantage. Yet Sir Walter's advantages were not to shine. He had good prospects, but he squandered them with gambling and women. Lady Margery knew this, and they did not see eye to eye on this or other matters. However, while she lived, he had the use of her wealth.'

'So, he killed her for her money?' Sir Thomas said.

'No! Because he knew that as soon as she breathed her last, he would have nothing. If he had fathered a child with her, the son would become the lord of her demesne, but if she died, her money and property went to her family. Which I think means young Gilbert. Sir Walter has nothing. Perhaps he can claim the right to be the boy's guardian, but if he tries, Lady Margery's family will no doubt fight the case. He is too much of a spendthrift to be a safe guardian. In any case, he is one man who had absolutely no interest in seeing her dead. He bullied her and beat her, and two days before she died, he took her seal. With that he hoped to defraud her tenants and take the money for himself.'

'It was my right!' Sir Walter spat. He looked like a school bully brought to judgement.

'No,' I said coolly. 'It was your decision to try to defraud your wife's family, but it was not your right.'

I continued. 'Her death came too soon. His plans were broken asunder as a result. However, there was one last avenue to pursue: Lady Elizabeth's seal. His wife took it so that she could, on behalf of the Queen, control Lady Elizabeth's correspondence. If he could find Lady Elizabeth's seal, he could use it. Either he could sell it back to the Princess, or he could give it to the Coroner to prove that Lady Elizabeth had plotted against her sister. It would be a forged letter, of course, but Sir Walter wouldn't let a detail like that get in his way.'

'You speak proudly enough now,' Sir Walter said. 'You're little more than a peasant with straw and mud between your toes! Beware when you walk on a quiet road without anyone watching!'

Blount quickly stepped forward and grabbed my arm anxiously.

'What are you doing?' I hissed.

'Please, Jack! Don't lose your temper. If you attack him here, there are too many witnesses,' Blount said, loudly enough for all to hear. 'You cannot fight him here and now, Jack!'

'I won't,' I said. I was a little confused by his act, until I realized that he had just demonstrated to all present that I was a lethal enemy. I stared at Sir Walter, who was watching Blount and me with sudden alarm, before continuing.

'I will ignore the rudeness of that interruption for now. I won't bicker with fraudsters. However, Sir Walter had no reason to try to kill his wife. That responsibility lies with another.'

'If Sir Walter did not wish to see his wife dead, who did?'

The calm voice was quiet, but it carried like a banshee's scream in that room. None of the men turned to look at Princess Elizabeth but me. I smiled at her as coolly as I could.

'My Lady, I am embarrassed to admit that a lot of the men in this chamber have come to the conclusion that only one person wanted Lady Margery dead, and that was you. They think that because she was selected as a spy for your sister—'

'*Half*-sister,' she murmured.

'Of course,' I bowed. 'They felt sure that because of that, you wanted Lady Margery dead. Especially since she had taken your seal.'

'I see.'

'I don't,' Sir Henry said. 'Surely that gave the Princess here a distinct motive to have the woman killed? She has the men in her household. Any one of them could have escaped from the gatehouse and come here to commit murder, and returned later.'

'They could, yes, but since they were all equally aware that the Princess was friendly with Lady Margery, they would hardly have murdered her.'

'What?' Sir Henry blurted. 'But surely they hated each other?'

'No, Sir. As I said, they had been friends since childhood. Lady Margery was considerably older, but used to know Lady Elizabeth's family well, and had played with Lady Elizabeth as a child.'

Lady Elizabeth nodded. 'I looked on her as an older sister. Her family and my mother's were friends for many years.'

'Murdering Lady Margery was not a way to court her favour,' I said. 'No, this was nothing to do with the Lady Elizabeth,' I said, bowing to her again, in case she had been in any doubt as to my loyalties.

'Quite so,' she said.

'Perhaps you would explain about the seal?'

'Of course,' she said, and pulled out a seal on a chain about her neck. 'It is here.'

There was a grunt of disbelief from Lady Anne, and her father leaned forward with a frown on his face. 'But Lady Margery had it, and—'

'And you thought that her murderer had used it on the document you waved about?' Lady Elizabeth said curtly. 'Do you truly believe that I would seek to remove my half-sister from the throne, from where she rightfully rules her kingdom? Do I look like a traitor? Besides, if I were to do such a thing, would I be so base and foolish a knave that I would allow the message to be committed to paper? Would I allow it to pass through the garrison of my prison, assuming that it would succeed? Do I look to be so dull-witted?'

For all that her tone was calm and unemotional, the anger was there for all to see; it was simply held in check for now.

'No, my Lady,' I said. 'That is why the seal was always so problematic. No one here realized that you still held it in your safe keeping. Lady Margery refused to consider removing it, so, after taking it in public, she returned it to you in private. Which is why your ladies-in-waiting were so upset to hear that she had died. They, like you, knew that she was more an ally than a gaoler.'

Blount was faster on the uptake than the others. 'Lady Margery passed it back to the Princess?'

I took a haughty line with him. 'The Lady Elizabeth is just there, Master. You can ask her.'

He glanced at her, and then coloured as he realized his rudeness, and quickly bowed low. 'Your Highness, forgive me. This is all such a surprise.'

'Quite,' she said, with a level of sardonic amusement I had never heard in a lady so young before.

'So,' I continued, 'there was no royal seal about Lady Margery when she was killed.'

'But if there was no seal,' Lady Anne said, 'why did she die?'

Her father nodded. Then his head shot up and he turned to stare at Sir Walter. 'Do you mean that Sir Walter killed his own wife to steal the seal?'

I sighed. 'Sir Henry, don't forget, he knew that if he killed her, he would lose everything. Why would he kill her? No, he took her seal two days before Lady Margery was murdered. Afterwards, he hunted high and low for the Princess's seal, but that was because he thought that he would be rewarded by Lady Elizabeth or her enemies, were he successful.'

'Then who killed the poor woman?' Sir Henry said.

'There are others here who have their own motives,' I said. 'For one, there is Harvey.'

'Who?' Sir Walter said.

'Sir, Harvey is a renegade priest, or so he would describe himself. However, he is an altogether more clever fellow than that. He is working for someone else.'

'Hold hard!' Blount said urgently, glancing at Sir Thomas.

'I believe that Harvey had himself installed here as priest in order to maintain contact with the Lady Elizabeth. He, as her confessor, was able to win over her confidence, naturally. He is a deeply kind, amiable, open-hearted man. That is apparent to all who meet him.'

Blount was shaking his head and mouthing something, but

although I smiled at him and nodded accommodatingly, I did not stop. 'He was certainly a keen pair of ears when someone wished to speak with him. As he would be. A spy has a duty to listen to all who wish to open their mouths before him.'

Sir Thomas had joined Blount and was glaring at me fixedly. There was none of the affable gentleman about him now. He exuded a dangerous calmness, like the peaceful winds before a great storm.

'The thing is, none realized that he reports to another strong character: Harvey was installed here at the behest of Sir Thomas Parry. Sir Thomas was not satisfied that the interests of the realm were adequately guarded, and wanted his own pair of eyes and ears here. Everything that has happened here has been related to him without the interference of another man's bias.'

'At least he had no reason to want to see the lady murdered,' Sir Thomas said.

'No. Of course he wouldn't,' I said. 'Besides, he's one of the only people who was not seen anywhere near the scene on the day of the murder. It was all the others about here who were visible and present and had the opportunity to kill her. And so we come to the poor squire, whom we all know so well. Many are the people who told of his affair with Lady Margery. All spoke of her flirtatiousness with younger men. All those who knew nothing of her, anyway. Even her husband suspected her, and I saw him threatening the squire in the court. However, the squire had nothing further from his mind. His love was reserved for his beloved, who sadly died in childbirth.'

Lady Anne's face hardened at the mention of him and 'his beloved'. I hastened onwards. 'But there is one other who did want to control the situation here. And this is the person who murdered poor Lady Margery.'

I paused and looked about the room. Sir Walter stood very still; Blount was glaring at me now, promising violence to come; Lady Elizabeth stared at me as though suspecting that I could be moon-crazed; Bedingfield looked utterly confused and the Coroner simply furious.

But I didn't care about any of them. Instead, I stared at Anne.

'You did it for the best of reasons, I know,' I said. 'But you shouldn't have killed her.'

'Her?' Lady Elizabeth said with genuine surprise.

Lady Anne was calm; standing before me she looked almost as regal as the Princess behind her.

'There was no one else, was there? Obviously, I couldn't have done it. Master Blount here was in the yard, as was the squire. Sir Walter was about that part of the palace, but he had no wish to kill her off. One-Eye, Huff, was near, but he wasn't bright enough to stage the scene. Because that was what you did, wasn't it? You waited until Sir Walter arrived, and then you flung down the pewter so that anyone coming would find him. However, you hadn't expected him to run off so quickly. You'd thought that he would be appalled to find his wife dead, whereas in fact he was only desperate to run away to think. With her gone, his little fraud was irrelevant. Most important, he stood to lose everything. No, the only person there who was keen to remove Lady Margery was you, because you could see how unhappy your father was.'

'Who couldn't see it? He was mortified to have to guard the sister to the Queen. Father had been here before, looking after the Queen's mother. He was as loyal as any when Queen Mary asked for support against Lady Jane. Everyone acclaimed her as the new Queen, but not my father. While others wavered, he declared for Mary wholeheartedly. And as reward, she gave him this poisoned chalice: the chance to guard her own sister. Fail, and he could be viewed as a supporter of the rebels; succeed, and he would be tainted with the job of gaoler for years to come. What sort of a position is that? Poor Father didn't ask to be sent here to monitor Lady Elizabeth. He was imposed on, without the finances or the rewards commensurate with the position.'

'So you decided to implicate Lady Elizabeth in a plot.'

'Well, I had heard that Lady Margery kept a seal on her necklace. It made sense to me to borrow it and create a letter . . .'

I saw Princess Elizabeth's eyes sharpen at that.

'So you wrote a letter, purporting to come from Lady

Elizabeth, and you needed the seal. You went to the passage and waited, and when Lady Margery appeared, you stepped behind her in the gloom, took her chin in one hand and drew your knife across her throat, killing her immediately.'

Lady Anne looked away, as if my angry stare was painful.

'Then, when you were sure she was dead, you looked for the seal – but it wasn't there.'

'No. Only the Crucifix.'

That made me frown for an instant. Something grated. I peered over her shoulder at the Princess and saw that her eyes were narrowed as she listened intently. 'And you wrote out the letter. But your forgery failed, because it was not the Princess's seal,' I said sternly, glancing at the Coroner. 'No matter that some declared it genuine.'

'I am not responsible for that,' the Coroner said quickly. 'How would I recognize one seal above another? It looked authentic to me.'

'You should, perhaps, have made certain by asking others who might know it well, rather than leaping to conclusions,' I said.

'What of the clatter of plates that you heard?' Blount said.

'That was all a part of the stage-acting. Lady Anne realized it would be difficult to put the blame on anyone. So she hatched a ploy. She wanted Sir Walter to be persuaded to leave. He had made himself entirely unwelcome with all the staff, after all. So she had an idea. She took a pewter plate or bowl, and waited at the top of the stairs. When someone came, she hoped it would be him.'

'No, she sent a boy to fetch me,' Sir Walter said, eyeing Lady Anne with loathing. 'The boy said it was my wife who called me. I hurried to her, not knowing what she wanted, and when I arrived, I found her dead. Then this plate rattled down the stairs, and I was convinced that I would be accused of the murder, so I left her and hurried out to the yard. There I met Matthew Huff, and told him to go and find my wife as though he was the First Finder. I said that there would be money in it for him, and he was nothing loath.'

'It was your wife sent the boy for you,' Lady Anne said quietly. She was still looking at me with bemusement, as if astonished that I could have put together all the evidence to conclude my story. 'She wanted to speak with you about something. I heard her in the yard instructing the boy to find you. I killed her and waited for you. When you arrived, I threw the plate down the stairs.'

'And you came back just as I found the body,' I said.

'I felt bad to see you appear,' she said. She gave a graceful little shrug of her delicate shoulders. 'It seemed kinder to save you at the time. Besides, I never liked Huff. He was not a pleasant character.'

'You still let me think you thought I could have committed the murder,' I said a little heatedly.

'I could hardly let you see that I knew you had not done it because *I* had, could I?' she said.

Bedingfield stood. Neither of us had paid him any attention for the last while, but now I felt truly sorry for him. His face was pale and drawn, like a man who has become inflicted with a poison or the plague. His eyes were raw as though he had been weeping for a week, and the lines about his face looked to have become graven more deeply than ever I had noticed before. 'Master Blackjack: *enough!* Lady Elizabeth, Sir Walter, Coroner, Sir Thomas, can I beg a few moments of your time? I crave a favour. I . . . this is an enormous surprise, as you will understand. However, to place the responsibility for a murder on a young lady's shoulders, a young lady who could have expected a long and joyous life, that is a grave undertaking. Better by far to allow her to leave.'

'What would you have us do, Sir Henry?' Sir Walter said in his sneering tone. 'Leave a murderess to depart hence and find another victim?'

'No! She will never commit such an offence again, I am sure,' Sir Henry said hollowly. 'Leave her to go from here. I will stand trial in her place and allow justice to take its course.'

Lady Elizabeth stood with a flounce of silken skirts. 'Sir Henry, you are asking us to participate in a shabby deception. I can understand the desire of a father to protect his daughter, but you cannot expect me to acquiesce in such an arrangement.' She looked at me, standing with her chin a little raised. I thought for a moment she was going to address me. Instead, she turned with a loud rustling of silks and walked from the room.

'That is that,' Sir Thomas said. 'I am sorry, Sir Henry, but without the Princess's support, there is no way we could agree to any form of concealment. What would the word of each of us be against that of the Princess? Even if we wished to help you, it would be impossible.'

Sir Henry nodded, his head remaining low. He was suddenly an old man, and I felt sorry to see him brought so low. Lady Anne stood at his side, pale, perilously beautiful, but unbending. She had caused this disaster, but she would not apologize for it. It was for others to react as they wished.

I left the room feeling very low. I had done my best to show who was guilty, but it was not a source of pleasure or pride, only of sadness.

I walked about the palace that afternoon, avoiding everyone. Master Blount seemed to hold me responsible for the death, or perhaps for placing the blame firmly upon another when he thought it was my own act. The Princess's face kept returning to me. How she looked so pale, how her eyes had narrowed. There was something I had missed. Perhaps it was the lack of nutrition, I thought.

But I didn't want to mingle with people from the palace. Later I ordered the groom to fetch me a pony; I mounted it and left the palace, heading for Woodstock.

Yes, I know that there were still ruffians about, but most were in Woodstock's gaol by that time, and I had need of fresh air and a sense of freedom.

There were bodies piled by the gatehouse, outside the court-yard for those who had tried to hold the palace against Parry's men, and others inside, nearer the chapel, for those who had served Bedingfield and Parry to the death. There were not so very many, thankfully. Even those I had seen with apparently grievous injuries had, many of them, lived. Some, of course, would soon succumb to infections or just the simple shock of their wounds, but many may yet survive long enough to dance a jig from a rope.

I'd had enough of death and blood. The reek of blood from

a wound, as it grows sour and sickly in the sun, has to be
smelled to be believed. It's horribly like rancid pork, and after
the last days, I swore I'd never eat pork again. Only ham or
bacon for me in future.

I jogged along the road without thinking. With my mind
empty, I entered Woodstock, the horseshoes clattering every
so often on stones or cobbles. The pony seemed to know its
way around here, and I wasn't concentrating. My head felt
entirely empty, as though I'd been working so hard that every
thought had been sucked from it. My heart felt oddly similar,
leaving a hollowness in my breast, as if all emotions had also
been torn from me. I was little more than an exhausted husk.

The pony stopped. I looked up to see that we were outside
the tavern. There was the sound of chatter from inside, but it
was a lot quieter now than last time I came, when Parry had
his bravoes in there with him. Now it was clearly more an
evening with the local peasants and a few travellers. That was
all to the good as far as I was concerned. I threw the reins to
a waiting stableboy, weighed my purse in my hand, and entered.

It was dark. They had only recently thrown some fresh logs
on the fire, and the smoke billowed into the room as I opened
the door. A number of men coughed meaningfully as I stood
in the doorway, but the conversation returned as I made my
way across the room to the bar area. There was a young maid
with a face rather like my pony's, who was filling leather pots
with beer, and I waited quite patiently while she laboriously
turned the tap on the barrel for each one. Someone must have
advised her against spilling beer, because she took enormous
care over every pot, and I found myself glancing around the
room with casual boredom as I waited. Usually, I would have
leched over the maid's arse as she bent, but today I had other
things on my mind.

The smoke was beginning to clear. There were men at many
of the tables, although the area that had been taken up by
Parry's men was singular by their absence. It seemed as though
the locals dared not move in and take over that part of the
inn, or perhaps it was that the people who lived here had gone
to the same tables since time immemorial, and when Parry
arrived, he and his party were forced into the only corner that

was deserted. Even now, there were no more than three men there. Two sat with their backs to me. The third was leaning back, and seemed interested in me.

He looked familiar. I put it down to the fact that he was with Parry's band and thought no more of him, especially since the maid had finished serving her pots and was gazing at me expectantly, rather like a pony seeing a carrot.

'I'll have a pint of beer,' I said. She turned and went through her careful manoeuvres again, and I watched while the thirst peaked and had me almost dribbling. Yet all the while I was seeing Bedingfield's face as his daughter spoke, how she went so pale as she told of her plan, and how the Princess's face sharpened with her attention. It was a trio of melancholy, I thought.

By the time the barmaid had set the pot on the bar, I was so thirsty that it was hard not to snatch it from her. I picked it up, and as I raised it to my lips, something jarred my elbow and a quarter of my pot was thrown all over me.

Furious, I turned to face whoever had knocked me, and then froze.

'Hello, Jack,' Thomas Falkes said.

Now, I know that many, being confronted by the cuckolded husband of the light-heeled maid you've been regularly spurring to a gallop, would throw the rest of the beer in his face and take to their heels, but it's not that easy, you see. I ran through that possibility in my mind in an instant. First, I knew he had two fly characters with him, and who could say whether they were faster than me or not? Then again, my pony was somewhere with the stableboy. The damn fool could have had the saddle off by now, which meant I would have to forgo the pleasure of a four-legged assistant and hope to make my way alone. That was unlikely to guarantee my safety, since they could leave one man here to get a horse readied while the other pair could continue to chase me down. It was not a pleasant consideration, I assure you, but it was better to remain inside a large inn than tempt fate by walking outside.

So I smiled coolly instead. 'Master Falkes. I hope I see you well, sir?'

'I am very well, Master Blackjack. Why, how strange to find you here. Any man might think you were trying to avoid me.'

'No, not in the least,' I said, trying to sound loftily disinterested. 'I have been kept busy.'

'Really? Even without my woman, eh?' he said, and jabbed an unfriendly elbow into my flank. I refused to react, beyond a mild hiss.

'Aren't you going to buy me some beer, then?'

I smiled thinly at that, but there seemed to be little chance to refuse. The maid soon had three more pints set out, because the blasted man demanded refreshment for his men too.

They all knew. It was in their eyes. They were going to drink my purse dry, and then outside I'd be gutted and left for the ravens. I'd seen it all too often before. There were no friends of mine in the tavern, nobody I could call on for help in escaping them. All I needed was the time to fetch a horse or pony, and a few minutes' head start, and I'd be in the palace – and once there, I'd be safe. 'I need to pluck a rose,' I said.

'I could do with a piss as well,' said Thomas's man on my left. Suddenly I recognized him. It was the man who had stared at me that first time I had met Parry here at the inn. He must have followed me all the way from London. He looked a healthy fellow, the sort who could engage in a knife fight before breakfast, and come back afterwards for a duel with swords. There are some men who have faces that have no fat on them, with skin like leather that's been tanned too long, all wrinkled and worn. But his arms and chest looked as feeble as a ship's cable.

I hadn't planned on company, so I stayed a while. That cost me another quartet of beer, and all the while I was surrounded. Falkes stood on my right, while the man who had followed me stood on my left. The third man was behind me all the time, and he was the one I most disliked. Not seeing him, not knowing what he was doing, was unnerving. I drank my beer slowly, savouring it like a man who's set for the rope and knows it will be the last beer he drinks.

'You must need to wet the weeds by now,' Falkes said. 'You said you wanted to point your pizzle before that pint.'

'I'm all right for now.'

'You should come outside,' the man on my left said. The man behind me pushed me in the back, and I stumbled forward.

Then I had an idea. '*Don't* do that again!' I shouted at the top of my voice. The other patrons of the inn stopped in their games to look up. The maid gave me a look over her shoulder, and the innkeeper appeared in the doorway.

There was another shove, this time harder, and I threw caution to the winds. My pot of ale I threw forward, and it struck the serving maid full in the face. She stood bolt upright in a trice, beer dripping, wearing an expression of unholy rage. I preferred her in full horsey appearance to this. 'This man keeps barging into me,' I said by way of explanation, but she wasn't listening. She picked up a wooden tray, and even as I realized that Falkes had a dagger in his hand, and that the others were reaching for me, I heard a loud crack, and Falkes's eyes narrowed in a wince of agony. He half turned to the maid, but before he could, the tray swung again, this time slamming into his face, smashing his nose and knocking him cold.

I heard a knife drawn, and struggled to release myself from the two sturdy figures, but before I could there was a general scraping of stools as the entire clientele rose to their feet. Some looked anxious at becoming involved, but they were in the minority. For the rest, all carried knives of different lengths, and many held cudgels too, and they were advancing.

If I had been one of the two, I would have stabbed me quickly and been away, but these two were not so resolute or determined, I suppose, for they began to move away from the bar, still gripping my arms.

That was when I heard a loud crunch, and the man on my left suddenly wasn't there. When I glanced around, I saw that the maid was now standing on the bar, and she had taken an almighty swing with her tray, bringing it down on the head of the man who now lay on the ground, moaning softly to himself. I smiled and looked at the man on the right. He gazed at me, with the thought *What am I doing here?* clearly running through his mind, when the slight whistling noise of a cracked tray moving through the air at speed could be heard. Suddenly, both my arms were free, and I grinned, just for a moment.

Because then the stupid maid brought the damned tray down on *my* head, and that was the last I knew.

I came to with the firm conviction that everyone was determined to break my pate for me. My head was unbearably painful and the bright light threatened to make the top of my skull unscrew itself so my brain could run away and hide. When I opened my eyes just a little slit, I was nearly blinded by the pair of rushlights on the table near me. I had an overwhelming desire to throw up just then. It took a major effort of will to swallow and keep the bile at bay. If you are asked, I would recommend that you refuse an offer of being hit on the head by a slight-looking bar maid with a heavy tray. Ask for a slow-strangling from a rope in preference.

Trying to move proved to be painful. My hands were not bound, which was, from personal experience, a positive sign. I opened my eyes again, and this time I was confronted with an open window and doorway. Both were searingly bright, and I had to avert my face.

Doing so brought into focus the figure sitting on a stool nearby. Jonathan Harvey was contentedly sinking a quart of the loathsome cider they brewed in this area. 'Feeling better?' he asked.

I looked about me carefully, trying not to jerk my head in case a sharp movement caused it to fall off. 'What happened?'

'Ah, your friend Falkes? I came here and discovered you and he were in close contact. In fact, there were four of you on the ground. Not the best place for a fellow with a new jack, really. Still, you're looking more yourself now.'

'What happened to Falkes?'

'Oh, he is in gaol at present. I helped the local beadle to shift him and his companions. At the moment they are being held against a surety for brawling. You were to be held, but I explained that Princess Elizabeth is keen to see you, and the problem of Falkes retreated somewhat. The locals here rather like the Princess. Especially since her presence means a constant trade for the town. They don't like foreigners coming here and starting fights, either. They consider that it is their prerogative to start fights in their own town.'

He drained his pot, set it on the table at his side, and held out his hand. 'I think you should come with me.'

I was grateful for his hand. Without it, I could not have climbed to my feet. 'Thank you.'

'It is fine, my friend,' he said. He put an arm about my shoulder on the way to the door, and I glanced back to see the landlord standing at the corner of the bar, a big pot of ale in his fist. On his face was an expression of genuine fear, which surprised me. He should surely have been glad to see me leaving the bar, since I was the cause of his latest brawl. Then again, he probably feared Lady Elizabeth's wrath if she were to hear I had been set upon by his barmaid. I lifted my hand to my head and encountered a lump the size of a good-sized goose egg. The mere touch felt as if I'd driven a spike into my skull, and I took my hand away again very swiftly.

Outside was my pony and Harvey's, both held by a groom. He gave us the reins, and I made him give me a leg up. There was no chance of my being able to clamber aboard in my current condition. I took the reins, tried to quash the latest feeling of queasiness, and pulled the beast's head round to the causeway that led to the palace. We rode on, and when we were a half mile from the town, Harvey spoke again.

'You resolved the problems very swiftly there at the palace,' he said.

'What was your part in it?'

'Mine? Small enough. I inveigled my way into Sir Thomas Parry's group, and have been attempting to do my best to further my master's ambitions.'

'So you wanted to help Parry and Lady Elizabeth?' I said, but I could not help throwing a look at him. There was something . . . I don't know, something measuring in his eyes that didn't agree with his general demeanour. I wondered where the gaol was, fleetingly, but then Harvey's face brought back the look on the landlord's features. A reluctance, a resentment, a feeling that he was conspiring in something he didn't . . .

'I think when we get back, I will eat. I hope they have a decent leg of pork or lamb today. I have been fed on too much fish and thin gruel in the last weeks,' Harvey said.

'Yes. Some meat would be welcome,' I said. 'A capon for me, I think. I could eat it whole. Ow!' My head was jerked as I spoke, the pony stumbling slightly on a loose cobble, and I winced at the pain of it. I was not feeling entirely myself. That blow on the head was enough to leave me feeling disorientated. The slow movement of the pony, jogging along, was enough to jolt my injuries with every step, and as I continued now, the mere idea of food was enough to make me want to heave.

'Especially when it comes to the information I've been fed,' Harvey said, and chuckled to himself. 'Anyone would look at the palace of Woodstock and think that the place was a haven for fools and the criminally lunatic, would they not?'

'Only the sort of fools who'd think it amusing to take their rest in a place that was as wet as the bogs all about it,' I said with feeling, wincing again. It really was easier to ride with my eyes closed. There was little need to keep them open, in any case. The pony knew its way. If it were to get lost, Harvey would be able to pull us back into line. I allowed my eyelids to fall slowly over my eyes and enjoyed the sensation of the sun on my head, until there was a jerk again, and both eyes snapped open. 'Ow!'

And then I looked over my shoulder. To my horror, Harvey had drawn his sword, and was even now within striking distance.

'What are you doing?'

He smiled – a little sadly, I like to think. 'The thing is, Master Blackjack, you are a threat to too many people. My master, the Queen, and many others. My master asked me to work out what you were doing here, and it was soon clear enough what your mission was: to murder Lady Margery. My master had his suspicions about you during the rebellion, and when he heard you were to come up here, he set his mind to working out why. That was why he sent me too. It was the merest good fortune that I became friendly with Sir Thomas Parry. And then I learned you are to be his assassin. Well, I am sorry, but since I am already employed by Bishop Gardiner to smooth out the little bumps in the way of his political ambition, I think you are a superfluous addition to my profession.' He looked at me apologetically. 'That means I have to kill you.'

'But – wait! How did you forge the letter?'

'Someone with a pleasing enough hand.'

'The seal? But the Princess had it all the while!'

'I had hoped you would accuse the fool Sir Walter, since he bruised his wife's neck when he pulled her own seal from her, but you didn't have the wits. No, I expected to find it when I killed Lady Margery, but it wasn't on her new crucifix or in her purse. I hoped, after the inquest when you and I visited Princess Elizabeth's chamber, that I might find it then, but unfortunately her manservants had their eyes on me all the time. It was only when we went back, when you and I went to her chamber with the injured boy, that I succeeded. While I was supposedly fortifying her bedchamber, I found a drawer in her writing table. I was in her chamber for some length of time, wasn't I?' he smiled. 'When the attack happened, the men were supposed to find the seal and accuse her of writing the letter, but she realized, I suppose, and hid it somewhere herself.'

Now, all this was a complete shock to me, as you may believe. While he spoke, my mouth fell open, and I tried to reason with him. It wasn't easy. My head was pounding painfully, my belly recoiled from the idea of a fast movement, and I had thought Harvey was a friend; I wasn't ready for the declaration that he was about to murder me. Since it was at the behest, if not the direct orders, of the Lord Chancellor himself, however, I was less surprised, I suppose. I had met Gardiner. I hadn't liked him.

Now I liked him a great deal less.

'Let's just think about . . .' I said, but my words ended in a rather squeaky bleat as his sword whirled through the air and missed me by a mere six inches. 'No! *Stop!*' I said, but then the blade was heading towards my, well, my head. I ducked, the sword struck the pony at the rear of the cantle, luckily where the leather protected the beast's back, and the blade skittered off, catching my upper buttock.

The pony was startled. That's nothing to how I felt.

I let out a loud yelp as I felt the sting of the blade, and then I was aware of blood running freely. The sensation of my own blood leaking is not one that I have ever enjoyed. I ducked as the blade sang through the air, and if you don't believe me when I say it sang, all I can say is you haven't heard a blade pass only a couple of inches from your skull. Harvey swore and swung again, and this time I felt something give.

I think that there was some reinforcement at the back of the saddle, and his blade had weakened it. Whether it had or not, suddenly I found the rear of the saddle gave me no support. I spoke under my breath at some length about the parentage of the saddle-maker, but then the blade came again, and I clapped spurs to my pony's flanks and crouched low, hoping for the best.

In the distance, perhaps a mile away, I could see smoke in the sky, which I hoped came from the palace chimneys, and I aimed myself at them, trying not to think about the three feet of steel that was being aimed at me. I was so low over the brute's neck that I was almost one with it. All I could smell was horse sweat, and the beating of hoofs slammed at my skull like an army of smiths practising with two-pound hammers in sequence. There was a stream, and we splashed through the shallow waters like horse racers, great plumes of water being thrown up on either side, drenching us all. Then I saw movement, and he was there beside me, his sword held aloft.

I kicked my feet free from the stirrups and as his blade came at me, I was already falling.

I had never really thought about how painful falling from a horse could be. I suppose if I had thought about things, I might have tried to spring lightly from the saddle, landing on the far side of the horse, tumbling gently to the ground and rolling like an acrobat. But I'm not an acrobat; I was injured, and I didn't think much beyond getting out of reach of that damned sword. I started thinking that the Coroner could have fun working out the value of the weapon that decapitated me, but then my mind was taken up with another thought. It was this: hitting the ground at full gallop hurts. It hurts a lot.

One foot struck first, and I felt pain like a flash of lightning as it kicked an immovable rock. The anguish rose to the knee, and then paused to make its presence felt. I would have howled, but by then the ground was rushing up towards my face with alarming speed. I had time – just – to curl myself into a ball, protecting my head with my arms, I think, but the top of my head, where that evil harpy had hit me with her wooden board, still took a lot of the brunt of the fall. I bounced, rolled and wailed, and thankfully much of it was over watery marshland at the side of the causeway. Not that it made me feel any better.

I became aware that I had stopped moving. I was lying on my back, staring up at the sky with a kind of relief: I must be dead, after all. No one could have survived a fall like that. And then I realized that water was trickling on my face. It was raining.

Somehow that made me realize I wasn't dead yet. Still, I wasn't going to bother moving. My neck was surely broken, and the agony that would ensue were I to try to stand made the experiment undesirable. Besides, I was about to die, I thought, and as I did, I saw Harvey approaching on foot.

'You should have let me do it quietly, as I was going to,' he said, and there was a tone of regret in his voice. 'You have thwarted my plans, and now you know I killed her, I can't let you live.'

'Why do you have to do this?' I said.

'Oh, it's the way of things,' he said. 'Bye, Jack.'

I closed my eyes as he hefted his sword. He drew it back to stab, but I couldn't watch. There was a slight gasp, a muffled sound like a stocking of sand hitting a brick, and I had the most awful feeling of pain, although it wasn't in my breast, it was in my leg.

Warily, I opened my eyes and found Harvey was kneeling on my thigh. He gave me a frowning look, as though trying to remember my name, and then he dropped his sword with a clatter, and gradually slipped sideways. Even then, when he was lying at my side, his eyes had a contemplative surprise in them.

I had a sudden panic that he had stabbed me and I hadn't noticed. I felt all over my body, gently patting with both hands.

'He didn't touch you, you fool. Are you going to lie there all day?' Atwood asked in a conversational tone. 'I'm happy

to ride back and have a couple of cups of wine, if you want to
stay here. Otherwise, get up! People want to see you.'

Atwood twirled a long stocking in one hand as he spoke.
Rather than have him hit me as well, I essayed sitting upright.

It was not pleasant. Every limb appeared to have lost significant quantities of flesh. Those parts of my jack that had been
unstained before were now showing signs of wear. There was
a rip that corresponded to what felt like a tear in my breast;
a thick mark of peat-like mud at the hip had ruined that part
of the jack while also bruising my lower flank. All in all, I
was in a dreadful state. I managed to rise to a crouch, and
hobbled in the direction of my pony and Harvey's horse, while
Atwood threw Harvey's body over his horse and bound it
there. When I reached my pony, I was unable to catch it, and
in the end Atwood, laughing uproariously at my predicament,
trotted over and held my mount while I tried to climb up into
the saddle, but it was no good. With a bad grace, considering
the amusement I'd given him, Atwood dismounted, helped me
up, and then remounted and led my pony and me to the palace.

As we approached the gates, I could see that the bodies
outside were already being loaded on to a wagon. Five men
from the Coroner's party were picking up the almost naked
figures, having stripped them of all usable clothing, swinging
them back and forth, and then releasing them. As I watched,
a party missed with their projectile, and the figure struck the
side-boards. To the jeers and cat calls of the men on the walls,
the men concerned took the body by wrists and ankles, and
began to swing again.

I didn't watch. The roar of cheering told me that they had
probably succeeded, and the next pair of men were moving
up with their own body.

Inside the palace, I reluctantly dropped from my horse, and
instantly collapsed on my arse in the dirt. There I sat for some
time, jarred and aching, watching about me. Atwood dismounted
and walked to Harvey, cutting him free. The man slid to the
ground, and stood there, watching everyone carefully. Atwood
stood before him, smiling, his long knife unsheathed.

'You took your time.'

It was Blount, of course. He was behind me, and I wrenched my neck turning to squint at him.

'Where have you been? Brawling in a midden?'

I stopped the three first responses that sprung into my mind. After all, in my current condition he could kick me to London and back and I wouldn't be able to raise a finger to stop him. And my head hurt. 'So how long have you been using Atwood?'

'He's been a useful informer.'

'And when you realized Harvey was here, you thought you could have a problem? How long did it take you to work out he was a danger?'

'Sir Thomas Parry knew that Harvey was planted on us from the outset. It was obvious. Besides, I have my men keeping an eye on Gardiner. A fellow like that can change his coat at the drop of the wrong hat. Harvey was seen in Gardiner's presence several times. He did have training from his time as a churchman; he could read and write, plan and plot. It seemed a fair bet that he was on the side of the Lord Chancellor. From that, it was only a case of working out what his purpose was.'

'So you . . .' My jaw was flapping unnecessarily. He had given me a sudden thought. It was clear, sharp and obvious. I shut my mouth with a snap of teeth. Through them, I said, 'So you knew before you invited me here that there was a risk to me from Harvey?'

'We needed you to draw him out. I had to see what he was up to.'

'And what was he up to?'

'Harvey was trying to ensure that no matter what, his master stayed secure.'

'Good for him. Where is the Lady Anne?' I asked, and when he told me, I started off in that direction. 'Come with me.'

'Wait! What are you doing?'

'Seeing her. And bring the forged letter, too,' I said.

Blount eyed me without pleasure, but finally called to the Bear and sent him to fetch it.

Groaning, swearing and complaining under my breath, I led the way to the hall. We passed through the screens and out to the other side where a staircase led up to Lady Anne's chamber. There we stopped and knocked. It was opened by a young, grim-faced warrior with a long-bladed knife already drawn and ready. Seeing Blount, he stood back a little in a significantly less threatening manner. Blount murmured a few words, received a nod, and then he led me up the staircase to the first storey.

Inside was Lady Anne, pale, but determined.

I ignored the people of higher status in the room such as my own master, and hobbled to the stool. There I sat, feeling the cut in my buttock where Harvey had slashed at me. It stung.

I was in no mood to beat about the bush. 'Lady Anne, the confession you gave us was a total fabrication, wasn't it?'

She stared at me and in her eyes I saw again that same ruthless determination that had so impressed me on the first occasion I had met her.

'What do you mean?'

'I mean you realized your father was in danger, and you sought to take the blame from his shoulders.'

'I have no idea what—'

'First, Lady Anne, you were out in the courtyard, the inner court, with your father before Lady Margery was killed, weren't you? You separated, and he carried on towards the chamber where Lady Margery was killed, while you went to your room or somewhere else where you had business. You knew your father had been into the room where Lady Margery was discovered. As soon as you discovered her body, you thought to yourself that your father must have killed her, didn't you?'

'I don't know what you are talking about,' she said firmly.

I spoke to Blount now. She was not going to help me. 'You see, her father has had a dreadful time. At first it was the Princess herself, because she is several rungs further up the ladder of intelligence than he; then her maids were appalling, because they were loyal, devoted, educated – and intelligent, too! What was Sir Henry to do? He did all he could, and in the end he took the final step of removing the chief lady-in-waiting and replaced her with a woman he thought would be more amenable to his instruction. He brought Lady Margery to take over the key duties. But then he learned that the woman was a friend and associate of Princess Elizabeth from ten and more years ago. Her family were close to the Boleyns, and Lady Margery had played with the Princess when they were young. So now, in trying to find a spy who would keep him informed, instead he had installed a woman who would be ever more determined to aid her.'

'What of it?' Blount said.

'Even the second necklace was given to her by Lady Elizabeth,' I said.

A thought suddenly occurred to me. It came from that moment when I had seen her conceal her keys between her breasts. 'The crucifix. Did you see it?'

'Yes,' she said. 'What of it?'

'You must have known she did not have the seal. A woman will always judge another's jewellery. You must have seen that the crucifix lay on her breast. If the seal was there, it would have been obvious. But the original necklace would have concealed her father's signet behind her bodice.'

Lady Anne did not argue.

'After installing Lady Margery, Lady Anne must have been regularly regaled with stories of the intolerable woman, I imagine, and how she was making Sir Henry's life all the more difficult. Where is the letter?'

Blount passed me the document that had been the cause of so much trouble. I tapped my chin with it, eyeing Lady Anne all the while. 'You were quick to assert that you forged this. You said you had the seal and wrote and sealed it yourself, did you not?'

'Well, I . . .'

'Lady Anne, read it to me.'

'What?'

'You heard, I believe. Read it to me.'

She took it when I passed the document to her, but she did not open it.

'Will you not, then? In that case, would you take a reed from the clerk behind you? I would like you to forge Lady Elizabeth's signature for me.'

'This is ridiculous!' she flamed. 'Why do you demand this?'

'Because I do not think you could copy the Princess's hand. I'm not certain you can read or write, let alone copy a signature. You never had this paper in your hand. It is vastly more competent as a forgery than anything you could produce. Your family is not fully convinced of learning, is it? Your father can read, just, but his signature is feeble at best, and he never saw much point in having you educated beyond the necessary essentials, did he? Perhaps if you were a son he would consider it, but not a daughter. What good would reading do you?'

'I am perfectly capable.'

'Then take up a reed and copy that signature.'

She sat with her chin high, gazing at me with those beautiful, clear eyes of hers, but not speaking.

'My Lady,' I said wearily, 'you never thought of the other aspect of all this. If you were incapable of forging that letter, how much more incapable was your father? He could never have written that note himself, and even had he wanted it done, he could never have thought up so devious a scheme as producing this letter. Finally, he is not so untruthful as to seek to destroy a young woman by a deception of this nature. It is not in him to be so manipulative.'

At last I thought I was getting through to her. There was a flicker in her eye, and an uncertain look up at Blount behind me.

'Lady Anne,' I said. 'If you don't tell us the truth, it may not matter. You can go to the execution block, and soon after, no doubt, your father will follow you. But someone else has fabricated this whole situation. Would it not be infinitely better to see *him* punished?'

Blount eyed me as I hobbled stiffly from her room and down a flight of stairs. It was not easy going, but made no effort to help me. His mind was fixed on our conversation with Lady Anne. 'How much of that did you know?'

'That she could not read or write? I was guessing. But when you look at her father, can you honestly imagine that he would give a better education to a daughter than he had himself enjoyed? He never believed education to be vital. Why would he waste it on a daughter?'

'But it is a long way from saying that to thinking that his

daughter was incapable of forging a signature, and she may still have been able to read the note and make sure.'

'She could not have murdered Lady Margery and come back so swiftly. If she had done so, her hands would have been covered in gore, as would her clothing. Yet there was nothing on her. She did not steal the seal and—'

'Lady Elizabeth told us that the seal was never stolen, though.'

'Did you study the seal on this letter? You should.'

'I would not recognize her seal if it was put in front of me.'

'Nor would I.'

'Then what—'

I stopped him peremptorily with a raised hand. 'If someone wished to put the blame for a letter on the Princess, how could they do so, if she had no seal? If someone wished to make sure that the Princess was accused of a crime such as plotting against her sister, they would have to give proof that she had used her seal. If the seal was lost or stolen, clearly she could not use it. But if someone stole the seal, used it and then returned it to the Princess, how could she clear her own good name?'

Blount stared at me.

'Yes, Harvey stole the seal from Lady Elizabeth, and then put it back before the Princess noticed.'

'I see.'

But he had not noticed the flaw in the sequence. The men who had broken into the Princess's chambers and ransacked the place to find the seal had discovered nothing.

'Do you want to confront her now?'

'No! What I want is a long sleep, a physician, plenty of brandy, the ministrations of Sal or Kitty, and a rapid journey home. I want you to talk to Sir Thomas and tell him all about this. But for now, let's go and see the Princess and Sir Henry Bedingfield and put the whole matter before them. Then, perhaps, we can all go home.'

In the great blue-ceilinged chamber we were confronted by a pair of strong youths with suspicious eyes, who gripped short polearms across their bodies ready to attack us. A third stood a little behind the throne-like chair on which the Lady Elizabeth sat.

She was the picture of elegance. As we waited, she read a letter, set it aside, and held out her left hand for the next. At one side a clerk shovelled papers into her hand, while at the other a second took the letters and installed them safely into a satchel in some order best known, no doubt, to him. She glanced up once, and then only to look me up and down with an expression of mild shock rather than disapproval.

The last letter read, she waved a hand. The guards left the chamber, eyeing us mistrustfully, and the Princess turned to us. She had the sort of look in her eye that her father would have had while looking at an unproductive and irritating wife. I imagined it was the sort of look he used to give Anne Boleyn after hearing she was sharing her bed with another man. It lacked a certain friendliness and warmth.

'Well?'

'You were clever to have me see your seal. It showed that the thing had not left your hands, and that invalidated the letter forged by Lady Anne. You managed it very well, Your Highness,' I said.

'What?'

'The concealment. Not many noticed that the seal on the documents was genuine. Only I and my master here.'

She lifted her chin slightly. 'I do not follow you.'

'Lady Margery was an old friend. When her husband stole her seal from her, he snapped the chain on which it was held. When that happened she realized your seal was not safe on a cord or thong about her throat, didn't she? She was supposed to retain the seal in her own safekeeping, but she knew that was not safe. Especially with her avaricious husband. However, she was your friend. Harvey, like most, thought it still hung about her throat, but it didn't, did it? *You* already had it. Harvey wanted to create a forgery signed with a genuine mark from your seal. What could he do? He came here with me and the injured boy, and realized you might have it still. He searched and found it. He didn't even have to remove it. Instead he sealed the letter he had prepared so that when the forgery was produced, you could be held to account. Except – fortunately – the murderer had not thought of the inefficiency – that is to say, the honesty – of Sir Henry. He might be a boring old buffoon, but he is as honest as the day is long. So he would not believe that the letter was genuine when you said it was not.'

'An interesting theory.'

'And the only one that fits the facts. When I say that my latest injuries were caused by a servant of Bishop Gardiner, and that he was paid to see to it that you were threatened with death for plotting against Her Majesty the Queen, perhaps you will realize the narrowness of the thread on which your life is balanced,' I said.

'Who was this?'

'Jonathan Harvey, Princess. A man who is devious, dangerous – and captured.'

'How did you know, when you demonstrated to us all that it was Lady Anne who was responsible?'

'It was a thought that occurred to me: of all those who had the opportunity to kill Lady Margery, only one was never apparently near her. That set me thinking: if I were to plan a murder, surely I would make sure that my own movements were not witnessed by others. In short, if I were a murderer, I would be as invisible as he apparently was.'

Her expression told me all I needed to know. Master Blount was gazing at me with every sign of admiration – or surprise.

I continued. 'Lady Elizabeth, you have been duped by a very dishonest man. He gave the appearance of being a friend, I know, but he was no friend to you or to me.'

She squirmed slightly in her seat. Her eyes were very firmly fixed on mine. She gave no indication of fear, but the way she did not blink told me how anxious she must be.

'This is your death warrant, my Lady. If your sister should see it, she will recognize your seal and signature, I am sure.'

I held the letter up, and as she watched, I held it to a candle flame. The parchment caught fire, the wax from the seal melting and running, flaring briefly, and then the whole paper was alight and I dropped it to the floor. I stopped Blount from standing on it until I was certain that it was all burned, and then I ground the ashes to dust. 'It is done. My Lady, you must be more untrusting and suspicious.'

She looked at me, then at Blount. 'I am most grateful to you, Master Jack. How can I repay you?'

I was tempted to inquire how full was her money chest, but just then I was too weary to bother. 'Lady, your thanks is all I need. I wanted to see justice done, and prevent the perversion of justice by seeing Lady Anne and Sir Henry suffer. There is already enough suffering in the kingdom.'

'Then go, and take my blessings with you.'

I hesitated. 'There is one question, if I may?'

She graciously inclined her head. 'I think I owe you enough to justify a response, Master Blackjack.'

'It is this. Harvey told me that he found the seal and told the men-at-arms they might discover it. How was it that they did not succeed?'

She smiled then, a great smile of delight. 'I and my ladies knew it would be found, so when I went to the chapel while they hunted, I took the seal with me and concealed it.'

'Where?'

'In the little stoup of Holy water by the door. I felt that if it were guarded in Holy Water, it could not incriminate me. And, you see, I was right!'

EPILOGUE

It was two days later that I jogged along from Woodstock to take the London road. Master Blount was with me, and his two companions, but they were all who accompanied us. Harvey was to remain at Woodstock, accused of murder, and would soon be visited by the Justices of Gaol Delivery. After that, I felt his life expectancy would reduce rapidly.

'So you mean to say that you did not, after all, murder Lady Margery?' Blount said again.

'It was too soon for me. I was still studying her and the palace to see how best to do so,' I said loftily.

Will, behind me, snorted. I chose to ignore his rudeness.

'So why did Harvey kill Lady Margery? He could simply have robbed her.'

'And have the fact that she had been robbed made so plain at the outset? It was easier to leave her death as a mystery, and hope that it would confuse matters still more. Besides, once the discovery of the forged letter came into the open, it was safe to think that the murder would become irrelevant. The Queen would not care who had killed Margery, were she to learn that her half-sister had tried to kill her.'

Will grunted. 'That makes sense. Once Harvey had planted the idea of a plot against her rule, she would naturally forget about some gentlewoman's death.'

'What will happen to young Gilbert?' I asked.

Blount shrugged. 'I believe that the Percy clan have asked for him to be returned to them. No doubt they will look after the boy.'

'And Sir Walter?'

'He'll disappear. Join a minor lord, or travel to Europe to seek a war. The sooner he leaves the kingdom, the happier I'll be.'

'Squire George is the man I feel most sorry for,' I said. 'He made the mistake of falling in love, marrying without permission, and now he's lost everything.'

'He'll cope,' Blount said unfeelingly. 'He's young. He'll find another woman and make a new life.'

His lack of sympathy grated on me, but for now I could shrug it off. Falkes was in a gaol at Woodstock still, and would be unlikely to be released for a while. By the time he was freed, it was likely that his little empire in London would have been taken over by a business rival, which meant I was unlikely to have to worry about him. Meanwhile, Jen would be without a protector. That meant I could hope for some more horizontal coursing without fear. Blount had that very morning handed me a heavy purse to join the ones that Sir Thomas and the Princess had given me.

'A high-born lady wanted you to know that she appreciated your help,' he said.

It still lay against my belly, under my shirt – a pleasantly weighty purse that went well with the other that she had given me earlier, and the one Sir Thomas had given me. So it was a battered, bruised, but contented Jack who rode back towards town.

I gave little thought to my surroundings as we entered a town on our second day's ride. It was familiar, but I thought little of it. We entered an inn, gave our mounts to the grooms, and entered in time to ask for some food. After our repast, I heard the sound of raucous pleasure in a back room. Wandering out to seek the source, my purses rattling happily, I found a game of dice in full flow.

I have always enjoyed dice. Barging my way through the yokels and tatterdemalions who were ringing the game, I stood and peered down. It was loud, and these fools were easy prey for a fellow from London.

But I didn't like the way that a man at the other side of the room suddenly stared. He looked horribly familiar, somehow. Then the game ceased and there was a sharp silence. I felt men drawing near behind me, and two men before me drew knives.

'Hey! You're the man sold us that good luck potion!'

'Shit!' I said, and took to my heels.

Lightning Source UK Ltd.
Milton Keynes UK
UKHW01f0424150818
327267UK00001B/29/P